HORROR HOUSE DETECTIVE

Printed in the United States of America

Published by Silverthought Press
www.silverthought.com

Cover design by Paul Hughes

ISBN: 978-0-9841738-1-5

HORROR HOUSE DETECTIVE
BY MICHAEL GOLD

[silverthought]
PHILADELPHIA / NEW YORK

This book is dedicated to my father—a man of honor, courtesy, generosity and quiet warmth.

TABLE OF CONTENTS

SPECIAL NOTE:

This is a work of fiction. Any resemblance to anyone living or dead is purely coincidental. So, Uncle David, you're not a model for any characters in the book. Please don't get mad.

BIRTH OF THE WEIRD

I met The Weirdness when I was a young boy.

It started when I was 5 or 6 years old. Most kids don't remember much of what happened before then. But gradually, a feeling came on when I started to notice things around me.

Dad didn't say much. He was short, only about five feet, six inches tall, but his chest was a rubber band of muscle. The shoulders were great bunched-up mountain ridges and the arms were like cannons. Purple scars ran up and down up the forearms, like worms crawling out of the ground to escape the rain.

I asked him once, "Daddy, how did you get those?"

His eyes bulged out. His lips tightened. He looked at me like I had done something terribly wrong. He looked at me like I was from Mars. He looked at me as if to say, "It's not your place to ask." I was terrified by that look.

The man I called "Dad" was one tough guy. I knew this because of the look, but other than that, I didn't really experience it myself.

First, there was all that muscle, but I had never seen him use it except to haul plywood from the house into his station wagon.

Second, the way he carried himself was in direct contradiction to the way his face was set along that firm jaw line. He wisped about the house trying to pretend he wasn't really there most of the time. The newspaper was a great place to hide. The cool, dark basement was even better.

I wondered why he was like this. I didn't make the connection that the shortest direction from point to point is a straight line. That would be my mother. She had basically ceded the raising of my younger brother to me. I was 6 years old at the time and he was 2. I didn't even know what was going on half the time and now I had to change diapers and feed a squalling toddler with whatever was available to my 6-year-old abilities. Or I was afraid he might starve.

I had to worry about figuring out first grade and taking care of Derek. There were many days when I came home from school to a house where he was wandering around alone in a soiled diaper. I changed him on the diaper pad. He was often screaming and kicking me. I tried not to take it personally.

After the diaper change, he was still crying. He must have been hungry, hungry, hungry. I didn't know what to feed him, so I gave him foods I liked and could prepare. He ate a lot of bananas and Cheerios and apple sauce. Other than that, I was at sea. I wondered where my mother was. I wondered about a mother who left a 2-year-old boy alone.

My mother was like a field general with an army of three— Dad, me, and my little brother. She didn't speak. She gave orders. If she told us to do something, she assumed we would carry out her will. She didn't need to follow up.

She would make dinner most nights, but when Mom cooked, it was an experiment in terror. She made a lousy pot roast, for instance. We sat around the table, my father, brother, and I, looking at the brown, dead meat. Its flatness alone was depressing enough. The boiled potatoes next to the roast were hard nuggets that could break your teeth.

We were ordered to eat all of it. I had to steel myself against gagging each time the food came close to my less than eager mouth.

Mother spent most of her time with the Ozone Park Ladies' Garden Club, presiding over the planting and blooming of tulips and irises and sunflowers in back yards all over southern Queens. She was the Stalin of gardening. If you didn't plant what she liked, who knows? You may find yourself suddenly disinvited from membership in the garden club. A whispering campaign may commence about your fitness as a wife and a mother. And there is nothing around here that's as tyrannical as the opinion of your garden club sisters. If you persist in your opinions about what should go in your garden, a neighborhood dog may find its way past your backyard fence and dig up all your beautiful flowers, leaving a scorched earth of soil in its wake. The Mob has studied her methods.

Mother was only five feet tall, but her face was like a weapon. The red hair put people off right off the bat. It reminded people of blood. The nose was a gun pointed in your direction. The mouth was a finely-sculpted arsenal of atomic bullets. The premature jowls hanging off the cheeks didn't encourage anybody, either. She may have looked like a squirrel hiding nuts, but she seemed ready to spit them right at your head. People were afraid of her. My father only seemed relaxed when he asked Mother to call businessmen who owed him money. When Dad had exhausted all methods and couldn't seem to extract the money from his customers, he turned to my mother. She could really work a man over in just five minutes on the phone. Father was happy, I guess, that she wasn't directing her fire at him at the moment.

Father didn't seem any more relaxed when Mom was gone. He pulled some food out of the refrigerator—turkey, cheese, white bread, lettuce, mayo, a chocolate-covered doughnut, and a bottle of cream soda—and carried all the goods down the thick wooden steps to the basement and closed the door with his foot.

I was not invited, and neither was my brother. We looked at each other, me in my brown shorts and my brother in his diaper and tee-shirt. We knew we were on our own. If we cried about it, no one would comfort us. We knew we would have to raise ourselves. There was a dark side which called out to us ("Luke, you don't know the power of the Dark Side!"), but if we embraced it, we would be lost. So we tried our best with the scarce brains we had.

Brother's name is Derek. He didn't look like a Derek. He was more like a Joe or a Jack. But leave it to my mother to distort the nature of things. She was the direct source of The Weirdness, I think, but she was afflicted with it too.

Father didn't have any say in naming my brother. I knew this because Mother had told me, many times. She was proud that Father had no power in the house, glad that she was the ruler of her little kingdom.

My father may have been a rough and tumble man in the world of plywood and hammers, of concrete and glass, a man who could build houses and who competed in the cut and thrust of the real estate business in this toughest of cities, but at home he had completely subjugated himself to Mother. This is the first of the mysteries I confronted in my young life, and there would be many more.

So this is what I mean by The Weirdness. The Weirdness is not a person or an evil malignant cancer, but I feel it as a physical force. Reality is bent. Instead of the nuclear picture of an American family of four, smiling at the camera, all happy together, the sun splashing behind us, we were somehow not regular, not normal, in ways you may not be able to define.

It continued with my name. In school, my fellow students laughed and pointed when they heard my name called with the roll.

My first name's Harold. It's not the coolest name. People make fun of it, kids especially. You hear the story about Old Weird Harold? And so on. But it's a solid name, a lot better than my last name. By calling me Harold, my parents tried to make me classy like a British schoolboy, but it didn't take.

The Derek thing was another effort to be British. Mother told us Brother was named after Derek Jacobi, the great English actor with that most crisp of accents. Surprisingly, Derek did not obtain the cherished English accent by some kind of magical telepathy with Mr. Jacobi. He sounded more like that great nasal king of Queens—Joey Ramone.

Then there's my last name—Schreiber. You sit in a class with kids with names like O'Connor, Catalano, and Kelly, and you're just going to catch it. They gave me several choice names—Shrub, Shrubber and Shremp.

By seventh grade, I'd had enough of it. If a guy got too persistent with the names, I called him out in the schoolyard. The kid may have been bigger, he may have been tougher, but I had rage on my side—rage against The Weirdness. I won three out of three fights on the bleak gray asphalt playground during that first year of junior high school.

My strategy was always to rush right in and punch the guy flat in the nose. I could usually draw blood right away. That usually stunned him. Then, while he was contemplating the fact that his nostrils had been opened, I slugged the guy in the stomach. Then a shot right in the forehead, and another punch in the nose.

The other thing I did was not stop. I just kept punching, like a piston, all over the face—cheeks, eyes, mouth. You push his lips against his lower teeth and he's going to bleed there too. Pretty soon the onlookers are going to yell or scream that he's bleeding and to fight back, dammit, you're bigger than Shrubber is, and your opponent is confused and scared. He asks you to stop and you do. You don't need a formal surrender because you need to leave the guy with what little dignity he has left. You insist on shaking hands because there is an unspoken promise in that. The boy will never call you names again.

And pretty soon most of the guys just called me Harold. There were a few exceptions, of course (there are always exceptions), and I'll get to them later.

Still, The Weirdness persisted. Things just didn't feel quite right. Like the time my mother made my brother Derek eat eight ounces of peas at dinner. He protested he didn't like peas. The smell, he said, he couldn't take the smell. I didn't like them either, not one bit, but I just shut up and forced them down.

Derek was 6 years old at the time. He cried that he hated them. Mother wouldn't hear it.

"You're going to eat every single one of those peas!" she yelled at him.

"Mom, that's three servings," my 10-year-old mouth protested.

"Don't you ever talk back to me!" Mother shouted.

Father looked on, said nothing, tried to make himself disappear.

Derek, crying, ate the peas, one at a time. The tears mixed with the peas and made them even saltier.

He ate all the peas, God bless him. After the last pea, his mouth opened like an anti-aircraft gun and he promptly sprayed vomit all over the kitchen tablecloth, a huge flow of green muck on Mother's white linen. It was just like *The Exorcist*, except I think Derek had more to vomit than Linda Blair ever did.

"You've ruined my tablecloth!" Mother screeched. "You're going to clean it all up, Derek!"

I took Derek by the shoulders and pulled him out of there, to the bathroom, to clean him up—to wash his face and tangled brown hair in the sink.

By the time Derek and I returned from the bathroom, both my mother and father had disappeared. Like I said, Mother just expected you to do what she said. She couldn't bother herself with minor details like overseeing the work she wanted done.

I told him: "Derek, go brush your teeth and go read a book in bed."

"What about the mess?" he said, his eyes still red and watery.

"I'll take care of it."

I soaked the green out of the tablecloth with hot water and lots of bleach in the square basement sink, then put it in the washing machine. The cloth still had a pale green cast to it, so I put more bleach on it, and ran it through the machine again.

After two hours, the tablecloth was no longer green in any way, but a bright, shiny white that you couldn't look at without being blinded.

Despite all my kindnesses to my brother, he was attacked by The Weirdness, too. We started fighting when he was 8 years old. I was 12.

I should have seen it coming. He drew a picture of himself with an "X" at each significant point in his face—eyes, nose, mouth. He threw some extra "X's" over the rest of his face. It looked as if a chicken had scratched him everywhere with its clawed feet.

He brought it home from school and showed it to me proudly, as if he had made a rainbow.

When my mother yelled at him, he hid his head inside his shirt, like he was a turtle. This made Mom even madder, and she started ranting at Derek, saying things like, "What's wrong with you? You need to buck up, boy!" One time, after one of these lectures, he started banging his bare forehead on the nearest available table.

This was one of the most disturbing things any of us had ever seen. We all stared at him, my father, mother, and me. Dad backed out of the room, slowly, with his face to us, as if he knew someone was going to pull out a gun if his back was turned.

I tried to comfort Derek. I went over to his side and tried to hug him and make him stop punching his head on the wood, spilling soft words in his ear.

"Go away, fuckhead!" he screamed.

There is little that is worse than having your hug rejected by your little brother, with the possible exception that you have been called a fuckhead.

At other times, Derek went into my room and took all the clothes, which I had carefully folded myself, out of my drawers and kicked them around the room in piles. He drew grotesque pictures on my walls, of himself impaled on the Empire State Building's great spire, of the Statue of Liberty, one of my favorite places in the whole world, with her torch burning the city and a gleeful smile on her face (He was a really good artist—the sneer on Lady Liberty was quite effective). He took my Boy Scout merit badges, ripped them off the corkboard on my wall, and rubbed dirt on them (Yes, I have joined the Boy Scouts by this time. It's my only way to fight off the dark side. The Boy Scouts are the Jedi Knights of Queens, as far as I'm concerned). I cleaned the merit badges over and over again, digging the soil out of every little ridge, and put them back on the corkboard in the correct order in which I had won them.

When I was doing my homework, Derek might saunter casually over and bite me on the shoulder. He often drew blood. We would start to fight.

Or he would start punching me for no earthly reason when I was reading a book or watching the New York Giants or the Knicks by myself. This happened when Mom and Dad weren't home and soon they weren't home a lot, with Derek acting like a rabid pit bull. He was my younger brother and I tried to restrain myself for that reason, but with the rain of punches pouring down, another part of my brain took over and I felt murderous myself. I pounded him and wrestled him down on the floor, with my legs corralling his chest and me swinging at him like Larry Holmes on a bad day.

I gave my brother black eyes and bloody noses and torn-up mouths. When Mother came home, I was blamed. I tried to explain that I didn't start it, he started it, but there was no debate about this. Mother always took Derek's side. It was as if she was trying to defend him to make up for her permanent vacation from raising him correctly. Derek took comfort from her scoldings of me and smiled with vicious triumph.

It looked like Derek had been raised in back-alley Queens by wolves. And maybe he had been. Maybe I just didn't know well enough how to raise a psychologically healthy kid. I was just a kid too. But then again, when you've basically lost the interest of your mother, you might go nuts at an early age too.

The parents were sufficiently disturbed after several months to send Derek to a psychiatrist with an affiliation at the Creedmoor Hospital. Creedmoor is the lunatic asylum and it's a brightly colored slab of giant beige bricks rising up happily between two parkways within the swamps of Queens.

Creedmoor—the name whispers madness. It reminded me of that warning to the two hikers from *An American Werewolf in London*—"Stay off the moors." Because that's where the werewolves lurk. They'll eat you alive. And take your soul too.

A moor is part open country, where your mind can lose its sense of itself in the vast expanse. Or it can be a bog—a place where dead trees gather and deteriorate. Either way, you're screwed on a moor. Heathcliff lost it on the moors.

As for the "Creed" part of the name, that's innocent enough. The family that owned the land before selling it to the state was named Creed.

In 1870, the Creeds sold part of their farm to the New York State National Guard and the National Rifle Association. The place became a rifle range. When bullet technology improved, the bullets started traveling farther, off the range and sometimes into neighbors' yards. People got tired of this and the range was abandoned. In 1908, the New York State Commission for Lunacy opened the Farm Colony of Brooklyn State Hospital (source: New York Office of Mental Health). The name was later changed to Creedmoor. As far as the patients were concerned, the bullets were still flying, but they were invisible.

Derek visited the psychiatrist once a week. It wasn't enough. His mind was melting. During one meeting, he challenged the psychiatrist to a duel. With pistols. The psychiatrist, name of Pitsky, tried to be patient, but he was old and Derek had far more energy than he did.

The following anecdotal incidents were related to us:

- Derek turned off all the lights in Pitsky's office during a visit.
- Derek knocked down a lamp.
- Derek argued with the psychiatrist about who was the best team—the Yankees or the Mets (This is a constant sore point in Queens). Derek liked the Yankees (They win). Pitsky liked

the Mets. Derek threatened to urinate on Pitsky's head. (Perhaps Pitsky shouldn't have ventured an opinion.)

■ Derek threw a book on clinical depression at Pitsky after Pitsky asked, "How do you feel about your mother?" The book hit Pitsky square in the chest.

■ Derek took a delicate vase of brightly colored flowers from Pitsky's desk and squeezed it between his hands until it broke. Apparently, Pitsky had fallen asleep during the session and Derek got upset. Derek took several stitches in each hand. (We gave points to Pitsky for honesty, then wondered if we should sue him.)

■ Pitsky asked my parents to sign papers to commit Derek to Creedmoor for more serious treatment and psychiatric observation. My parents agreed.

The next time I saw Derek it was behind two inches of glass interwoven with a steel web so you couldn't break it. The room he inhabited was completely white. There was not a trace of color in the nine-by-seven unit. The mattress had a plastic cover and no sheets (so he couldn't hang himself). He was 9 years old.

Derek wore a white hospital gown, soiled with what looked like streaks of dust from the floor. His eyes were brown clouds. He walked with a halting gait. He recognized us, and said hello, but did not smile, perhaps could not smile.

The drugs did this. I couldn't pronounce their names and I didn't know what good they were doing. I saw that whatever my brother was, he had become a shell of a boy, a doll from Weirdland, not a real, living kid who throws footballs or builds model airplanes or rides his bicycle to the candy store. Derek had been turned into a zombie.

My parents swooned. Mother cried, loudly. Father's lips tightened and I could hear him hold his breath in pain.

My father really needed to escape after this episode. He bought a series of boats (Business was good at the time). First we got a little speedboat. Then he said we needed a bigger boat. We got a 23-footer. That wasn't big enough either. So Dad bought a 28-foot cabin cruiser. Mother refused to go out in the thing, said it was a waste of money and time. It was a big boat for only him and me. Yet Mom did not make him sell it. Maybe she saw that even Father had a breaking point.

Father seemed grateful for her resistance to go on the boat. He didn't ask again. I was invited out with him every time.

We went out whether it was sunny or cloudy. Father only got upset if it was raining on the weekend. He seemed to take it personally, as if God were singling him out for punishment.

Out on the water, the southern bays of Long Island, and the ocean, The Weirdness departed for a bit of time. Father guided the boat over the waves and I enjoyed seeing the huge wake we made from the engines.

When we visited the Great South Bay, we saw that the water was only six feet deep and it was so clear that you could see the bottom. Fish raced away from us and the sand had waves of its own, pushed by the tides.

Dad's face actually seemed to shine when he was at the helm of the boat, steering the cabin cruiser, looking at the water and seeming to drink it all in with great gulps of his eyes. He taught me how to steer the ship, with as much care and tenderness as he was capable of. I was unsure, tentative, but he was patient and supportive.

Father stopped the engines and he let the boat drift among the none-too-powerful waves. We ate our lunch together, in silence. When we finished our meal, he might talk about the quality of the sandwich, or the details of putting up a house. I treasured these words, any words, that came out of his mouth.

At home, I threw myself into the Boy Scouts, to block out The Weirdness.

By the time I was 13, I earned the many merit badges you needed to become an Eagle Scout. You can earn merit badges for achievements in first aid, citizenship in the community, nation, and world, communications, personal fitness, emergency preparedness, lifesaving, environmental science, personal management, swimming, hiking, cycling, camping, and family life. But earning merit badges isn't enough. You must demonstrate Scout spirit, service and leadership. Only two percent of all Scouts have become Eagle Scouts, out of 83 million Scouts since 1911 (source: Wikipedia).

I followed the Scouts' creed to the letter. A Scout is loyal to his country and his employers. He sticks with them through "thick and thin" against anyone who is their enemy. A Scout must be useful and help others, even if he needs to give up his own pleasure or comfort or safety to do it. A Scout is courteous, polite to all. A Scout obeys orders.

Earning that merit badge for family life was tricky. I did it by wearing two personalities. One, I offered grace and obedience in front of my mother, despite the steel in her manner. I didn't argue with her about God when she told me daily I needed to follow His Ways more (She was a fervent believer). When she told me to do something, I performed the task immediately. I did what I was told.

Two, I tried to train my body like I was Captain America. When the alarm clock went off three hours before school started, I hit the floor and did 100 push-ups. I ran miles on the flat streets of southern Queens, or swam endless laps at the local gym in Ozone Park. I took boxing lessons and punched a heavy bag.

Sometimes that wasn't enough. After I showered and ate breakfast, I might run the three miles to junior high school instead of having my dad drive me.

After school, I hit the books, then worked on earning merit badges. It was a grueling schedule, yet I needed to fill my time in order to screen out the black voices braying at me, whispering sweet nothings, offering me the chance to earn quick money by running errands and doing jobs for the local social club, where the men seemed to do nothing but sit in front of their building all day, playing cards and drinking beer, and eating fat sandwiches filled with delicious red deli meats, from pastrami to roast beef, layered with rich cheese and wide, obese rolls of bread dough.

I saw them call over kids to do things for them all the time.

"Hey, kid, want to buy me a roast beef sandwich? Here's five bucks. Tell them I want rye bread and put provolone cheese and mayo on it."

"Hey, kid, can you go to the garage down the street and tell Frankie he needs to fix the jukebox in here again?" (They have music in the place too! These guys can do whatever they want!) "Here's a buck. Run."

"Hey, kid, want to wash my car in the back? I'll give you ten bucks. There's soap and water in a bucket in the alley."

"Hey, kid, take my shoes over to the store and get 'em shined. I'll give you a fiver."

The mystery men took the sun and read the paper—sports pages mostly. Why are the Mets so bad? The magic of 1969 is long gone. Are the Jets ever going to find a decent quarterback? Richard Todd is no Joe Namath. Can you believe how bad the Giants are? Always bet against them. Walt Frazier, Willis Reed, and Bill Bradley are history. And now the Knicks suck. The Yankees? They're rich and therefore feared, but they are not loved.

It looked like a great life. Sometimes I found my head pulling the rest of my body over to that side of the street. It almost made me drunk to see how happy the men were, how comfortable they were in their own bodies.

My intensity let up in the deep, dark night and that's when the black spirits came at me. Dream images of Derek in his Creedmoor gown and bare feet walking right by me on the street, staring straight ahead, saying nothing, not even acknowledging me as his brother, acting like a stranger. Or he was trying to crack me over the head with a vase. In these black visions of the night, he smashed through the glass door of our house with a fist. Or he ran right through the glass, the shards spraying out like water drops from a shower head. He punched me in the eye. I punched back too. I hit him again and again, never hurting him.

I sweated it all out in my sleep. When I woke up in the morning, my pillowcase was soaked. Mother yelled at me for ruining the pillowcase. I apologized with my head down.

Dad started to wake up to the fact that I was troubled too. I was less obvious about it than Derek, but there was some writhing beast in me and Dad saw a little of it. He invented another escape for us. He and I started to go bowling on weekends in the winter. Queens used to be a hotbed of bowling. On Saturdays, Dad would take me to the Woodhaven Lanes and we bowled game after game. There were dozens of happy people around us, kids having bowling birthday parties, men drinking beer and weaving down the lanes, and some of the guys from the social club, sitting back like they owned the place. Maybe they did.

I was happy to be surrounded by these people, but knew I was not part of them. The game of bowling itself was appealing enough for me. My father and I really worked to knock down as many pins as possible. There was an animal satisfaction in destroying their prim little pyramid arrangements with a ball of molded plastic as heavy as a stack of wood slats bundled together. The bowling ball is a weapon of the gods. My father felt it too.

The year after I earned my Eagle Scout rank, Derek, all of 10 years old, escaped from Creedmoor. It was late September. The nights were getting shorter and colder and wetter.

Pitsky called us to his office in Forest Hills, wouldn't tell us what was wrong on the phone. My parents shivered in two leather-backed chairs, with me on the couch. The office was a rectangle and full of psychiatry books sitting on oak wood shelves. Derek had thrown one of these books at Pitsky.

"I am very sorry to have to tell you this," Pitsky said. My mother started to cry. She thought Pitsky was going to tell her that Derek was dead. We always think the worst.

"Your son has evacuated the facility." I noticed the language. Pitsky was talking as if Derek were fleeing a hurricane and not that the medical and security personnel failed utterly in making sure nothing like this ever happened.

I wondered if this had occurred before. Were there dozens of psychos wandering around the wet bog of the moor in hospital gowns, rocketing from tree to tree or falling in the mud or attacking people walking by with their little dachshunds?

"When did this happen?" Mother said.

"Last night, sometime before dinner."

That was Friday. Pitsky called us on Saturday morning, about seven AM. It was now eight o'clock in the morning. That meant Derek had been missing for at least twelve hours. I wondered if maybe they waited to call, hoping they could find him so they wouldn't have to call our family.

"Where is he?" my mother asked, starting to get angry. Pitsky had no idea what was about to hit him.

Pitsky's mouth froze for a moment. "We have been unable to retrieve him." Like Derek was a stick of wood.

"What do you mean?" Mother yelled.

Pitsky's mouth unfroze. The words started spilling out of him like manure from a horse. "We don't know where he is. We're trying to find him. We have the city police out looking for him. We're very concerned."

I imagined two guys with enormous bellies wiping doughnut dust from their mouths while they plodded through the woods around the hospital.

Mother released her primary weapon. "You're concerned? You're CONCERNED?"

"I'm very sorry. We're doing what we can."

"He's 10 years old! He could get hurt. Somebody could snatch him right up and he'd be gone without a trace. He could hurt himself."

"Listen, we're doing our best to—"

"Whatever you're doing is completely nothing. You call the governor and you tell him you need help."

"Ma'am, that's really not appropriate here."

"I know Morton Halperin. I'm calling his office as soon as we get home." Morton Halperin was our Congressman.

"I know Steve Lee at the Long Island Press. This will make a great story for the newspapers and the TV."

"No, no, that's not necessary. We have a plan for these types of situations. We're executing it now."

"So this has happened before? How many loony tunes do you have running around out there? (I agreed with my mother for once.) Your plan is worth crap. Pure crap." Mother's jowls were working overtime now and they looked like they were going to explode.

Pitsky tried to act imperious, to try to cow my mother. He raised himself up from behind his desk and stood, both hands on the desk, knuckles pointed outward, his Einstein hair seeming to levitate to the ceiling. He looked like a silverback gorilla.

"We have activated numerous personnel and we are working on the problem, all hands on deck. Mrs. Schreiber, the best thing for you to do is go home and stay calm," Pitsky intoned with all the authority he could muster, which, at that point, wasn't much.

My mother stood right up and puffed out her considerable middle. She pointed at Pitsky with a stubby finger that might as well have been a .45 Magnum handgun.

"You have no right to tell me to remain calm. You have no idea what it feels like when it's your child." (If only she had been as protective in changing the boy's diapers.)

"I have sons of my own," Pitsky said, defensive, but beginning to shrink back already.

Mother yelled at the top of her very large lungs. "I'm going to call everyone I can about you! You're a liar. You're a criminal. You're a pig!"

With that, Pitsky looked shaken, ashen. My father did something I never expected him to do. He spoke.

"Let's go, Ruth."

"I am not going, Abe!"

"It's time to go," he said, calmly.

"No!" she said, like she was a toddler screaming at her parents.

"I'm leaving," he said quietly. He started to walk out of the office. My mother was somehow moved by this. She nudged Abe's hand so he would hold it. They began to leave together, their backs toward the psychiatrist.

Mother turned one more time, hand firmly in Abe's massive paw, and pointed her gun finger at the doctor.

"You find him. That's all. Just find him."

Pitsky looked relieved.

Everyone had forgotten I was there. They didn't come back for me until after a little scrap of confrontation with the incompetent calling himself a psychiatrist on the walls of his office.

I looked around at all his diplomas. I marched confidently up to his desk, all of 14 years old.

"Where was he last seen?" I asked.

Pitsky didn't take me seriously. Who was I, a cop? This was in my favor.

"He was in the exercise yard at five o'clock."

"So he escaped from there?"

"We don't think so. The fence is twelve feet high and has barbed wire on top. He would have been seen, obviously."

"Obviously."

Pitsky's tiny eyes widened with surprise. He had weathered the whiplash storm that was my mother. He didn't expect sarcastic guff from a 14-year-old kid, an Eagle Scout no less. I was a little surprised at myself. But I felt a change within me because of Derek's disappearance.

When my mother called to me to come along, I turned to go. Then on the way out, I looked at Pitsky and the plastic electrical plate for the light and turned off the switch, just like Derek did. I laughed a crazy laugh, at the weirdness of it all.

I decided to try to find him.

I was expected to haul myself home to an empty house after ninth grade classes were over and I used this to my advantage.

I got on the city bus to Creedmoor. The ride took about 20 minutes. We went from the stand-alone houses of Ozone Park

(What kind of real estate moron names a place after a pollutant?) and Woodhaven to the elegant, understated wealth of the mansions of Forest Hills Gardens, then the sea of apartment buildings spraying outward from Kew Gardens to Briarwood, stopped only by the parkways crisscrossing eastern Queens, taking commuters to their cherished little patches of grass on Long Island. The bus worked its way slowly along Hillside Avenue as it ran toward the outer edges of the city. It stopped at a booth about 20 yards away from the facility.

The Long Island Expressway skirts Creedmoor. You can see the hospital's three-towered beige bricks jutting up from the grass off the road.

From Hillside Avenue, the hospital looked like Everest looming above my 14-year-old eyes. The wind kicked back my brown hair. The center was a little intimidating. I had been there before to see Derek with Abe and Ruth. Now I was alone and wondering what the hell I was doing.

The windows were banded by metal strips so patients couldn't jump out, I imagined. The front had security guards.

As I walked by the entrance, a couple of security men were yakking. They glanced at me, figured I wasn't much of a threat, and went back to their conversation.

I walked completely around the center, looking at the question of how my brother got out of the place. The fence was a complex mesh of steel and iron. The walk took about an hour. I noticed that much of the facility was surrounded by the back yards of houses. I hiked over fences from back yard to back yard. Nobody was around to challenge me. In some places, I saw woods and some boggy land. No houses.

The lateness of the time caught up with me. I quit for the bus and ride home, thinking about my brother.

The next day I went back after school again. I homed in on the exercise yard. There was a wooded area next to the yard.

I walked through the woods to the fence in front of the yard. On the edge of the yard, near the building, there was a basketball court, rutted and with no nets on the orange metal rims (Was somebody going to jump high enough to unhook the nets from the rims and use them to hang themselves?). The rest of the yard was a dusty field, frayed from the walking of the countless number of Queens residents troubled enough to land in there.

The September wind blew the dust in little puffs so the view in front of me was a brown cloud. I had no method to what I was doing. I stared at the yard for a while. Then it was time to go home.

For six weeks, I went to the fence by the yard, staring at the field as if it would throw up a clue. I never saw a cop kicking through the grass. Pitsky's plan to find my brother was working perfectly.

My mother made her calls, with no result. Halperin the Congressman was unresponsive. Steve Lee, from the *Long Island Press*, was unmoved. He talked politely to my mother and hung up the phone. The big New York papers didn't even cover the story. There were too many other, bigger things going on than a 10-year-old kid's escape from an out-of-the-way mental hospital in sleepy eastern Queens. More than 2,000 people had been murdered in the city during the year. A guy had just killed his girlfriend and boiled her down to the bones. The cops had found them in a locker in Grand Central. A 19-year-old man was strangled and partially eaten by his pet python. And the topper? "Headless Body Found In Topless Bar"—*New York Post*. The economy wasn't much better than that—the city was on its knees.

Mother ruminated on whether she should write a letter to the governor. As if he had nothing better to do. He had all the time in the world to stop working on saving the city from financial disaster to help out Ruth Schreiber, one midget voter from Queens.

Dad's meaty forearms, more tense than usual, retreated to the basement. There was a bowling moratorium on in the house.

In early November, it occurred to me to walk around the fence of the building again. I walked gingerly through the trees. Little mirrors of water speckled the ground. They were black except for when the sunlight danced in uninvited. I walked near them, looking at my face. There was nothing there.

I wandered back to the fence, kicking at the grass. The ground there was very uneven. It rolled up and down like a miniature prairie. I walked back and forth 50 yards in each direction.

On the third go-round, I tripped over an especially high mound, fell and scraped my face on the fence. I was about to get mad. Then I noticed that the mound was total dirt, no grass on it at all.

I started digging at the soil. The sun's music was dying around me. I worked deliberately, clawing the dirt. The lights from the exercise yard flashed on. I didn't think to bring a flashlight. I had just violated the Scouts' main motto—be prepared.

But I didn't care. I had just discovered the base of the fence and the hole under it. I stuck my hand into the hole. A rabbit wouldn't have made that. It was too big. The space was about three feet across. Big enough for a 10-year-old boy to crawl through.

The hole swung upward to inside the fence. It was possible that Derek hadn't spaded out that hole, but unlikely.

I stopped. There was no use trying to dig further. I didn't want to break into the grounds of a mental hospital.

I turned around and faced the woods. The shortest space between two points is a straight line. I walked with my eyes downward through the woods. That was the path he may have taken. It led straight out to Hillside Avenue. But he had no money. Where would he go? What would he do? He'd been gone for more than six weeks. How could he possibly survive for that long?

A flashlight blinded me.

"Hey, it's a kid," the guy behind the flash said. He lowered the light.

I looked at them, my eyes working to get right. Two men in blue. Their ID bars glinted with false promise.

"What are you doing here?"

"Who wants to know?"

"Little tough guy, huh? I'll pop you for trespassing, shithead."

Only a certain kind of new, young cop would talk that way, the kind that joined the force for the gun and the power. He thought the gun gave him the right to make threats, to sound like a B-movie actor. Stupidity was written all over this guy. He was especially thick.

Suddenly an idea occurred to me that was so ridiculous I thought it might actually work. I didn't know if it was The Weirdness or something else, but I was on fire with bad words.

"Arrest me."

The cops arrived at my side. They were a lot taller than me. I was 14 years old and five foot, three inches tall. They must have gone six feet, easy.

"What's your name, cop?"

"Paradiso, you little fucker. And your name is what? Whoremonger? Homobrain?"

"I can't think of a worse name for a cop. Who calls a 14-year-old kid a whoremonger? You must be one stupid cop."

I was baiting him and he was so moronic his mouth was closing in on the hook.

"Hey, Sal, let up on him. He's just a kid." That was the other cop, name badge said Mulligan.

"Pete, he's mine. It's my collar." His hand, as firm as a fullback's, grasped the collar of my button-down school shirt.

"I don't care about the collar, Sal. He's mocking you. You can't tell?"

"He's a little snot. And he's going to pay."

"For what? Walking in the woods?"

"We're at Creedmoor, Pete. The kid is trespassing."

"That's right, screwhead, I'm trespassing."

Paradiso's hand tightened on my collar. His hands, slimy with wood grease, rubbed against my neck.

"You stink to high holy heaven, Paradiso. What bar they have to haul you out of to get you down here?"

"That's it, you little shit! I'm taking you in!"

His fist met my eye, not in a good way.

"Sal, are you crazy? He's a juvenile!"

"I don't care! Any kid who can talk like that deserves a punch."

Paradiso pushed me out of the woods and toward Hillside Avenue, where the car's red top was whirling like the teacup at an amusement park.

Despite the pain of the slug, I was smiling. The Weirdness had broken through the wall and was enveloping me.

"Hey, Paradiso. You forgot to frisk me. You didn't follow police procedure. What are you, just out of the academy? I could have shot you twelve times before now."

He pushed me down in the dirt and frisked me as I lay on my stomach. He came up with nothing but my house keys and John Adams High School ID card.

"Harold Schreiber, you're in a shit storm of trouble," Paradiso declared.

"I don't think so."

Paradiso gripped me by the right shoulder. Mulligan sighed and took my shoulder on the left side. I looked up at them. They were both young, not much more than 22 or 23.

Paradiso pushed me against the trunk of the car, cuffed me. Shoppers walking by on Hillside stopped and gawked. The red light from an enormous drug store lit up my face for the pedestrians. I laughed like any two-bit punk would.

As I got paraded through the precinct house, cops looked up from their desks with something resembling surprise. Even in this town, the arrest of a 14-year-old was a little different. My black eye raised a few eyebrows too.

Mulligan peeled off as soon as we walked through the room. At the booking desk, I looked at Paradiso's face—still angry. A detective walked by, crisp in a smooth-looking suit. The handcuffs were a little big on me, but my arms were pinned back and it didn't feel good.

"Hey, Sal," the detective said.

"Yeah?"

"This kid's an Eagle Scout."

"Wha? How do you know?"

The detective pinched my shirt collar. "See this little pin?"

Paradiso, eyes gunning all over the desk for the right papers to fill out, looked up, his eyes slightly unglued.

"Yeah. So?"

"It means he must have done something really bad for you to cuff him and arrest him."

"Trespassing. At Creedmoor."

"You've got to be kidding me, Sal."

I turned my face away so Paradiso couldn't see me smile.

"I'll add assault too."

"It looks like he was the one assaulted."

"I got it covered, Detective."

The detective rolled his eyes and walked away. I was counting on being arrested, so I was glad he didn't make more of a deal about this.

We proceeded with the arrest paperwork.

I was taken to a juvenile holding cell. A guard stood outside. She looked pretty tough, with close-cropped hair and lots of muscle. Her name was Kingaski and she must have moonlighted as a wrestler on the pro circuit.

"We're going to call your parents, kid," Paradiso said.

"I want to make a phone call."

"We call your parents first." If my parents were called first, my idea would fail.

"No. You arrested me. I'm allowed a phone call."

Everything in my plan depended on the outcome of this confrontation.

"You're just a kid. Who you gonna call?"

"A friend."

"Who?"

"I have a right to call somebody."

Paradiso stared at me through the bars. He wanted to tear me apart. And he could have, too.

"You make me sick, you little snot."

The guard, her eyelids fluttering, spoke up. "The kid's within his rights, Sally."

Sal yelled, "OK, OK!" He gestured to Kingaski to open the cell. "Take him to his little phone call," he told her and walked away.

"I'm calling your parents, Schreiber."

Kingaski and I walked down the hall to a black phone on a desk. There were no other juveniles here this night. Our shoes echoed off the walls of the empty cells.

Kingaski stood over me as I made the call.

The phone rang.

"Lee here."

"Mr. Lee?"

"Yeah?"

"My name is Harold Schreiber. You know my mother, Ruth."

"Yeah, so?"

"I've just been arrested for trespassing at Creedmoor."

Lee didn't get it right away.

"That's pretty ordinary."

"My brother was committed there. He escaped about six weeks ago."

I didn't want to say any more because I didn't want to tip my hand to the guard.

I wished I could see Lee's face. I tried to imagine his eyes as he started to understand.

"Where are you?"

"612th Precinct. Can you come over?"

The guard intervened. "That's enough, kid."

"I gotta go, Mr. Lee. Come fast."

My parents arrived about 15 minutes later. I was sitting in the back of the cell, feeling the cool concrete of the wall. I wondered if Derek touched the walls of his cell too, exploring, trying to learn something from his environment. Or did he sit there and methodically sketch out his escape?

Lee didn't seem within 20 miles of there.

"What did you do?" Mother demanded. I shouldn't have expected a hello. "What shame have you brought on me now?"

I stepped up to the front of the cell, thrusting my black half-moon eye in front of me like Exhibit A.

My mother stepped back. "Oh my God. Have you been fighting?"

"I just went for a walk." I was pushing the Boy Scout ethic to always tell the truth.

My father's wood crate barrel shoulders sank a little. He sighed, but he was still level-headed, thinking about the next step.

"Let's get you out of here, Harold."

Kingaski silently opened the cell. I stepped out.

Mother slapped me hard on the face. I took it silently and looked away. Thankfully it was on the other side from the black eye.

"You're a disgrace!"

My father took my shoulder like he was a cop and walked us ahead of Mother. She hustled to keep up.

The three of us walked through the islands of cops sitting at desks, processing arrests or just drinking coffee. I was more upset by Lee's failure to come than Mother's slap.

I started shuffling, trying to slow down our pace, hoping, hoping, hoping that Lee would arrive. The double doors to the station house were 100 feet away.

I stared at the darkness outside. My face started to burn from the slap. The black eye felt like a piece of burned meat.

Through the doors there was a burst of lightning. Two men rode through the opening. One was wearing a plaid sports jacket, loud, that didn't match his tie of big red boxes. The other, with jeans and a huge belly covered by a lime green button-down shirt, had a camera. A news camera.

Steve Lee didn't say anything, just pointed dramatically and the photographer snapped off a half-dozen shots with the three Schreibers coming toward the door.

Lee walked up to me, said, "Hi, Ruth. We have to talk to Harold here."

Mother tensed up again. She felt assaulted on all sides. If this kept up, someone was going to get seriously hurt.

"Steve, what's this all about? What kind of trouble is Harold in?"

"That's the story, Ruth. He's not in trouble at all. It's everybody else who is."

"I don't understand."

"You hungry, kid?" Lee asked me.

By this time, some of the cops were sort of aware of what was happening. The desk sergeant yelled, "Get the hell out of here!" Ah, the charmers of Queens.

"I'm pretty hungry."

"Let's get some dinner at the T-Bone Diner on Queens Boulevard. All of us together."

The front page of the *Long Island Press* the next day had an eight-inch picture of my parents and me coming out of the station house. I was leading with my shiner. Mom and Dad looked stunned and uncomprehending.

"COPS NIX SCOUT'S SIB SEARCH!" I love the New York tabloids.

The subhead underneath explained it better: "Kid Hunting For Lost Brother Arrested."

I spilled my Eagle Scout guts to Lee and he digested it all. The story had everything I told him. The incompetent psychiatrist Pitsky, Derek's escape, the lack of follow-up by the cops to find him, my effort to locate him, my discovery of the little tunnel under the fence, Paradiso's confrontation with me, and the cop's very solid punch.

The next day was even better. The *Post* and the *Daily News* both covered the story on Page 3. The *Times* had me on the front page of its city section. The television stations followed—local channels 2, 4, 5, 7, and 11 all did short features on me. Derek was hot.

Mother and Father were bewildered by all the attention at first, but Mother got used to it, fast. The mayor called and told my Mom that he was going to get more men on the investigation. All the charges against me were dropped.

She talked about the mayor's call for days. The mayor called her!

Our state assembly representative promised to investigate the escape and the anemic recovery effort.

Mother gave interviews on her living room couch, with me sitting next to her. She served tea and coffee and cookies and acted very polite, yet quietly pained. She wore a black dress and teared up a little when she talked about Derek. She pointed to my black eye and the red area where she slapped me and said the cops had done this to her son, her little Eagle Scout. And all I was trying to do was find my brother. Oh, she was good and shameless. The reporters and camera men loved her.

I was glad about the attention for Derek's sake, but the media people wore me down. I just wanted to find Derek. I knew this would help, this was the original idea behind getting arrested, but I just wanted to get my brother back and re-enter my bubble as a kid. The Weirdness was coming in hard now, and I felt crowded. It was easier arguing with Paradiso and getting arrested than sitting through interview after interview with blow-dry, phony TV reporters.

Ruth was making noises about pursuing a civil suit against Paradiso for hitting me, but I asked her to quit it. The cops were already embarrassed and angry. We needed them on our side as much as possible and a lawsuit would make things much worse between us. I lied and told Mom that the punch wasn't that bad.

The manhunt was on. Cops scratched through the woods around Creedmoor, fanned out all over Hillside Avenue and the surrounding neighborhoods. The police visited local churches to see if a kid had stopped by for a meal. They talked to restaurant owners to find out if Derek had poached discarded food from their back alleys.

The cops checked the train stations at Jamaica, near our house, and Penn Station in Manhattan. They talked to the Port Authority Bus Station clerks, but I wondered why they bothered. Derek had no money on him. Where would he get the cash to buy a bus or train ticket?

The massive response effort went on for two weeks. They came up with nothing, zero, zip, nada. The Weirdness was working overtime on this case.

The media quickly lost interest, as they are prone to do. The heat lost, the police quietly cut back their efforts again.

I wanted to go back to my old life, but it was very difficult for me to accept that Derek had completely vanished. The fact of his disappearance bent reality so severely for me that I was very troubled. How could this be? It was a constant pain in my head.

I tried to carry on like usual and go to school and do my homework and Boy Scout jobs, but I felt like a ghost of myself.

One night, getting on into December, with no one home, as usual, I walked into my room and he was there, sitting on the bed, his feet on the brown carpet. It was like getting hit with the hammer of Thor.

Derek had dyed his dark hair white-blond, a strategy right out of *The Outsiders*. I had read it in English class the previous year. Ponyboy had used a dye job to hide himself from a world hunting for him. My brother was proving himself more clever than anyone had imagined.

He wore a thick black leather motorcycle jacket with metal zippers on it, making him look much older than his 10 years. His eyes were rimmed red and his cheeks were so awfully skinny. Worse, his nose had a deep red groove running along the slope. It was a good trick. Make an obvious scar, so people will look at you, but never connect you with a missing kid from a mental hospital.

We didn't say hello. We just looked at each other in recognition.

"Where'd you get that scar?" I asked, even though I suspected a bad answer that would confirm my fears about his mental stability.

Derek laughed. "I made it myself. Stole a big steak knife from a house store."

I stood in my doorway, unsure of the next move. "Where'd you get money to buy that jacket?"

"Stole it, you stupid fuck. Just ripped it off the rack and ran."

I didn't like his tone for a lot of reasons. An insult from your brother can wound you like no other. But besides that, there was a lot of aggression in his voice, especially from a 10-year-old kid, and I had a bad feeling The Weirdness was taking us in its grip.

"How are you eating?"

He smiled at his own cleverness. "Bakeries toss out a lot of day-old bread. Seven-Eleven is good too. I can eat a Twinkie in the back in like five seconds."

I decided to sit down on the bed, acting as if Derek was my brother and we were just having a good old-time conversation.

I stared at my Boy Scout merit badges. They couldn't help me now. Derek stared at them too for a second or two. They may as well have been from Mars when it came to this meeting.

We stayed focused on the wall and talked, not looking at each other.

"You're a good little Boy Scout. Mom's bitch."

I tried to ignore that most horrifying of insults, but it made me flinch inside.

"Maybe you should think about going back to the hospital," I said in the most gentle voice I could conjure up.

"Hah! You crazy?"

"Mom and Dad are worried about you."

"That's a laugh, you little bitch. Mom doesn't care. And Dad's completely out of it."

"No, they're really worried."

He turned to face me.

"And you. You turned me into a clown."

"I was worried. I was trying to find you."

"I didn't want to be *found*."

"So, why'd you come here now?"

"You think it's easy with all the cops out there?"

"You fooled 'em, Derek. They've lost interest."

"There's still a few jerks after me."

I sighed, the kind of sigh when you feel you're in an impossible spot.

"What do you want?"

I didn't see it coming. I should have. The punch landed on my ear, mashing it against my skull. I fell over onto the floor from the impact. There was a lot of hate in that punch.

Derek was on top of me, punching me in the nose and the cheek where the cop had taken his pleasure. When brothers fight, a lot of times you're both holding back. Some of the fight is theater, some of it is just to prove who's the one on the top of the hierarchy. Neither of you fights with all the viciousness you're capable of, because you both know you're brothers to the end.

That wasn't the case here. Derek swung with everything he had. One of the zippers of his jacket cut open a piece of my face. He hit me in the throat, taking my breath.

I tried to get up, but he had me pinned down tightly. He hit me square on the forehead.

The Weirdness was rolling in like thick molasses now. I tried to ward off the blows, but Derek had anger and real madness on his side. I considered the situation in a microsecond.

I stopped being rational. I had to get up. I kicked my knees up into his back, rocking him forward, but not moving him enough. I turned onto one side and got enough room to push my arm up off the floor. Brother kept hitting me on the skull, in the eye, the neck, the jaw, but now he couldn't stop my 14-year-old body from rising.

I jumped up with him still half on me. He slid off my hip and now we faced each other like two boxers in the ring. I was damaged, but I could still punch.

Derek was panting with the effort. I tagged Brother with a hook punch in the stomach, took all the air out of him. Then I made a long arc of my arm and kissed his mouth with my fist. Blood came trickling out of the teeth, made little capillary streams over the lips.

He hit me with another couple of punches in the chest and the head, but he was losing power. I smiled, against my own instincts, and struck my brother in the nose, right on the fresh scar. Blood streamed out. I grabbed Derek by the throat and choked the air out of him. I threw him against the cork board with my merit badges. He grabbed me and we both fell into it and down on the brown carpet. The merit badge display exploded like a mini-supernova, the little awards flying outward into the air and down on the brown carpet every which way.

I sat up, exhausted, next to the wall where the merit badge board had been so nicely arranged. Derek's black jacket was against my arm. He breathed in short little gasps. Then in a sitting up position he punched me as hard as he could in the stomach. It wasn't an easy blow to make and he didn't have a lot of leverage.

But it surprised me and that's all Brother needed. I sank down a little toward the floor and he got up. He had taken a lot of punishment. Anybody else, they'd be face-down on the floor, not wanting to get up. But he was using The Weirdness, going with its energy. He stood up, his nose and mouth awash with glossy red blood, and stood over me.

I thought he would say something. This would have been a good moment for a little speech, like "Don't ever try to find me again." Or "Leave me the fuck alone."

But he didn't open his mouth. My brother just looked down at me, blood starting to run over the collar of the black leather jacket, and walked out of the house.

I thought about calling the police. Even if they did catch Derek, I wasn't sure he would or could really be helped. I had a feeling that Derek would take any capture very badly. They'd drug him up in Creedmoor and he'd become a zombie. He could eventually fake his way through the doctors' regimen again and look for another opening and find another way out of there. He escaped once and I realized, under the influence of many of his punches, that he knew the place as prison. And I might easily start another media circus that would do nobody any good at all, except my mother.

I went to the bathroom and cleaned up. I had a new shiner, with a stub of flesh opening in the middle, flowering a little glob of blood. I held my right index finger on the cut until it stopped flowing. Other than that, I looked OK. The cut from Derek's jacket zipper was relatively easy to explain as an accident playing football in the schoolyard.

After that, I found Mother's make-up kit and brushed a dull matte product over the black eye. I didn't want to deal with any questions from my parents.

The merit badge board was next. I tried to put them back in the exact positions I had them in, but I couldn't seem to get the badges in the right arrangement. They looked a little haphazard to me now, a crazy-quilt. I couldn't put my finger on what it was, but the board didn't have that perfect little symmetry it used to have. This issue would drive me a little nuts for the next four years.

I tried to do my homework but had a lot of trouble concentrating. I looked at the school books, but the sentences looked like Sumerian etchings from 5,000 years ago. Nothing was getting in.

I heard the front door swing open downstairs. Two people walked into the kitchen. Then a shout.

"Harold!"

I walked down the steps to the kitchen. My parents were on the opposite side of the room and stood at its edges, as if the linoleum was contaminated and they'd get infected with some terrible disease if they came any closer to the atrocity standing in the middle of the floor.

It was a half-gallon milk carton turned upside down on the floor, the top opened to make four corners so the carton could stand straight up. Milk was pooling into a white lake around the container.

"Did you do this?" Mother demanded.

I wanted to say, "Why would I do this?"

I decided to be Polite Harold, the Harold who had earned his Eagle Scout badge by appearing humble and polite and respectful to his mother, even though she had slapped him in a police station.

"No."

"Well then, who did?"

"I don't know."

"Don't lie to me, Harold! You're lying!"

Father looked at the milk and at me and he gave me a look that said, "I don't think you did this, but what can I do?"

"Derek did it."

The anger in Mother's face bubbled up like lava. She forgot her horror about the milk and walked through the lake like a soldier forging ahead through a swamp. Her hand came up to slap me right where Derek's jacket zipper had sliced through the skin.

The Weirdness took me in its grip. The hand came down. I speared it at the wrist, in mid-air.

She looked at me with disbelief. I said nothing, just held her arm by the wrist and stared at her with all the defiance I could muster.

She wriggled her hand out of my grip and ran off to the master bedroom, screaming, "Abe, our son is a liar! He's such a liar!"

Dad looked at me, said quietly, "Harold, better clean this all up." Then he turned to go to the bedroom to comfort his wife.

I sopped up the milk on the linoleum with an endless number of paper towels.

I would live in their house and things between Mother and Father and me would change. Mom never tried to slap me again, but she never stopped working on me either, trying to make me respectable in her eyes.

I knew Derek was gone, but I had a feeling The Weirdness would be staying around for quite a while.

HORROR HOUSE DETECTIVE

This town is what I call a tomato. She looks great on the outside, even beautiful at times. But when you taste her lips, it feels like somebody just died. You know she's going to dump you for some guy with a bigger clip of cash.

One tomato that came my way back then was college. I went to the local commuter university after high school, but I found myself gagging from the daily pecks it left on my nose and cheeks. So I dropped out to put down wood flooring and build houses. My dad ran the business.

We called it Queens Flooring—not too creative, but descriptive. Mostly, we laid down sub-floors and parquet wood floors as contractors to the main housing contractor. Occasionally, if a good property came our way, we built entire houses on our own and sold them on speculation.

Dad and I had been working together for about two years when we ran into a very weird piece of real estate. Derek was out there somewhere, had been for years, but I knew he didn't want to be found.

Mom wanted me to be a doctor. She shoved all this medicine crap at me in high school and I swallowed the stuff whole. Boy, did I take it.

At the local college, I loved my courses in history and English. One of my favorite classes was in the history of the city, from the streets to the newspapers to the politicians. We studied the big personalities, from mayors to publishers, preachers to sinners, great moralists to prominent deviants, who sometimes were all mixed up in one soul. I aced the course. It's important to know the enemy.

But then I ran into a wall called organic chemistry. In class the symbols and equations started coming at me like bees drunk on tequila. I wanted to stand up on my chair and scream my lungs out. I wanted to take a baseball bat to the chalk board. Instead I drummed my pencil on the counter in the lab and thought about how to get the hell out of there.

So Mom's dream came crumbling down. I dropped out of college. Only good thing about school was I met this nice Southern girl, named Ravidinsky. Polish. I'll get to her later.

I thought about joining the Marines. I grew up as we lost in Vietnam. It didn't square with my feelings about how things should go, to say the least. My history classes gave me a good grounding in World War Two. Now, that was a good war. The United States knew what it was doing then. The big Rambo Vietnam movie had come out about four years earlier. It gave me some ideas, which I had yet to realize. I was a young man and I thought defending my country was a job that needed to be done.

The local recruiter wanted me to sign up. He said I looked like I would make a good soldier. But I let my mother talk me out of it. Another mistake made because of Mom. I joined the United States Naval Reserve instead. It was a compromise I made on behalf of Mom. I got to do something for my country a weekend a month without obviously risking my life.

And I took up Dad's work. I was surprised that I liked it so much.

The reason I'm writing about this is what happened when Donny Troy tried to sell us on building a house on some property in the Gardens. The Garden district isn't like the rest of the city. The area's very pretty. The houses are set far apart. There's a large private park in the middle of the neighborhood, and football fields worth of green grass. The quiet would scare you. A lot of the big money boys live there, but it's still inside the city line.

I met up with Donny by accident at the T-Bone, the late-night diner. It's on the main boulevard, which runs like a giant knife wound through Queens. The T-Bone is about a ten-minute drive from my house in one direction and the Gardens are in the other.

We still lived in Ozone Park, in the Flats. The name says a lot about the neighborhood. The Flats is middle class, mostly row houses, some stand-alone homes. The kids played stickball in the street, and freeze tag and Johnny-On-The-Pony. Our house was on a corner lot. It was a little more expensive, a little better-kept than the rest. But it was still in the Flats and not in the Gardens.

Midnight, and my date had washed out. She was a girl from the local union office, Irene Something. Nice legs, but a little too tight in the brain. She called me at seven, when I had just come out of the shower. It had been a long, hot day on the job and I wanted to look nice for Irene. I had some pride. Irene told me she couldn't make it. Her girlfriend was in trouble. Like I couldn't figure out that dodge.

So I took a couple of quick pops at the bar down the street. The place bored me. The action on Thursday night was like nothing. Two old-time rummies were sitting at the end of the old oak bar drooling. Looking at them was fascinating. Like I told you, this tomato will break your heart every time.

I wasn't ready to go home and hear my mom snoring all through the house. And my dad, he might have been waiting up for me in the kitchen, reading the paper or drinking coffee. I was 23 years old; you'd think the old man would have let me alone. He didn't ask any questions, but he had this way of making me feel guilty just by looking at me.

The diner counter felt warm and uncomfortable. The air conditioning was out again. Early May, and we were having a heat wave. This tomato of a town gives you a slap anytime.

I was eating a bagel with a slab of cream cheese when someone's paw slammed into my shoulder. I don't like being touched. I wheeled around on the stool and was ready to hit the creep who started in.

"Schreiber! How is it you're so skinny, but you got those big arms?"

Even though I saw it was Donny, I still wanted to hit him. I don't like it when anybody calls me Schreiber. I have enough of a burden with Harold. Schreiber is over the top.

"I don't know, Donny, but either one is big enough to smack you right in the eye."

When we were in seventh grade, winter term, Donny had organized a bunch of boys to chase me after school. It had something to do with my last name. So I turned and threw a rock and hit Donny flush in the face. He rushed me, the other kids cheering him on. I rounded my fist at him like a comet, the shoulder following through, like Dad and the local boxing club had taught me.

Donny went down in the snow. He looked confused. I narrowed my eyes at Donny's crowd and pulled my fists up near my face. They walked off, quiet and dumb. After that, Donny made himself my best friend. Though we spent time together, I never let myself trust him. I already had a best friend. His name was Al. A man should not have two best friends.

"Very good, my man, very good. You seen your brother around?"

My brother was a running joke among people who knew me. It really frosted my mood.

"Cut it out, Donny. He's been gone for years. You know the story."

He got fake-sincere right away.

"All right, Harold. Can I talk to you about something?"

Ordinarily, this would have stood as an invitation for me to leave. But I felt trapped. We let these things happen, even if we don't want to admit it.

I could sense The Weirdness coming on, creeping up.

"I want to eat my bagel. Alone. Call our office in the morning."

"Schreiber, I've got a hot property to sell. I want you to see it."

I smiled, which scared him. Maybe because I had my hand curled into a fist when I said it.

"Call me Schreiber again, Donny."

"What is it with you? That's your name."

"My name is Harold. Just leave it at that."

He made a mock bowing gesture. "Yes, my lord."

"What do you want?"

"In the Gardens there's a house. Beautiful old place. It's on a corner lot, set off from the other houses. Lots of grass on all sides. But the owners let it go. A guy named Craft is representing the family. They're tired of the property and they'll sell it, cheap. I'm advertising the house in the paper, but I'll give you a crack at it."

I knew the Gardens pretty well. Dad had built two houses there, and laid down floors for a half-dozen more.

"Nothing in the Gardens sells cheap. What's the address?"

"1236 Yale Place." The original developer had named the streets for Ivy League schools. He thought that would attract the snobby rich. What a jerk.

I smiled again. "I know the place, Donny. It's huge and it's a total wreck."

"You and your dad can fix anything up."

"Donny, we'd have to knock it down to the foundation and start over completely. That's a lot of money right there."

"But this deal is perfect for you guys."

I took a bite of my bagel, got cream cheese on my chin. I wiped it off with the paper napkin and took a quick load of my coffee.

"You don't need me, Donny."

"Come on, Harold. Come see it with me. I'll buy you a steak dinner."

"I want New York Strip, rare and bloody. And I name the place."

"OK."

"And we both bring a date."

"OK, OK. Let's go."

"Let me finish my bagel and coffee."

We drove our own cars to the Gardens. I didn't want to be stuck in a car with Donny.

Not only was the house at Yale Place a mess of falling gables and crumbling brick, but it seemed as if the city had abandoned the place too. The normally reliable orange street light was busted out and had never been replaced.

The structure was three stories high and it was a beauty when it had first been born into the world. But now, it looked like an old hooker dressed in rags begging on the street.

Donny was out of his car first and working on his sales pitch before my engine had even turned off.

"You're gonna love this place, Harold."

"Donny, cut it. Tell me why I should like this deal."

He simultaneously gestured and hustled to the front door. The door had ruts punched in the wood. I was thinking that some kids must have taken some shots at the door, with something heavy. It could have been a tire iron.

Donny fumbled with the key and the lock resisted his advances. The key stuck in the lock and wouldn't move.

"Just give me a sec, Harold."

"The lock's frozen. You'll need to bust it out to get in."

"No, I can get in. I did it this afternoon."

After five minutes of time I could have better spent staring down my father, Donny still hadn't opened the lock. He kicked the door.

I found a fallen brick in the hedge next to the steps leading up to the front porch. Donny saw me and stepped aside, a little mad about what I was going to do, but shamed into letting me do it. I slammed the brick down on the knob and it broke off. The inside piece fell the other way and the lock was broken.

The house wasn't a house. It was more like a random arrangement of pieces of wood. There were holes in the floorboards. The staircase had a banister but no steps. You could see into the basement from the foyer. It looked like a black hole.

Donny sprayed his flashlight in front of him. He stepped into the kitchen, the flashlight guiding us. The floor was mostly intact. It was white marble, almost certainly northern Italian.

"Look at this floor. It's gorgeous!"

"It also has mouse droppings."

"That can be cleaned up easily."

The floor under Donny buckled a little. He re-balanced himself like a subway rider.

"Donny, this house is unstable. And we should go."

"There's something else I want to show you."

Through a long hallway, Donny's flashlight escorted us into the library. We walked on the sub-floor. The fine oak that must have been here had probably been stripped out long ago.

The library was bigger than my house. Thousands of moldering books still stood on the shelves. Finely crafted chairs were placed in a square in the middle of the room. The chairs had been lubricated with water and mold. The fabric on many of them had been eaten away, revealing the wood foundations underneath. That anyone had been allowed to let the chairs go to this level of degradation offended me.

Thousands of newspapers were stacked around the room as well, tied in bundles. The piles varied in height. Some went to six feet. Others were about two to three feet high. It seemed as if the owner couldn't decide that the papers should have a uniform height. The stacks looked like little newspaper families waiting for the bus.

A lot of the newspapers were wet too. On the far side of the room, several of the piles of newspapers had fallen off a book shelf. The books and papers were all mixed together in a soggy, pulpy mass. I could hear water lapping somewhere in the room.

The library had a puddle in it somewhere among all the papers, which was eroding the wood floor.

The room reminded me of a pair of guys I had read about once. I think they were called the Collyer Brothers. They collected newspapers for years, decades, until their whole house was filled with papers. My father talked about them when he walked into a house that wasn't neat enough for his taste.

I heard something breathing behind the desk at that end of the room. The Weirdness was here.

"You hear that, Donny?"

"Yeah. It's probably a raccoon."

"It sounds a lot bigger than that. Let's get the hell out of here."

"You haven't seen the recreation room. It was a palace."

He took a step deeper into the library. The thing behind the desk rocketed past the chairs. It knocked over Donny and his flashlight. I was standing next to him, so I fell over too.

As I scrambled to get up, I heard the thing roar and tear into Donny's chest.

"Jesus Christ, Harold! Get this thing off of me!"

In the dark I couldn't even see the thing's head. I tried to find the flashlight.

"Harold, help me!"

I dipped around the floor and picked up the flashlight from the moldy carpet. I put the light on Donny. The thing that had knocked us down was trying to eat Donny's face. Its head looked like it had been wrapped in newspapers. But I couldn't spend much time thinking about appearances. Donny was screaming. Blood ran down his face from his forehead and cheeks.

The light stopped the thing from chewing on Donny's head. It crouched and stared at me. The creature, or whatever it was, seemed to be covered in newspaper. Headlines and sentences and photographs ran over its body like they had been tattooed there. The paper was wrapped tightly around its whole body, from head to toe, like a mummy. He had long fingernails, so long they curled into claws. The beast lunged and took me down too.

I jammed the flashlight in the mummy's jaw. It clawed me on the cheek. I hit it in what I thought was the area of the ear. The mummy fell back, breathing in that heavy way again.

Then the bastard ran for me and tried to leap on my chest. I ducked and used its momentum to throw it against the wall of books. The sound of the impact was like a rifle shot.

The heavy breathing started again. The sound trailed away from us. I used the light to try to get a line on the thing, but whatever it was had retreated to some other part of the house.

I didn't hear Donny. I found him with the flashlight. Lying on the floor, he didn't look like he was having a good time. Blood was trailing from his eyes. There were bite marks through his shirt, exposing the flesh underneath. Chunks of flesh had been dug out of his chest.

"Donny?"

I felt his wrist for a pulse. I thought there was a faint one, but I remembered I was no doctor. Organic chemistry class had taken care of that.

My next thought was: "How am I going to explain this?"

Donny groaned.

"Donny, I'm going to get help."

He turned over and curled up his knees as if to get a better sleeping position.

"Donny?"

I turned Donny so he was lying face-up. His cheeks had sunk in. He lay there very still, among the wet carpet, the piles of out-of-date newspapers and the collapsing bookshelves.

I tried chest compressions, but no air escaped from Donny's mouth. I made my hands into a single fist and hammered it on Donny's chest, for several minutes. I even tried mouth-to-mouth resuscitation, God help me, and listened for the sound of a breath.

Life comes in many colors, but death is usually black and white to the police. I sat in a steel chair in the 612th precinct house and thought of what I could possibly say to the two brick-like faces looking at me in the room. They were big seeds in this tomato of a town.

"Your buddy was torn up pretty bad," a tough-guy lieutenant said to me, as he strolled around the room. Under the fluorescent light, the lieutenant's badge looked like it was on fire.

"I know."

The lieutenant sat down across the table from me, while his friend, a sergeant, stayed standing. He had a look that said to me he already knew who had killed Donny. This conversation was just a little detail.

"Any thoughts on who did it?"

Many thoughts ran through my mind. I considered how they would react if I told them a clawed beast wearing wet newspapers like Saran Wrap had killed Donny Troy.

"There was a guy in the house."

"Yeah? What did he look like?"

"It was pretty dark. It was hard to get a good look. He had very sharp fingernails."

The lieutenant's contempt for me grew, if such a thing was possible.

"You're a funny guy, Schreiber."

"I don't like it when people call me that."

"Get used to it. You're going to be hearing it a lot."

I looked up at the ceiling.

"Nobody's going to help you up there," the other detective said. He leaned against a confident wall.

"I didn't kill Donny Troy."

"Hey, Brennan, you hear that? Schreiber didn't kill Donny Troy," the lieutenant said to the standing detective. "Let's just let him go now. The murder's been solved!"

Brennan laughed. He laughed in a way that chilled me. It was the laugh of a kid who had pulled a prank on another kid, maybe something like stepping on the back of his sneaker, or mashing a snowball in his mouth.

"Why would I come here on my own to tell you my friend was murdered? How come I didn't get in a car and drive all night to Pennsylvania?"

The lieutenant looked at me with narrow eyes. I looked at his badge. His name was Hope. This wasn't a good sign.

"It's original, I admit that. I can't figure it out. But I don't have to, Schreiber. We can put you at the scene. You've got claw marks on your face. So I figure you and Troy got into some kind of fight and he fought like hell. Troy's a big man, bigger than you. But you're stronger. I can see it in your arms. Cannons. What, do you lift weights?"

"I build houses. We haul a lot of lumber."

"We have a file on you. It says you were arrested nine years ago for trespassing at Creedmoor."

This was getting better and better.

"I was looking for my brother, who'd escaped. Which you guys weren't. And the charges were dropped."

"That was quite a stunt you pulled, getting the newspapers and TV people involved in the case."

I said nothing.

"Your brother involved in this?"

"No!" I shouted. "I don't even know where the hell he is."

"Your high school yearbook says you wanted to go into the Marines."

"How'd you get a hold of that?"

"The desk man went to your high school, graduated same year as you. He told us."

You have to wonder about a guy who remembers what other people had listed in their high school yearbooks.

"So why didn't you go into the Marines, Schreiber? Didn't think you could take it?"

It was my turn to look somewhere else again. I chose the door. I imagined the looks on the cops' faces if I said my mom talked me out of it.

"I got into college."

"But you screwed that up, too, right? Couldn't make it? So the frustration builds and builds through the years. And hanging around your old neighborhood doesn't help. So finally you just let it all loose on your buddy, your oldest friend."

"He's not my oldest friend. And you have a problem," I said. "That's the worst motive I ever heard."

"Give me time. I'll come up with a better one."

I'd had enough and I let them have it.

"I run a business with my father. He came up from the street. In the ghetto he grew up in, the streets stank from the factories and the garbage all year. When it rained, the sewage ran in the gutters. He worked in a slaughterhouse when he was just 14 years old. He has scars on his arms where the meat hooks got into him by accident. He had to drop out of school to bring home money to feed his nine brothers and sisters. My father worked too hard on me for me to throw it away on something as stupid as killing Donny Troy."

The lieutenant was unimpressed. He lit a cigarette.

"You actually say that like you mean it. He must have taught you how to lie good too. You have to lie in business all the time."

"You're on thin ice now."

"I'm on thin ice? I'm on thin ice?" I really punched his buttons there.

With the cigarette trapped between his teeth, Hope hit me in the jaw. I tasted the blood running out of the side of my mouth.

"Nice shot."

"I've got other ones."

"Me too."

Sergeant Brennan, leaning against the wall, came over and punched me in the chest. I wished I had a name like that.

Brennan's was a clean hit and it put me on the floor. I took a deep breath and stayed there for a minute. The concrete was nice and cool.

"Get up, Schreiber."

I did as I was told.

The most horrifying sight I caught from the holding pen was a single look from my father. Before the guard let him in to the cell, he took hold of my eyes and gave me a visual slap I'll never forget. I felt like a piece of tough meat in the slaughterhouse Dad used to work in as a boy. The tough meat gets the sharpest knife.

He motioned for me to sit down on the bunk. I did and he sat next to me. The light from outside the cell bounced off his hairless head. That head was a granite rock, the eyes like uncut diamonds. His arms and shoulders still contained generous amounts of muscle underneath his finely-cut navy suit, bought from a cousin's shop at a 20 percent discount.

We didn't speak for what seemed like a long time.

First thing he said was, "Your mother called the ambulance. She told them she's going into shock. They took her to Parkway Hospital for observation."

This was going to be rough.

"I put up the business and the house for your bail. The judge says you seem an unlikely flight risk. You did come in to the precinct house to report it. That carried some weight. We called Tommy Mallon. He's a very good man."

Tommy Mallon was an ex-cop and the family's lawyer. I wished I had a name like Mallon.

"Tommy says it's a good sign they're giving you bail."

"I've heard that."

Dad turned and faced me square in the bunk. "You know how much this is going to cost us?"

I gave the same look back to him. "No, I don't."

He looked at me for seconds and turned away. "I don't either. But it could be a lot."

"Dad, I did not kill Donny Troy."

He sucked in a deep breath.

"I believe you, Harold. But what were you doing with Donny Troy? He's an idiot."

"He wanted to sell us on a property at Yale Place."

"Harold, again, Donny Troy is an idiot."

"I get it, Dad."

"What was the property?"

"1236 Yale Place."

"The Paper Mansion?"

"The family was called Paper?"

"No, Harold. The family was named Drew. They died out fifty, sixty years ago. We call it the Paper Mansion because of what's inside."

"Yeah, that's pretty clear."

"Let's go home."

I sat in our living room for three days. Dad wouldn't let me go to work. The Weirdness was floating out there. I knew it, but could do nothing about it.

Al Manning, my best friend, had heard about Donnie and me, and he had called for me several times at our office, my dad told me. I wasn't allowed to call him back. Mom was terrified to be around me, so she stayed in the hospital. I wasn't allowed to go to the hospital either, because of Mother's delicate condition.

I read the papers, every single article, in every single section, except for the style page. I looked at the sunshine blaze through our picture window. I tried to ignore Mother's plants, which were set all around the living room shelves. I wished I had a dog. A golden retriever would have been good. It might have distracted me from the house on Yale Place.

I kept thinking about that night. It clawed at my mind. What was that thing that attacked us?

On the fourth day, I started pacing the living room. After two hours, I couldn't stand to even be inside my skin. I called Al. Al and I knew each other from first grade. He could punch and he could play basketball. We had talked about going into the Marines together. His mother talked him out of it too. What is it about these moms?

"Hey, Al."

"Hey, Harold. How are you? I've been trying to call you. I heard about Donny and you in the Gardens."

"I know. I didn't kill Donny. You know that."

"I wanted to kill him a few times."

"You up for a project?"

"What kind of project?"

"I need to go back to the house."

"That's crazy, Harold. It's a crime scene. I don't know who'll kill you first—the police or your old man."

"We have to go there. We gotta find out who—or what—killed Donny. That's the only way I'm going to clear this whole thing up."

"You want to go now? I gotta go to work." Al worked in his dad's concrete business. The Manning family's house and business was in the Flats, like ours.

"No, no. We'll go tonight. My dad's got a Masonic meeting. He won't be around."

"I don't know, Harold. This sounds nuts."

"I'll pick you up at nine o'clock."

"Harold!"

I hung up the phone.

Police tape is intimidating until you cut it with your mom's kitchen knife. I sliced off just two edges so we could wrap the tape back on the front door without announcing that somebody had broken into a crime scene. As Al and I felt our way through the hallway, flashlights in hand, I thought of that old movie where Abbott and Costello meet Frankenstein.

We walked through the long hall where Donny and I had been four nights before. The sub-floor squeaked as we went.

"This is stupid," Al whispered.

"I know."

"I can think of about a dozen other ways we could have done this better."

"Like what?"

"We should have called Joe and Howie, get the boys together for this."

He was right, but you get too many guys involved and things get loud. People talk.

The door to the library had police tape across it as well. I cut just enough. When we went in, the huge room felt empty.

A sound like a gentle whirlpool bath came to us from behind the stacks of newspapers.

"I'm glad I brought a gun," Al said.

"Me too." I didn't own a gun. Dad wouldn't allow one in the house.

We treaded very slowly and carefully to the whirlpool sound, weaving our way through the newspaper stacks. About five feet from the sound, the floor melted away like muddy sand at the edge of the ocean.

I took another step and my shoe almost came off in the muck.

"Al, don't move."

"What's wrong?"

"The floor feels like there's something wet and sticky on top of it."

We trained our flashlights on the muck. A pool of water, about three, four feet across stirred in front of us. There were a few things floating in the pool, dark masses of floating pulpy stuff here and there. They looked like newspapers, saturated with water.

"You gotta be kidding," Al said.

"Al, throw a penny in it."

So he did. It sank. I took a bundle of newspapers and threw it in the pool. It wasn't the quietest thing I ever did. The water and muck swallowed it up. A bright yellow pinprick of light seemed to be coming from the bottom of the water. We crouched down to look at the sinking newsprint.

"You see that, Al?"

"Yeah. Very strange."

A low growl traveled across the room. I pointed to Al to move away from the pool. You could duck-walk like Groucho Marx through the maze of newspaper stacks. Al sneaked behind the stacks about two feet away from the bookshelves. I headed in the opposite direction, around the other side of the library.

The growl grew louder.

We could hear the thing move toward the pool. He knew the territory and his walk was confident. The beast's footfalls made squishy sounds on the floor, as if he had shoes full of water. I don't know why I came to think of the creature as male, but it's my prejudice, I guess.

As he arrived at the little pool, he stopped making sounds. I was about 15 feet away from him, behind a stack of papers, with only my head above the pile.

The creature was sniffing and digging at the side of the pool. He seemed disappointed with something. Aren't we all?

Then he looked up, and fixed his eyes on me. I looked back. He squinted, like he wasn't pleased with what he was seeing.

I drew my mother's kitchen knife from my suit, as quietly as possible. I briefly considered throwing it at his forehead, but discarded the idea. If we engaged in close quarters combat again, I would need Mom's special, very sharp knife.

From across the room, I could see Al staring at the creature. Al's mouth was open wider than the time I saw him eat three hamburgers at once at the T-Bone Diner, and the gun in his right hand was shaking like the Tilt-A-Whirl ride.

Al's rattling attracted the creature. The thing turned from me and lunged at Al. He fired and missed. The beast landed in front of Al and got into a fighting crouch.

I jumped over the row of newspapers, turned on my flashlight and waved my knife. The creature turned toward me. Al steadied himself and got ready to shoot.

"Now, Rupert, you don't want to treat our guests in this fashion."

The three of us turned in the direction of the voice.

The voice came from the door of the library. I put my flashlight on it.

"Sir, I'm afraid you have temporarily blinded me. Please lower your flashlight."

I did, but then I had some trouble taking in the sight of the person behind the voice. He walked toward us.

The door was about 50 feet from where we were standing. It took the voice at least 10 seconds to get to us. The creature stayed in his crouch, eyes on Al, who kept his gun aimed at Rupert's newspaper head.

"Gentlemen, please put down your weapons. Rupert is quite harmless."

"He ate a good chunk of a man's face four nights ago. I think he's much more than that."

The voice arrived. And damn it all, he was also wrapped in newspaper, from head to toe.

"If someone came into your home unannounced, what would you do? Rupert," the second newspaper creature said, "go play in the pool." Rupert made one growl in protest, then jumped across the floor, dove into his little pond and disappeared.

"Who the hell are you?" I asked, gently.

"You, sir, have no manners. You trespass in my house, twice. You bring weapons. It's as if you are urinating in my very own fireplace. Tut, tut."

I was trying to listen, but the creature's appearance was dizzying. Even in the dark, with a simple flashlight illuminating him, this second thing looked as bizarre as Rupert. He had the shape of a man, but his skin was newspaper. Headlines and news stories and pictures wrapped around him. On his forehead, the headline described the election of William McKinley to the presidency in 1896. On the right side of his chest, two headlines crossed unevenly. One of the headlines featured a masthead of the old *New York Courier*, a newspaper that died in 1929, when it merged with the *Sentinel*.

Patches of newsprint swirled all over the thing. His stomach tended to focus on science stories, from Einstein's theory of relativity to the discovery of radium. A tennis champion from 1914 held his trophy in a photo stuck on the man's knee. From head to toe, he looked like one of those papier-mâché projects you did in first grade, with the paper soaked in glue and water and plastered on a balloon to make a model planet. My brother would have loved this guy.

I was a little jangled, and so was Al. The Weirdness was playing serious games with my mind. I drew in a breath, exhaled quickly like I was smoking. I tried to ignore the man's appearance. I looked in his eyes, which were like milk, with a black inky center, and talked to him like someone who had done a bad job on a building project. I knew how to do that.

"This house has been abandoned for years. Take a look around you, pal. The place is falling apart. You're missing floors, and stairs. The chairs in here are completely ruined."

"That may be true. Nevertheless, it is home to Rupert and me."

"That thing killed a man."

"Rupert was simply defending his territory."

"And who are you? Do you have a name?"

"Again, manners, you barbarian. We must work on those. Ah, well, I see I shall have to introduce myself. My name is Drew."

Al stepped into it. "Drew, you ever look in the mirror? You look a little different than most of us."

"Ah, yes, my appearance. I suppose I must explain myself to you two troglodytes."

"That would be nice," said Al, who could not stop staring. I was doing the same. I noticed that Drew had very sharp teeth, like Rupert, and claw-like fingernails—the longest I had ever seen—curling out from his fingers to at least six inches.

Drew sat down in a casual way on one of the rotting chairs and crossed his legs like a genteel talk show host.

"Sit down, gentlemen."

We sat. My chair was wet. I thought of my suit pants. I thought of the dry cleaning bill.

Drew continued to look at us, while Al and I trained our flashlights on his face.

"Please, sirs, lower your flashlights."

We complied. Drew continued to sit silently, letting the drama build. Al and I were starting to lose our patience.

"Who, what are you?" I said.

"I am a product of nature. I am the result of certain organic processes."

"That doesn't tell us a whole lot," Al said.

"Yes, of course. With my superior intelligence, I should have known you would not understand. This house is not just where Rupert and I live. It is our mother, our nurturer."

"What is he talking about?" Al shouted at me. I think he wanted to shoot Drew on the grounds of pomposity alone.

I remembered something from organic chemistry. "Drew and Rupert are brothers, right?"

Drew nodded.

"And they were born in the muck of that pool behind us. The newspapers were the material they were formed from."

"Now, I don't know what you're talking about, Harold," Al said.

Drew nodded in approval. "Harold, very good. A proper English name."

"I have to hear this Harold stuff from a guy made of newspapers?" I thought, and then tossed it away. We had bigger problems to figure out.

"Al, we're made of genes, DNA. That's the material nature had to work with in making us. All nature had to work with here was the paper in the house."

Biology class had been good for something.

"That's completely nuts," Al said.

"That may sound 'nuts' to you, as you say," Drew said, "but your friend is substantially correct."

"But why?" Al asked. "Why did this happen here?"

Drew shook his head as if he had suffered too much already in our presence.

"I don't know why," I said, "but I think I know how. There's an energy source feeding the pool. You remember, Al, we saw that yellow light coming from the pool?"

"Yeah," he said.

"That's the energy source. The heat from the pool creates energy. The heat acted on the paper in some way I don't understand. It created life."

"OK. I don't really get it," Al said. "But how do they eat?"

Drew rolled his eyes at the ceiling.

"The energy in the pool feeds them."

"How?"

"I'm not sure. I'm guessing they either drink from the pool, or absorb the energy in the water through their newspaper skin somehow."

Drew smiled a little newspaper smile and looked gravely at Al. I didn't like that look.

It told me something.

A low growl came from the pool. Rupert hurled himself out of the water, beads of moisture flowing off his newspaper head and shoulders. At the edge of the pool, he crouched and showed his teeth, which had the look of tiny knives. Veins of news stories flowed through his molars.

I cast my eyes on the rest of him with my flashlight. His calves were massive explosions of muscle. The shoulders were thick expanses of animal. Over the corded muscle ran editorials screaming for the United States to fight in World War I and 1920s news columns about immigration threats to the country. Rupert looked like a National Football League linebacker. If you put that together with the teeth and the claw-like fingernails, Rupert presented a very powerful front. He was much bigger than Drew. I looked him up and down. It's important to know as much about the enemy as possible.

When I scanned Rupert's neck, my flashlight dangled in front of his eyes. He stopped growling and put his hands in front of his eyes. There it was—a critical weakness of Rupert and Drew. I bet they were blind in light. They were born in darkness, raised in darkness. Light was useless, even dangerous to them.

Rupert didn't look happy. He looked at the library ceiling, escaping the beam from my flashlight. He leaped from the pool to the soles of my shoes in one quick move. I fingered Mom's kitchen knife. Al's revolver came out of his pocket like he was getting ready to shoot pigeons.

Drew saw it all and quickly moved to take back control of the situation.

"Rupert, this is not the time!" he shouted. I took note of the precise language Drew used. Perhaps there would be a time when he would unleash his brother on us.

"Al, may I call you Al? Al, violence is not the answer."

Al had the gun at his side, just out of reach of Rupert's long arm. I wondered who would be quicker. I didn't want to find out.

"As long as your brother is ready to fight, I'm holding on to this gun," Al said.

The heat in Rupert's head made him start shaking. The beast crouched on all fours just feet from Al and me. He got on his feet and brought up his chest like a chimpanzee getting ready for a fight. He loosed his arms like he was going to fly. His neck seemed to grow larger.

Rupert let go with an animal scream that bounced off the ceiling and ran around the walls. Al and I scrunched down like we were driving in a car that had hit a tree.

Drew sat there and let his brother scream. Low in his chair, Al kept the gun pointed at Rupert. I took Mom's knife out and grasped it firmly.

"Enough!" Drew yelled, cutting Rupert off in mid-yowl. Then Drew rose up out of his chair. He raked his nails across Rupert's newspaper face. Black blood ran out of the wound on Rupert's cheek.

Drew punched his brother square on the left side of his face. Black blood ran from the corner of Rupert's white eye. He collapsed to his knees, and his shoulders shrunk in on themselves.

"We can't do this now," Drew told the brother. Again, I noted the language. "We're going to come to an understanding with these men. And, my dear friend, you are going to stop this."

Rupert looked at his brother with what I understood to be anger and sadness at the same time. Even though Rupert was clearly bigger, Drew had something on him; he was more vicious in his elegant, refined way.

The beast stood up straight, his white eyes narrow and mean. He didn't like being second to his brother, that was certain. Then Rupert walked slowly from us, his feet squishing on the floor again. He walked to the door of the library, opened the door and left.

Drew sat down in his chair in the dark. Al and I kept our flashlights pointed at his waist, so we could see him without blinding him.

He thought he was again in command of the situation. I guess he was. I had made another mistake.

"Now, gentleman, we are quite finished, I believe."

"What does that mean?" I asked. Sometimes I ask a question because I want to find out more about that person, even if I already know the answer.

Drew rolled his white eyes. "You are to leave now and never come back. I did everything I could to keep Rupert from tearing you both apart. I succeeded this time. Next time, you will not be so fortunate."

"Wait a second," I said. "This isn't going to have a clean finish, like you want. The cops have got me hung up on a murder charge for what your brother did."

Drew spread his fingers out like five points and looked at his hand for a moment, as if he had just gotten a manicure. Al noticed it and looked at me. Drew's paper hand was drying out. That's why the brothers had to stay close to the pool. They needed water, just like we did, only in a more obvious way.

Putting his two paper hands together in the classic pyramid, I'm in charge style, the claw fingernails scraping against each other, Drew tried to take me down like a principal lecturing a seventh-grade kid who's just been caught throwing a spitball.

"Now, Harold, we have our own problems here. We have to worry about our survival, every day, and stay hidden, away from the armies of dirty men like you. Your world is not our world."

"I'm sorry," Al said, "but this isn't going to cut it for us."

Drew turned on him and I saw the power he had in him. I just didn't know where it came from.

"You two pitiable, misdirected fools are dismissed."

Mom's extra-special sharp kitchen knife would go unused this night.

"This isn't over, pulp man," I said.

Drew looked at me with that superior face again. I wanted to soak his smile in black ink.

"I'm afraid it is. Or you two will be dead. Now, go. Rupert is in a foul mood. You don't have much time."

I didn't see that we had much choice in the matter. I gestured to Al with my head that we should go. He had been ready to fight, and I was honored by his fierce drive to do the job. Al didn't like to give up, and this was giving up. I knew that we would have to come back, but we needed to plan things better. We had a better understanding of the situation. We would be better prepared next time.

Al and I got up. We walked to the library door. Al turned. "I just have to ask one more thing," he said.

"Oh, what do you want now?" Drew pouted.

"How is it that you know how to talk and your brother doesn't?"

Drew smiled. "I was born in paper and surrounded by it. I thought it would make sense to try to understand what the printed symbols on all these pages meant. I've read everything in this room. My friend chose another way."

On our way out the front door, Al and I heard a hissing sound from above. Rupert was crouched above the small space between the door and the ceiling, his feet on the door molding. He was ready to kill us, I knew. Both Al and I backed away from the door. We didn't want Rupert to land on us.

Al clicked the safety off his gun for the fourth or fifth time that night. Before he had a chance to shoot, I aimed the flashlight at Rupert's eyes and left it there.

"Ahhhhhhhhhhhhhhhhhhh!" Rupert yelled and threw his hands over his paper eyes without thinking where he was. He fell off the molding onto the sub-floor. I kept the flashlight on Rupert's face as we stepped over him.

"Eat some light, pulp man," I said. Rupert's voice turned into a demonic cry that would pierce your skin. It sounded like a rat after it's been poisoned.

He was still screaming in that unholy pitch as we walked out the door and off the property.

After all that action, I thought about getting a beer at some new joint I heard about on the boulevard, but I had to get to our house before my father did. Those Masonic meetings seemed to stretch on forever (What do they talk about for all that time? Creating a secret world government?), but I didn't want to take any chances. I took the roads very fast and Al didn't say a thing. I dropped him off, then sped home, thinking I would beat Dad into bed.

My old man was waiting for me in the kitchen. A cup of coffee sat in a saucer. The paper lay unread. Before I met Rupert, I thought that only my father could use a newspaper as a weapon.

He glanced at the headlines and dismissed them, pushing the paper to the far end of our kitchen table. The cup of coffee smelled very good. Dad slowly picked up the cup and drank from it, quietly. Then he set it down without saying a word. His eyes picked me up and drop-kicked me down a flight of stairs. He would have made an excellent assassin.

The silence was suffocating.

"You went out."

"Yeah."

"To the house."

"I called Al to get a drink. It's been a little slow here."

My father gestured for me to sit down next to his place at the head of the table. He folded his hands in front of the saucer. He appeared to stare at the table, but I knew where he was really looking.

"In business, it's important for partners to trust each other. Without trust, you have nothing. Don't insult me by lying."

"OK."

"Harold, why did you go to the house?"

"I don't think I need to explain myself to you."

My father came forward in his seat, again quietly.

"This isn't a case of you living under my roof and going out at all hours. I've never said anything about that. You're a man now. You show up ready to work in the morning, it's none of my business what you do at night."

"So why do you wait up for me?"

"Your mother worries when you'll be home. We lost your brother and she doesn't want to lose you. I'm a man. I understand these things better.

"But this is very different. You have a murder charge against you. You went to a crime scene. This is illegal."

"How do you know this?"

"One of the Masons followed you, at my request."

"You put a tail on me? Talk about trusting your partner!"

"You created the lack of trust in the first place, Harold."

"And what is it about the Masons? Maybe they really are a secret society, like some of those conspiracy nuts say."

My father looked at the floor. "We do what we have to do. This is survival."

It was my turn to look at the floor.

"Don't leave the house until I tell you to," my father said in a dry voice. "You're going to screw everything up."

The next day was torture by ten thousand ticks of boredom on the clock. Time itself seemed to stop. The sun came through the picture window. Men and women in suits walked to the train, for work. A few neighborhood kids in tee-shirts and ripped sneakers, cutting school, walked by on the way to the stores on the boulevard. One caught me looking at them. He gave me the finger. I returned his good will.

I ate breakfast. I ate lunch. I sat in the living room and looked at Mom's purchased sculptures of white porcelain dachshund puppies. She preferred them to real dogs.

My mother was still in the hospital, the only good news going. If she were home, I couldn't imagine the conversations we might have.

Finally, at one o'clock, something happened. A guy I had known from the local college stopped by.

He tried to knock on the door, but I had already opened it in an effort to creep out of the house and take a walk around the block. The boredom was eating at me.

"Hi, Norman."

"Harold, hey! You surprised me."

"I've been doing that a lot of that these days."

"What's that?"

"Never mind. Come on in. We can sit on the couch in the living room. My mother's not home."

"How are you doing?"

"I'm in my dad's business now. What's going on with you?"

"I'm majoring in accounting. It's solid."

"That's a smart move."

"I didn't come over to chat. I mean, I did, but I came over for a reason."

"Yeah, what's that?"

"Do you remember Helen?"

"No. Sorry."

"She was in sociology class with us."

"OK."

"She has cat's eye glasses. You borrowed her notes?"

"Oh, yeah. And I got a better grade on the final than she did. Now I remember, kind of. What's her last name? Wasn't she Polish, or Russian or something?"

"Ravidinsky."

"Helen Ravidinsky, that's it. Brown hair, brown eyes."

"Like you."

"Yeah. She was Polish, but she came from some screwy place. South Carolina or something like that."

"Right, Harold. She's got a little Southern accent. Her voice has a bit of a twang, but she's not one of these Southern-fried girls, if you know what I mean."

"You mean she's respectable."

"I mean she's from the South, but she's not really Southern. She asked me to give you this note. I ran into her on the train going from school."

"Thank you, Norman. You are a gentleman."

"What's that, Harold? I never heard you talk so politely."

"I picked it up from a guy I met. Strange guy."

"Strange how?"

"Strange enough."

"Well, Harold, I have to go. I have a class at 2 pm. Business statistics."

"Sounds like a barrel of monkeys."

Norman rolled his eyes. "It's all that and more."

He handed me the note and I walked him out the front door.

When Norman had left, I looked over the note from Helen Ravidinsky. The paper was folded ever so neatly in a blue card. I was glad it wasn't pink. This girl wasn't a delicate flower. The perfume on it was subtle and not overpowering. This girl had some class. I couldn't believe she was interested in me. When you get down to it, I'm a sweat bomb. I carry lumber. I put in sub-floors. I pour concrete. I work with construction unions.

The note told me that she had heard about the trouble I'd had with organic chemistry. She wrote that she had barely made it through organic chemistry, but she had passed. Helen was studying to become a nutritionist.

Anyway, Helen wrote, she didn't mean to go on, but she wondered what had happened to me after I left school. Did I want to meet her for coffee? She lived with her older sister in a neighborhood on the boulevard, just outside the Flats, and I could reach her at night at this phone number.

I was tempted to call her, but not with this trouble on my head. I put the thought of the Ravidinsky girl away, as much as I could. Now my clock was set back to boredom. There was an unfinished piece of chair waiting for me in the basement. Dad had a little workshop down there. So I closed myself off from the world and worked on cutting and shaping legs for the chair.

Dad came home early from a job, at about five o'clock. I heard him moving around the kitchen, making coffee and putting something in the oven for us to eat. I heard the phone ring, and let him get it.

About a half-hour later, he walked down the stairs. I tried to ignore him by concentrating on tapering one of the chair legs like the curve of a woman's calf. He tapped me on the shoulder.

"Hey, Pop."

"Hi." He was his usual cheery self. But under the circumstances, I didn't blame him.

Dad breathed in like he didn't want to get any more air. "There are some men here to see you, from the police department."

"Let me guess."

"Said their names were Hope and Brennan."

"I know who they are."

"They said someone broke into the Drew Mansion. The police tape was cut from the front door."

"Oh, hell."

"Oh, hell what?"

I suddenly remembered that Al and I had forgotten to re-attach the tape. We were so rattled by Rupert the Pulp Man's attempt on our lives that we left it dangling. Brilliant.

The detectives didn't wait for an invitation. They rumbled down the stairs, their feet smashing into the wood slats on the steps. My father turned toward them. His shoulders stiffened as if ready for a fight.

"Lieutenant Hope. Sergeant Brennan. Nice to see you again."

"Screw you, Schreiber. Now I got you on a murder rap and disturbing a crime scene."

"I would say the obvious thing, like 'prove it,' but in this case I don't think it's necessary."

"No, it's not," said Hope, "because you're freakin' guilty."

"What do you want?"

My father looked at me, his mouth open. He seemed shocked by my lack of respect.

"We're going to the house and we're taking you with us. We're going to take fingerprints off the police tape, walk through the crime scene in the library and make sure you didn't tamper with the evidence. Then we're going to arrest you again."

The boys muscled my father out of the way by walking into him like he wasn't there. He let them, quickly stepping to the side, his powerful shoulders slumping.

"Let's go upstairs." Brennan walked up first, then Hope gestured for me to go. He followed. It's a classic restraining move—one man in front, one in the back. I gave Hope some mental credit. He wasn't a total idiot.

In the kitchen, the two men squeezed me between them, then began to walk me out the door. My father, having arrived last, got upset.

"My son is innocent until proven guilty. And he's allowed legal counsel right now."

Hope laughed.

My father then did something I never expected. "I'm going with you."

Lieutenant Hope looked like he had been stuck in the eye by a pencil. "What?"

Dad waved his finger at the men. "This isn't the Soviet Union. And you aren't the secret police. You're not going to haul my son off to some old abandoned house and shoot him or beat him up or do God knows what out there. I'm calling our lawyer. And I'm going with you to the Drew place."

When Dad said the Drew place again, I understood that I had missed a very big thing about this case. My history course from college had taught me something that was relevant to the Paper Mansion, but I had forgotten it, until now. And I was really angry at myself because I realized that the pulp man named Drew had lied about an important thing, and I hadn't figured that out in time.

Brennan grimaced and Lieutenant Hope fingered his gun. I wanted to tell my father right there, "You see the two brick-heads I've been dealt?"

"You can't, Mr. Schreiber," Hope said. "Harold is not going to be taken off to some dead-end place. He's going with us to the crime scene." Suddenly I'm Harold to these balloon faces.

"I... I don't trust you," Dad said. It took a lot for him to say that.

"We're leaving, sir," Lieutenant Hope announced, "and you're not coming with us."

"It's OK, Dad. It's better this way."

"I'm calling our lawyer, Tommy Mallon, and I'm going over there."

"I'm telling you, Mr. Schreiber, in the clearest language possible. You will be arrested for disturbing a crime scene."

"You can't do this, Lieutenant. I'm getting the lawyer on the phone."

"You do that."

We walked out of the house, the two police goons close by my arms, with Dad furiously dialing the phone for Tommy Mallon.

They pushed me into the back seat of their car.

"Thanks, boys."

"Shut up," Brennan said.

"I love it when you talk to me that way."

He didn't say a word. I'd beaten him for the moment. While Hope drove, I fingered Mom's extra-sharp kitchen knife in my jacket pocket. They'd forgotten to frisk me. Despite my breezy attitude toward the cops, I was worried. This wasn't the way I planned to return to the Drew house. I had something very different in mind for dealing with the pulp men, and it certainly didn't involve these two knuckleheads. Again, we were going in unprepared.

By the time we closed in on 1236 Yale Place, the sun had melted past the horizon, trailing streaks of orange to the west.

"Here's the tape you cut," Hope told me as the goons muscled me through the door.

"You guys don't know what you're getting into."

Brennan punched me in the back of the head.

"What a great guy you are, Brennan. Will you send me flowers in the morning?"

He punched me again.

The house seemed even more dilapidated, even though Al and I had been there just the night before. The sub-floor sagged beneath our steps. A smell of deep decay seemed to envelop the hallways.

The dark and the stench and the falling-apart house seemed to unnerve my police friends a little. They were quietly trying to step on stable ground. I took the opportunity to say something.

"This is a mistake. We should be coming in here with a SWAT team. We need automatic weapons, flash grenades, night vision goggles."

"You need to seriously shut up, Schreiber," Hope said.

"Floodlights. We need floodlights."

"Shut up."

"Just remember that I'm warning you."

Brennan turned to me in the dark and hit me in the stomach with a very angry fist. I started to go down. Then Brennan clubbed me on the cheek with the flashlight. I landed on the sub-floor.

There was a gash on my face. Blood was flowing generously down my face to my neck. The bastard had ruined my shirt.

The blow to the stomach had left me pretty unbalanced. The two cops sort of half-carried me by my elbows to the library, the scene of my crime.

Brennan was elected to open the door to the library, while the lieutenant held me up. He brushed away the police tape I had cut and failed to re-attach to the moldings by the door. Once we stepped inside, the room was possessed of a profound silence.

Brennan and Hope walked over to where they had found Donnie's mutilated body. They dumped me into one of the ragged chairs. My head was full of stars, but I cared a lot about what was going to happen next. I just couldn't move very well.

The detectives pointed their flashlights at the outline of Donny's body and knelt down to inspect it further. I didn't understand what they could be looking for. But it didn't matter.

There are moments in our lives when we realize with great insight that we have made a terrible mistake. Unfortunately, these often take place when we are in mortal danger. There's very little we can do about making corrections at this point.

I realized this as Rupert and Drew leaped from the upper shelves of the library onto the heads of the two detectives.

Brennan's flashlight came tumbling down. One of the pulp men dug his long nails into Brennan's back and knocked his head on the floor with great enthusiasm, over and over. Brennan was screaming. The Weirdness was all around me now, in my head and taking over.

The other pulp man was punching and biting into Hope's shoulder and chest. Hope was screaming too.

Off in some distant land, I observed with clinical detachment that these two men were going to be killed. After that I would be killed. If I somehow got out of the library alive, I would be arrested for killing the two detectives. No matter how you looked at it, I had to keep them alive, despite the great odds against this outcome. So I had to organize myself quickly. I picked up Brennan's flashlight and pointed it like a gun at one of the pulp men.

From the chair, I shouted out, "Franklin Hancock Drew, Junior! You urinated in your fiancée's fireplace!" The man pummeling Brennan stopped and looked my way. Brennan wrestled with himself on the floor and moaned, then grew silent.

I popped the flash in the creature's eyes. It was Drew. He covered his face. Rupert stopped killing Lieutenant Hope for a few seconds as well.

"What did you say?" Drew asked.

"You told me your name, Mr. Drew. But I didn't realize you were telling me your last name. Your full name is Franklin Hancock Drew, Jr. You inherited a newspaper from your father and published it until 1929. It was called the *New York Courier.* You were a big-money guy, in high society. But you got very drunk one night and came late to a party at your fiancée's house. You urinated into a roaring fireplace, in front of the whole crowd. You disgraced yourself and embarrassed your fiancée. She broke off the engagement. Then you ran your newspaper into the ground with wild spending sprees and expensive publicity stunts which didn't pan out."

I had distracted Drew long enough. He liked hearing about himself. Brennan recovered a little bit. He shot Drew and hit him on the side of the chest. Black blood flew outward like little meteors. I took a little of it on my lips. It was like eating oil.

Drew staggered a little, but remained standing. Brennan shot him again, this time in the leg. Drew turned and clawed the gun out of Brennan's hand. Brennan gasped. Drew turned Brennan around on all fours and grabbed his head with both forearms. He was going to break the cop's neck.

Desperate to save the brick-head's life and mine, I clubbed Drew with the flashlight. He didn't see it coming, so I was able to knock him off Brennan.

Rupert had torn gashes in Hope's chest and leg. Hope was lying on the floor, helpless. The great beast was going in to the lieutenant's face with his teeth, like he had done to Donny. So I ripped Mom's kitchen knife out from the pocket of my jacket and stabbed Rupert in the back of the neck.

We heard the rat-being-poisoned scream again, but Rupert wasn't dead. He was very strong. He rolled over onto his back with Mom's kitchen knife still in him. So I brought the flashlight down onto his face, again and again, the light blazing. He screamed and screamed, like a car alarm that won't turn off. I slammed him hard a dozen times with the light driving into every corner of his eyes, and he finally shut up.

"Pulp boy, you are a pain in the ass!" I shouted at Rupert, even though he was probably dead or dying.

A voice shouted at me, very angry.

"You're a barbarian, Mr. Schreiber!"

The voice wanted my attention.

I turned around, on my knees, knife-less. Drew stood above me a few feet away, a little hunched and bleeding that bizarre black blood, but standing, which meant he could do quite a bit of damage.

I stood up.

"You're right about all that, Mr. Drew. But you let your own son kill a man the other night. You talk about barbarians."

"Mr. Schreiber, despite your crude appearance, I am impressed at your deductive powers. How did you know?"

"No grown-up brother would let another brother treat him the way you did last night. But a son will take a lot of crap from his father. Believe me, I know."

"You should see the way I'm going to treat you, Harold. Just like you treated my son."

Hope let loose a shot from the floor. It took off a piece of Drew's shoulder. Splintered newsprint flew into my face. Drew staggered and laughed.

Then he put his hands on my throat and shoved me up against one of the newspaper stacks, which fell over. Hope shot his weapon again, but missed. Brennan started firing too, but we were lost in stacks of newspaper.

I fell onto the stack, Drew over me. I tried pinching the underside of his wrists with my thumbs to open up his hands, a trick that works in ordinary fights, but not with Drew. I kneed him in the crotch, which stopped him from choking me long enough for me to slug him in the throat. It felt like layers and layers of tissue paper.

Drew, reflexes in control now, brought his hands to his own throat. I hit him in the stomach. It was like punching a phone book.

Drew, laughing and bleeding black blood all over my pants, punched me flush on the mouth. The dry cleaning bill for the pants kept going up. I tasted the old paper of Drew's hand on my tongue.

Somebody turned on the lights. How did the lights still work in this creeped-out joint? Drew screamed and covered his eyes. I threw him over and punched him in the throat, which seemed like the softest part of him. He moaned and I hit him again.

"What's going on here?"

I stopped hitting Drew. "Hi, Dad."

I was almost embarrassed, like when you've been caught stealing from the liquor cabinet when you're 16.

"Oh my God. What is that thing?"

"Dad, meet Franklin Hancock Drew, Jr., child of privilege, former newspaper publisher and now creature of the night."

"That doesn't even begin to sum it up, you pitiable lunkhead," Drew said, still covering his eyes.

Brennan pulled himself up into a sitting position. He was bleeding badly. Chest heaving, but aiming the gun as steady as he could at Drew, the brick-head didn't know when to quit. I admired him suddenly.

I still needed a few things from Drew before Brennan shot him, so I said: "Why did you try to kill us the other night? Why did you have your son kill Donny Troy? You could have hidden away when we came in."

"You trespassed, you big blob of meat. We had every right to kill you and your friend. You were in my house!"

"So why didn't you try to kill the cops when they came in the first time to investigate the crime scene?"

"I'm not stupid. We covered up the pool with newspapers and hid."

"So why not just hide again when we came in tonight?"

"Too many people, too many questions."

"The history books say you were buried in Paris."

"The press can make up anything. Journalists are quite creative. I should know. I was born in New York. I wanted to be buried in New York."

"You're under arrest, Mr. Drew," Brennan said, weakly. I looked over at Hope. Mumbling, he was fighting to stay conscious.

Drew, still covering his eyes, said, "That won't be necessary, officer. You're going to be dead. As will be everyone else in this room."

Brennan shot at Drew twice, missing both times, but killing the overhead light.

Suddenly free from blindness, Drew jumped on Brennan again. The gun skipped out of the brick-head's hand.

I leaped over a newspaper stack and tried to pull Drew off the brick-head. Drew had been shot three times, but was still wickedly strong.

I had distracted Drew long enough for Brennan to hit him in his newspaper nose. That allowed me to get my arms around Drew's neck and push two fingers into his throat. He started to gag and rolled over. Then he put his hands together like a hammer and socked me in the chin.

Drew took me down on the floor and laughed that crazy laugh of his again. "First I kill you, then I kill your father."

Something broke inside me. I wanted to say, "Pulp man, you're dead," but the words didn't come out. What did come out was my right fist, slugging. I hit Drew in the face. I hit him in the eye. That staggered him and I rose up. He recovered, but somebody hit him from behind with a heavy object. Drew took it smack on the back of his head. I was pleased. In the dark, I could make out the outline of my father, holding a table lamp on the follow-through, his slaughterhouse arms still deadly.

I hit Drew flush on the nose. I bashed him in the space between his eyes. I hit him in the throat. He took it all in. Despite the pulp man's great strength, he was a little shaky.

"You common worm," he gasped. "You little nothing. You nobody."

I hit him in the throat again. I put everything I had into the punch. He went down, his knees buckling in a crazy-leg dance.

My father put a flashlight in Drew's eyes. The pulp man spoke something softly, as if to a lover. We couldn't hear it.

I withdrew Mom's kitchen knife from the back of Rupert's neck. I used it to cut up the cords holding the newspaper bundles together. My father understood and we took the cords to bind up Drew and Rupert both.

Rupert was almost certainly dead and definitely not moving. But we didn't want to take any chances. You should lock up every detail. You never know when some little thing is going to go wrong on you, like detached police tape. Dad had taught me that. Now I worry about the little details every day.

My arms were very sore and my hands felt like they had been iced in a meat locker, but we did the job. That's what Dad had trained me to do—always finish the work.

Brennan pulled himself up into a sitting position, leaned against a newspaper stack. He was bleeding and possibly going into shock. My father tried to comfort him, but the brick-head's eyes were going blank. Hope didn't look good at all. Every time he breathed, blood came out of his nose and mouth. I felt like I had just kissed another tomato.

In the pure sunlight, the house looked dried out. The wood had lost its flexibility. The brick was spewing red dust in the warm wind. I pointed and the wrecking ball took its first swing. It didn't take long for the mansion to come down.

After the house was leveled and the debris cleared away, my father and I walked to the area that was the library. Drew's pool lay still. One of the science professors at my old local university said it was a geothermal vent.

To find out why anyone would ask that their body get dumped in a geothermal vent, I decided to try to find Drew's will. I looked for it in the New York Municipal Building's Hall of Records, the New York Public Library and the New York Historical Society.

I found Drew's will at the Historical Society archives. It took hours to find in the huge file about Mr. Drew.

The will contained Drew's dictation for the disposal of his remains. Drew had directed that upon his death his body should be delivered to the pool. At the time I didn't know if Drew knew what would happen to his body when it was dumped in the water. And the will didn't account for a son. Drew had no heirs when he died. So I wondered where the son came from.

At the Historical Society archives, I also found the architectural drawings for Drew's house. It clearly directed that the house would be built around the pool. The pool was a source of conversation and debate among Drew's friends, among other things. The historical record didn't indicate whether Drew ever put himself in the pool and bathed there.

The science professor had begged my father and me to let him study the pool. We listened, politely and patiently, and told him no. If it was possible to bury The Weirdness, we were going to try. Dad had the pool filled in with dense concrete, supplied by Al Manning's family business.

"There are some things you don't want to know," I told the professor.

However, there were still some important things I wanted to find out. So I went to the 612th Precinct to see the newly minted Lieutenant Brennan. The official police report had Brennan and Hope fighting off the two perpetrators and saving my father and me. That's the way things go in this tomato town. But I realized it was for the best. I didn't need publicity. I needed a girl.

The charges against me were quietly dropped. Everything was kept out of the papers. Hope survived Rupert's attack, barely, and would need months of rehabilitation. My dad sent him a big chocolate heart and lots of sports and bikini magazines.

The basement holding cell at the 612th Precinct was becoming quite familiar to me. I could trace the outlines. The thin bed was tight against the wall, the dark concrete cool even through your shoes.

The only change in the room was the five-foot-high plastic barrel tub in the middle of the room. In it stood Drew, handcuffed in the front like Houdini because his hands were too dangerous floating free. A metal ring pulled at Drew's waist, attached to a wall of the cell. The cops had set up some special rigging for their unusual prisoner.

The pulp man needed the tub of water to keep him from drying out. Brennan told me police-contracted biologists were putting nutrients into the water to try to replicate the nutrients in the pool in Drew's library, to keep him fed.

I saw that Drew's lethal fingernails had been cut to the very edge of his newspaper flesh, and his teeth had been filed down to little squares. That made me smile.

I was accompanied by Brennan, who told me the police doctor was giving Drew tranquilizers around the clock. He was partly human, and the tranquilizers seemed to work on him, a little. Even with Drew's hands and waist restrained, walled off behind ungiving iron bars, the cops took no chances with the pulp man breaking out.

"The tranquilizers should help make him somewhat agreeable in answering your questions," Brennan said.

We stood outside the cell. I couldn't stop myself from staring at his forehead, announcing McKinley's presidential win in 1896. History buff that I am, I wanted to read the story under the headline.

"Ah, it's the big block of meat, with his stooge. You sicken me," Drew said in a slightly thickened voice.

"I see you remember our last meeting, Frankie," I said, "with you ending up on the floor."

He splashed water at us with his handcuffed hands. We drew back and the water hit the floor. Even with tranquilizers in his newspaper veins, the pulp man was still pretty lively.

"You killed my son!" he rasped at me.

"Self-defense," Brennan said in a stiff police manner. Stitches tattooed his cheek, like mine. Brennan's breathing was a little shallow, but he was mostly whole.

"Why did you lie about that, by the way? Why tell us he's your brother?" I asked.

"You said that. I didn't. But it was a good way to obscure who we were."

The pulp man stood in the water, his shoulders bending suddenly down. He looked exhausted. "How is this going to end?" he said.

"We don't know exactly," the detective said. "We can't try you in public court. You'd cause a riot. This kind of thing throws society off-balance. We can't have that."

Brennan saw The Weirdness too and I was glad.

"Why is he here?" Drew said, nodding in my direction.

"I have a few questions," I said.

"You always have questions, barbarian."

"Always. There's no record of you having a son."

"I know what you are going to say. I did have a son. There was a quite beautiful common girl I met in Paris. I received the finest education there. I used to buy bread from this girl. She worked in a bakery, near my rooms. We spent some afternoons together, and some mornings too. She had my son, my only child."

"There's no record of him," I said.

"No, of course, there wouldn't be. I already had a reputation."

"According to the history, late in life you married a woman from the Lefaux family. They owned a European news service and several newspapers. They were very wealthy. How did you keep your son from them?"

"Things are easy when you are rich, you uneducated peasant. When he had grown up, I set Rupert up in one of my new mansions in New York. We gave him a management job at the *Courier*, under a different last name than mine."

"What happened to him?"

"Alas, he was killed in a fall from a horse while riding in the park. I had him buried near my father in the Green-Wood Cemetery in Brooklyn."

"So, how did he end up in the pool with you?" Brennan asked.

"Before I died, I had him dug up."

"I'm sorry?" I said, not sure of what I had just heard.

"You're slow, Harold, too slow. In the weeks before I died, I decided I wanted my boy with me, through eternity. A team of my people exhumed him and transported his body back to my mansion. They put him in the pool."

"So, you had no idea what would happen if you two went into the pool together?"

"I suspected the pool had interesting properties. There was that curious yellow light at the bottom. And it was warm all year round. I had scientists study its constituent elements. There was a thick, heated stew of oxygen and nitrogen and other minerals in there. But no, I did not know what was going to happen. I just wanted a final resting place that was interesting and comforting to me in life."

"But that didn't happen. You were given life again somehow. You came out of the pool with the same mind. But Rupert couldn't speak."

"Alas, something happened to him in the pool. He became something else. More of an animal than a man. But he was still my son."

"I don't get why the place was up for sale," I said.

Drew looked tired and sad. "We had a series of caretakers through the decades, after Rupert and I were resurrected. We needed a representative, to hide us from the outside world, to protect us. I had to defend the pool, at all costs. It was our food source. If we were discovered, we would die."

"So you had a caretaker recently?"

Drew sighed a long sigh. He was still the wealthy man of ease and luxury in his mind, far above peasants like us, with dirt under our fingernails at the end of the day. Drew didn't want to think about us, let alone answer our questions. The tranquilizer helped, though, making him somewhat compliant.

"We paid the caretakers a lot of money. We had four or five, I forget how many. I forget their names. But the last one, Craft, was not such a good employee."

"How's that?"

"Craft was not happy with his working conditions. I had grown tired of telling him to take care of the house, and watching out for Rupert. I was paying Craft a lot of money, too much money. But that wasn't enough for him."

"He kept the house functional for a while, right, like all the other caretakers? Craft paid the property taxes, paid the electric bill, kept the lights running for when he needed them on. But the place fell apart on you. You couldn't get repair work done. The contractors would see all those newspapers. They might find the pool in the library and there would be too many questions."

"I had to protect the pool. After some time, I cared about the pool more than anything. One must prioritize, after all."

"I gotta ask this question," Brennan said. "Why were all those newspapers in the house?"

"Rupert and I loved our newspaper, our wonderful and sacred *Courier*. We couldn't bear to part with any of the copies. Rupert collected them when he worked at the paper, kept them near us in the library. We continued collecting them after we came back out of the pool. We built a shrine, made of our newspapers, and then other papers—the *Tribune*, the *Herald*, the *Times*, the *Post*, the *News*. If the caretakers ever tried to throw them away, we would be angry."

"How did Craft feel about all this?" I asked.

Drew turned to Brennan. "Must I answer these ridiculous questions?"

Brennan nodded his head yes. Drew sighed again.

"Craft contacted a real estate broker. He said he was the selling agent, so he would get the money from a purchase."

"How did you find this out?"

"I read the newspapers," Drew said in his best superior voice. "They still come to the house. Craft made sure of that."

"You read the newspaper. What does this have to do with selling the house?" Brennan asked.

Drew looked besieged. I answered for him. "Donny Troy was representing Craft. He took out an ad in the real estate section of the paper to sell the property, but never told Craft. That's how Drew found out about Craft's move. He read about it in the newspaper."

"What happened to Craft?" Brennan said.

Drew stared at the ceiling. I knew that look. "I had Rupert take care of him."

Brennan and I looked at each other.

"Where's Craft now?" I asked.

"Drifting with the winds, fool. I'm tired of all your questions, Harold. Please leave me alone. My head hurts."

I had asked one too many questions, my usual problem. Brennan signaled for us to go.

"You get what you needed?" he asked.

"I wanted to know."

"Me, too. Of course I can't put it into the official report."

"No, of course not."

"We'll see if we can find any remains of Mr. Craft," Brennan said, "but I'm not optimistic."

"You're welcome to nose around the property, but we broke down the house to the foundation. The debris is in a lot in Ozone Park."

"I heard. Just doing your job."

"We can put a temporary stop work order on the project if you want to look around."

"I'll send somebody out to the property and the lot. They'll check out the sites and file a report, contact Craft's family."

Then the cop thought for a few seconds. "We still don't know how Drew and Rupert got to look like mummies, with all those newspapers plastered to them," Brennan said.

"Yeah. My only guess is that at one point, some of the stacks of newspapers fell in the pool. The bodies, the newspapers, they got mixed up together somehow."

"Drew probably doesn't even know," Brennan said.

I didn't have an answer to this last riddle. Brennan escorted me out of the station. He held the glass door open for me as I walked out, into the warm wind blowing through the trees in the late afternoon. I had to shield my eyes from the sun, especially after spending the time near Drew's dark cell.

I straightened out my finely-cut suit (purchased at Barney's, of course) and stepped into my car. I had called that Ravidinsky girl for a date. My mother, home from the hospital, asked if she was rich. I said no, but her dad owned a dry goods store in South Carolina, so she had some money.

"It's just as easy to marry a rich girl as a poor one," Mom said as I was getting ready to go.

"Right, Ma." I didn't want to talk about it. This Ravidinsky girl sounded like a winner and I didn't want my mother's voice to get inside my head. She had The Weirdness about her, always.

As I walked out the door, I said to her, "Hey, Ma, thanks for the kitchen knife."

"What? What did you do to my knife?"

I smiled. "Nothing, Ma, nothing at all."

Then she asked about the girl, forgetting about the knife, which was completely unlike her.

"What did you say her name was?"

"Helen. Helen Ravidinsky."

"Polish. That's no good."

"She's a classy girl, Ma. The real deal. Well-mannered, unlike me."

"This is trouble. Where are you taking her?"

"Dinner, and a walk in the park."

"Sounds serious."

"Then we're going bowling."

"Are you serious?"

"Always, Ma, always."

This town is still a tomato, but on this night she was also a lady.

THE WEIRDNESS VIRUS

Max hit Jon in the chest to resolve a tragic chocolate pudding accident. Richie tried to imitate a New York Jets defensive lineman and ran at Max at full speed in the living room, then wrestled him down on the carpet and held down his arms until he said, "Give." Jon body-slammed Mark down on a bed.

My four sons. After I married Helen, I thought that would tamp down The Weirdness for a while. My brother Derek had been missing for almost 20 years and the black drum he made in my heart still remained, beating low, but ever-present against the muscle. Sometimes I wondered whether he was dead.

So to fight against that dread, I wanted to have a normal life and I thought the more kids we had, the better. There was Richie, the oldest, the leader, blond and handsome, athletic, and sarcastic as hell. Then came the Three Stooges—all with brown hair and brown eyes—Max, skinny and a striver, always thinking hard about things, but shy and easily insulted. Third was Jon, who, when not fighting, liked to read philosophy books. Fourth was Mark, very quiet and sensitive, but stubborn as hell.

We also got a dog, a small, black dachshund, free, from Jerry Huberman, a guy I was friends with from high school. He bred them as a side business. Richie didn't want to have anything to do with the dog. He said she was completely useless. The three younger boys were crazy about her, though, and they decided to call her Gee Gee, as in "Gee, we got a dog! Gee!" I wanted to name her Gypsy, but the three boys couldn't agree on that. Gee Gee was a decision made in their favor, but a weird one. The boys seemed to have some sort of obsession over the letter "G." I wondered if they needed counseling. However, I was grateful they were able to make a mature group decision without coming to blows.

It's funny, because I loved my kids but they drove me completely crazy. I wished they would treat each other better. It pained me when they fought, which was often. I didn't understand why they had to fight over everything, from whose toy it was to a monkey doll to a game gone wrong.

Richie was 11 years old, Max, 9, Jon, 7, and Mark, 5, and I hadn't gotten a decent night's sleep in years. That alone took me into Weirdness territory. The economy was humming—there was money out there. The President had sex addiction problems, which was affecting the election, but the economy seemed not to notice.

"You just have to go out there and find the money, Schreiber," as my wife would say, her cat's eye glasses arching upward with her forehead. I hate that name—Schreiber. Hate it. But, there are only so many fights I can have with my wife. I concentrated on the money argument, tried to tell her that things aren't so great with the business, for reasons that have nothing to do with the general economy.

I walked around in a daze, up at four o'clock in the morning, hustling from minute one, trying to build my housing business, pushing myself to make money, support the family, feed the enormous appetites of my male offspring and grab the brass ring of financial security. Then when I came home from a day on the front lines of the never-ending business war, I had four small boys acting like the worst examples of mountain gorillas fighting for dominance you've ever seen on PBS.

Halloween is the absolute peak of hostilities for all of southern Queens and my boys got caught up in it. I hate Halloween. The kids in Queens think Halloween is a free "Get Out of My Parents' Rules for Good Behavior Jail" card. The normal rules of life are suspended. You can throw a barrage of eggs at total strangers, hit them with a sock full of chalk. Some adults complain that a bunch of kids wrapped their tree branches in toilet paper. If only that were the biggest crime!

Because there are other, much better things for a kid to do. Like throwing rocks at moving cars. Stealing more than usual from the local stores. And setting garbage cans on fire. Running into total strangers and tackling them on top of car hoods is also popular. Throwing Frisbees at people's heads is a tactic passed down from generation to generation as a hallowed tradition of the Ozone Park Rough Boys.

An adult in a business suit is particularly vulnerable. That's a red cape to the bulls stampeding through the neighborhood. You'll get egged or stoned or tackled, guaranteed.

The petty crimes were one thing. The costumes took the definition of terror to a whole new level. A Frankenstein outfit is like the pure innocence of Heidi compared to this parade of freaks. Manufactured head wounds with gaping crowns of blood were popular. An ax in the head with the inevitable red gusher was a big one too. The mask from the Scream movies appeared all too frequently (*Scream 3* had come out—Yay!). A guy named Pinhead was starring in *Hellraiser V: Inferno*. The kids of Queens, inspired, came out of their homes with little sticks of metal lining their rubber mask faces in grid patterns. Isn't that terrific? The Red Devil appeared in a few places in southern Queens, throwing live firecrackers at little kids who thought they were just going to get a lot of great candy wearing their thrilling little teddy bear, vampire, princess, and witch costumes.

The cops were out in force, don't get me wrong, but they were badly outnumbered. They were wary and tired already from taking care of the usual spatterings of New York City criminal activity on an everyday basis before they had to confront the teenagers taking absolute delight in acting like henchmen for the forces of darkness.

Halloween fell on a Tuesday this particular year. So people started celebrating on Saturday night to take advantage of the weekend. It would be like two Halloweens in four days—Saturday night and Tuesday night.

Max dressed up as Superman. He loved Superman. During summer weekends at the beach, he jumped around the dunes by himself, wearing a towel for a cape. He had a very rich fantasy life and this kind of scared me. Jon wanted to be Superman too. Max knew that Jon bought a Superman costume, because they went to the store together to buy them with their mother. Max complained at the time, and lost the argument with his mother. Now he renewed the argument with his mother in another part of the house.

They put on their costumes and Max argued with Jon, telling him he should be Batman. In Max's mind, Batman was clearly the junior partner to Superman. Jon insisted on Superman. Max did not like this. They argued more in the bunk-bed room they share. Max punched Jon in the chest. Jon defended himself. Max swung hard at Jon and pushed him onto the floor.

The sound of a kid falling heavily to the floor brought me from the kitchen to their room. The sight of two little Supermen fighting brought The Weirdness on too for me.

Daddy broke up the fight. I put myself between them. Max tried to hit Jon again and I caught his little fist with a curved palm and gave him the look of death. He started to cry. Jon was sobbing too. I had two crying Supermen on my hands.

"Max, your brother has the right to be Superman too. Now deal with it." I'm not the most sensitive father in the world. My fallback position was "I'm doing the best I can with four little maniacs under my roof." I could have blamed my less-than-stellar parenting skills on my mother, but as Richard Nixon said, that would be wrong.

Mark decided to be Luke Skywalker, with a Day-Glo light sword, which was just fine with everybody, thank God.

Richie, 11 years old, had already dashed out of the house, with a huge brown paper shopping bag for candy collection and no costume. He did not think it cool to wear a costume. And it was even more un-cool to be seen with your father. Helen and I prayed he would be safe. We told him he had two hours and to be home by nine.

The rest of the boys and I all marched out together to walk up and down blocks around our house, which was relatively safe from the marauding barbarians of the night. Still, in my casual slacks and a windbreaker, I carried a baseball bat, just in case. It's called "The Tennessee Thumper." The bat was made in Tullahoma, Tennessee, and it's thin at the grip and heavy on the end. The teenagers who saw me would know I had a more than effective way to retaliate against any aggression.

Max was still sniffling from his defeat at the hands of Jon and Daddy. But soon, he quickly dried up to focus on the serious business of getting candy from the neighbors.

The Saturday night on our neighborhood blocks went uneventfully, just some kids fired up to get candy, and I was grateful. We saw evidence of some attacks, eggs dashed on the sidewalk, toilet paper in a few trees, some chalk scratched into the streets. But we didn't see any problems while we were walking and I was relieved.

When we returned home later, I wanted the boys to go to bed, but they were all excited by their haul of candy. Helen and I watched as they poured their paper bags onto the kitchen table. Three Musketeers bars, Milky Ways, Mars Bars, Tootsie Pops, Sweet Tarts, Hershey's chocolates, Reese's Pieces, M&Ms, Mounds bars, Good & Plenty boxes, and other little confections came flooding out. Raisin boxes were tossed into the refrigerator immediately. They went into school lunch boxes over the next week. The boys can get raisins from their mother. They don't need a neighbor to give them raisins.

Mary Janes were tossed in the garbage. It's a peanut butter and molasses candy and not all that tasty to my kids, especially when you compare it to chocolate. Pennies came out too. Those went into the piggy banks for comic books and more candy at the shop up on the boulevard.

The boys wrote their names on their bags and scooped their booty back in. The bags went into the refrigerator. Each day three pieces of candy were to be consumed, under my wife's rules. Of course she couldn't watch them all the time, so they were sneaking some candy when the coast was clear.

Richie came home an hour later than his assigned time. Helen and I looked at each other as if to say, "What can you do?"

I give him a three-minute speech. He timed it by the cartoon cat clock on the wall in the kitchen. I had been completely ineffective in getting my point across.

The next day, Sunday, passed without any drama. The plain light of an October day kept the demons in their caves. The boys played football in the street.

When Monday came, the boys felt their own inner horrors even in the absence of Halloween's influence. School was like a black hole drawing them in with its gravitational power and they didn't like it one bit. Each of the four boys felt a certain little depression about having to slink in to classes, even Max. He would have preferred to read in some quiet place, not sit in the prison of school.

That Monday night, things were quiet. It was a little like one of those Middle Eastern cease fires. Both sides are sitting there, bristling with loaded weapons, filled with lust to shoot their guns. I didn't trust the false peace of Monday night because I knew what was coming.

Then Tuesday hit—the actual Halloween. It was a school night, but there were still parties and streams of random kids walking around the neighborhood in fright masks and ax-heads and rubber steak knives coated with a plentitude of fake blood.

The boys were not allowed to go out for this second night, but they ignored us. Richie ran out to find fun in whatever form he could discover. Max and Jon ran to the corner shop to buy comic books and football magazines.

On Wednesday, we woke up to a day that wasn't Halloween. The explosion of depravity had finally exhausted itself. I relaxed a little.

At seven at night, I put the television on in the den room. I settled into my black easy chair, the one that lays back. A rerun of *Law and Order* was on one of the cable channels. The one with Lennie Briscoe. The guy in the trench coat. He's tough and persistent. I wished I had him for a friend.

My enjoyment was abruptly finished by a scream from the dining room.

Helen ran in from the kitchen; I pushed myself out of my easy chair. We arrived simultaneously to see Jon holding his eyes with his hands. He sounded like he had been attacked by a pit viper.

The cause of his pain was immediately apparent. Max stood between the two of us, a spray-bottle of Windex in his right hand.

"What did you do?" I yelled.

Max said nothing, just stood there with his mouth open. We didn't really need an answer. He had sprayed Jon's eyes with the window cleaner, which my wife had unaccountably left on the dining room table. It was clear that if put in the right hands, anything could become a weapon in our house.

We hustled Jon off to the bathroom to wash out his eyes with New York City water. My wife relieved Max of the window cleaner. She sent him to bed.

I stuck Jon's head under the sink, turned his eyes toward the stream of water and turned on the faucet. The water distracted him from his crying. I turned his head for the other side. We repeated the procedure. I ran his head under the water for what seemed like several minutes.

"You OK?" I said.

He sniffled.

"Should we do it again?"

"OK."

We did it again. Then I dried his head with a towel. He seemed calm. His eyes looked normal.

My parents had come to our house for a pop-over visit. Their house is about 10 minutes from ours, in Ozone Park, the Flats. Mom and Dad arrived shortly after the Windex attack. Ruth walked into Max and Jon's bedroom. Max was lying under the covers with the lights on, ashamed.

Mother was wearing a gray dress and some kind of short hose that were supposed to function as socks, I think. She stood a few feet away from the bunk bed and said to Max, "So, look what you've done to your brother."

Her voice was dripping with contempt. Max cried out and tried to squeeze himself into a ball.

I stayed silent. I didn't know how to respond to Mother, but I suspected that perhaps this wasn't the best way to talk to my son.

I wasn't home when the next things happened over the next few days. Helen was. Jon beat up Mark. Max beat up Jon. Richie beat up Max. Afterward, when Richie wasn't paying attention, Max hit Richie in the eye, gave him a black one. Mark took a chair to get to the kitchen counter, pulled the biggest knife he could find out of Helen's butcher block, calmly walked out of the kitchen into the dining room and pointed the knife at Jon and yelled, "I'm gonna get you!"

The three other boys fled to the other side of the dining room. Mark stood at the entrance of the room and waved the knife in the air like a desperate criminal, cutting wide arcs at his enemy brothers. Helen ran to the three older boys, who were staring at their youngest brother with sudden, great fear.

How were we going to get out of this one?

Mark breathed heavily. Helen noticed that the corners of his eyes were dripping a heavy yellow pus. Did he have pinkeye?

Helen talked softly to him. "Sweetie, want some ice cream?"

"I want chocolate!" he demanded, holding the knife high up in the air, high enough to carve a line in my wife's stomach.

"OK. You can have chocolate."

"With fudge and sprinkles!"

"Yes. OK. I'll make it for you."

"They can't eat any!" he said, waving the knife in an uneasy arc.

"OK, honey. Only ice cream for you. None for them."

If only all fights could be solved with ice cream.

Helen took Mark to the doctor. He didn't have pinkeye. The doctor suggested Mark see an ophthalmologist. An appointment was made for the following week. The ophthalmologist was very busy.

Later in the week, Helen had to go to work. She had a part-time job as a dietitian at a local hospital. We needed the cash. The flooring part of my business was suffering because all of a sudden everybody wanted to put carpet over a simple plywood floor. I do parquet, which is beautiful. But if people want carpet, why do they need parquet? Carpets started to cover all of southern Queens. The parquet business tanked.

Helen walked into the house one afternoon to find all four boys playing tackle football in the living room. The living room is only 20 feet long and 15 feet wide.

The boys were only playing the running game, so that was one sign of intelligence. They didn't want to break the picture window fronting the house. Helen gaped as the boys drove who-ever was the ball carrier into the floor. (The family dog, the infa-mously named "Gee Gee," had retreated from her favorite sleep-ing spot and was hiding in the den room, sleeping on my easy chair.)

Helen saw this and started to cry and stamp her foot. My wife only cries when presidents get shot. The boys stopped, just looked at her.

Through her tears, Helen noticed that the boys had yellow pus coming from their eyes. They were all marched off to the eye doctor.

The eye doctor tested their eyes and there was nothing wrong with them. The eye doctor recommended additional tests, which were very expensive. We decided not to get the tests unless the boys continued to spew the pus.

By the weekend, my wife was a wreck from all the fighting. She retreated to the bedroom for a long nap. I took the boys for a drive to Jones Beach in Nassau County—the best beach in the golden suburbs. Even though it was early November, we all loved to walk on the beach. We went even in January. The water had a way of taking the fight out of the boys.

The dog asked to go too. As we were on our way out the door, Gee Gee ran up and looked at us with her big brown eyes, begging for the trip. She loved to ride in cars and the three younger boys were happy to take her. She knew it too. She stood on their laps and stuck her head out the window as we drove.

Before we went, I did a quick check of the boys' eyes. Just a little parent paranoia. They were pus-less. I breathed a little breath of relief.

As I steered the station wagon out of the Flats, we saw a man standing in a trench coat and black pants on the corner. He was wearing a fedora, which was out-of-date by 40 years. His face was shadowed by the hat. The man reminded me of Sam Spade. His head seemed to follow us as we drove toward him, then past him. Maybe I imagined it.

The boys pointed to him, excited, but whispering. They didn't want me to know something.

"Eh, what's that?" I asked from the driver's seat.

There was silence. I decided not to pursue the point. Maybe the guy was just some neighborhood eccentric. There are a lot of people in Queens who dress funny. You have guys wearing shorts and black socks and shoes, old women wearing bright red lipstick and low-cut blouses, their breasts searching for their rib cages, and a lot of old codgers demonstrating the power of checks and stripes to clash.

The wind at Jones Beach was moist and we all had to zip up our jackets when we stepped out of the car at the parking lot. The waves seemed huge and they rolled on, ignoring us.

The beach was very wide and clean. Richie had brought a football. He sent Max long and threw a tight 20-yard spiral. Max stumbled forward and for a second we thought he was going to hit the sand. He did, but caught the ball anyway. His smile was wide and beautiful. Max threw the ball back to Richie. Richie sent Jon out and directed Max to cover him.

Then they played two-on-two football, with Rich and Mark paired together and Max and Jon against. It was a silly game, not serious, because Mark was only five. The boys laughed when they were tackled. The dog ran after them, barking. She jumped on the boys' backs when they fell in the sand.

When they are like this, it's a thing of beauty.

We ate turkey sandwiches and bright red apples on a thick blanket. The wind kicked up and threw sand in our eyes, but the boys did not seem diminished by this little annoyance.

At four o'clock the zip went out of them and we walked to the car. Wind swept the sand into little piles on the parking lot. We quietly drove home. The three younger boys and the dog fell asleep. Richie sat in the front seat, his eyes staring at the road, bird-like, as if he were driving himself.

The peace in the house lasted for five days.

The next Saturday, I was loading flooring slats from the garage floor into the station wagon. One side of the living room borders the garage. So I was hauling the slats into the car for a job we had starting Monday and the living room wall sounded out a thump. There were several more thumps, and shouting. My wife started yelling. This was not your usual boys-just-jumping-on-the-couch kind of disturbance.

I ran into the den and made a sharp turn into the living room. The four boys were wrestling over a stuffed monkey doll named Yeknom. Yeknom had a chimpanzee face, a yellow shirt and red pants. He was about one foot tall. The monkey had been Richie's doll since he was about 4 years old, but now the question of his ownership was sketchy. Yeknom was "monkey" spelled back-wards. The doll was ragged and his legs had fallen off a few times, only to be saved by the sewing ministrations of my wife.

Max and Jon had started fighting over the doll. Richie broke them up and Max slapped Richie hard on the arm. I could see the welt on the bicep, flashing red. Richie threw Max against the wall. Max barreled into Richie.

That left Yeknom unattended. Mark picked him up. Jon tried to snatch up the monkey too. Mark and Jon started fighting. They all ended up in a big bunch, punching and wrestling until they fell into the wall as one tangled mass.

The dog grabbed the doll in its jaws and Richie dove on the dog. The dog screamed. Max tackled Richie. Jon threw himself on Max. Mark followed.

I shouted at them. "What the hell is wrong with you?"

I peeled layer upon layer of boy off boy. Gee Gee was buried underneath the pile. Once I uncovered her, she ran off, terrified, to the den room, to hide in the closet. Yeknom had lost a leg in the battle. He lay there, stunned and unable to move.

The boys stood there, out of breath, hair tangled, sweaty and looking somewhat deranged.

I repeated the question. "What are you doing?" Nobody could answer me.

Yellow pus leaked from their eyes. "That's it!" I shouted. "We're all going to the doctor!"

It was Saturday, so of course we had to make a lot of phone calls to find an eye doctor who would be willing to get off the golf course and see the boys. It took about an hour and a half of calls to find a guy.

But we did, and the boys got their tests, in an office on the north shore of Long Island. The doctor told us it could take a couple of weeks to get the results.

The boys cooled down for a while. On Sunday, after school, Jon and Max said they wanted to go to the candy store to buy more comic books and football magazines. Helen let them. They seemed to avoid direct conflict, but we noticed them stealing candy from each other's bags in the refrigerator. My wife and I figured they weren't hurting each other and we didn't want to start another fight by bringing up the stealing. When you're a parent, you make these kinds of unpleasant compromises all the time. Sometimes it feels like you're sliding down the deck of the *Titanic* as it lifts into the air for its final death throes.

When I got home at night, I was feeling stressed out from work. I started doing some binge eating. It involves a lot of shoveling food into your mouth. There was Helen's amazing fried chicken and mashed potatoes, loaded with butter. After that I went through half a box of Ritz crackers or saltines. Just to top it off, there were chocolate chip cookies, or doughnuts staring at me from the bottom shelf of the refrigerator.

After that, I figured I'd treat myself. I looked into the refrigerator again, at the boys' candy bags. I started digging in them. The Three Musketeers bars looked really good. The soft chocolate coating, the creamy filling. So I figured what the hell. I ate a few for dessert.

Two days later, I was walking in a little food market on Queens Boulevard. The place was near a job I was working on with my carpenters, in Forest Hills. Like many food markets in Queens, it doesn't have a lot of space. The aisles are very tight and you have to squeeze through them. Two people can't walk side-by-side. That's how squeezed in you feel. It was lunch time and I wanted a pastrami sandwich with mustard on rye bread. I was very hungry. As I walked up to the deli counter, a small guy in a white tee-shirt with a blue Yankees logo, tight muscles underneath, brushed past me. He was carrying a red plastic food basket and the basket banged into my knee.

Ordinarily, I might say, "Excuse me." I mean, you can start a fight in Queens any hour of the day. People do rude things all the time, like bump into each other or cut you in line at the store or steal your parking space. You have to let a lot of things go or you will be spending a good part of your day punching somebody and getting punched at in return. So you try to be actively calm.

But this guy. This guy! He walked by me like I wasn't even there. Like I'm freaking invisible or something.

He continued walking.

"Hey!"

He turned around in the aisle and looked at me. And I just knew he was stupid. He had little eyes, which I didn't trust, and an enormous honker of a nose, which looked like one of those joke disguises. And he had huge red pimples spraying out all over his face.

"You bumped into my leg!"

He turned around halfway. "So? It's still there."

At this point, two people might argue with each other for a minute or two and one of them walks away. I didn't want any part of that.

So I walked right up to him, my eyes blazing. He saw it coming, but maybe he was too shocked to do anything about it.

I slugged him right in the stomach. He went down very fast, but he still held onto that damn basket. The basket hit me in the knee again.

I was standing over the schmuck and he was angry. Sometimes in these cases, the hitter waits for the other guy to get up and they start fighting. I never understood that.

I dove onto the floor and started hitting the guy in the chest and shoulders. He tried to get up, but I was a lot bigger than him. I had my legs pinning down his arms.

I yelled at the guy, "My fist is still here too!"

The Chinese guy behind the deli counter was shouting at me. "Hey, you stop!"

I ignored that and pounded on the guy. He wormed his arms out from under my legs and stuck them up to say, "Stop! I surrender!"

"Fuck you!" I yelled. I hit him in the nose, and he started to bleed. This was very satisfying.

There were hands grabbing my back and waist. Three Chinese men, the owners of the store, pulled me off the lame Yankee tee-shirt man and pinned my arms up.

They stood me up, my arms in the air, and I punched my shoulders up and shook the men off.

The men shouted, "Go now! You go now! Don't ever come back!"

"Fine!"

I walked out of the store, but not before pulling down a whole row of apples off the shelf. I heard them bounce on the floor, which was a very pleasant sound.

I walked down the street to find another deli, head filled with hot blood, happy.

Cutting into my mood, a horrible thought rose from the front of my brain. I had just fought like one of my sons. The stomach shot, the hitting in the shoulders and chest. The legs holding down the arms. The only thing I'd done differently was popping the guy in the nose.

But I couldn't hold that realization for long, because my eyes were suddenly flooded with some kind of liquid. I took a tissue from the pocket of my jacket and dabbed it out. The stuff looked like thick mucus, but it was yellow. I had the same pus in my eyes as the boys. Holy, Oh My God, Damn It All To Hell, Crap.

I went to a pay phone to call the doctor who had done the tests on the boys. The phone rang like 800 times. Nobody picked up. It was lunch time. The quarters came spilling out of the coin slot. I picked them up and tried again.

After the seventh ring, a woman picked up the phone.

"Can I speak to Doctor Rivers?"

"He's not in today."

"I'm just trying to get test results on my sons. My name is Harold Schreiber. We were in on Saturday."

"Test results usually take two weeks. It's only Tuesday."

"I know, I know. I was just wondering if we could get the analysis speeded up. We have another case in the family."

"I'm sorry, Mr. Schreiber."

"Well, can you ask the doctor to call me back?"

"Yes. I'll take down your number."

Anxiety shivered through me. I stuffed it down and went back to the flooring job without eating.

When I came home, the boys were fighting in the living room, naturally. Helen was at her dietitian job. I let the boys go at it for a few minutes. I was too tired to break them up.

This time, it was the three younger boys versus Richie. Max tried to hit Richie in the chest. He laughed and punched Max hard in the shoulder. Jon jumped on Richie's back and managed to bring him down on the floor. Max got in a good shot to Richie's eye. Richie shook off Jon and hit Max in the eye. Mark threw himself on Richie and Richie spun him around and held him like he was a baby.

"You gonna hit me now? You gonna hit me now?" he shouted at Max and Jon, cradling his 5-year-old brother. Their eyes all had that sticky yellow stuff oozing onto their cheeks.

Now that the boys were all standing, the living room floor was clear. I looked down at a little black ball and I understood what they were fighting about.

Gee Gee was lying on her back by the couch, her legs clinging together in the air, struggling to get free of a rope I used sometimes to tie my wood slats together when I was getting ready for a job.

I got the story quickly from Max, breathing hard from the exertion of trying to retaliate against his older brother. Richie dove on the floor on top of the sleeping dog and hog-tied her like an animal being prepared for slaughter. The three younger boys saw it, didn't like it, and attacked their oldest brother.

As I listened, I had to restrain myself from hitting all of them in their pus-stained faces. I had to whisper to myself, "You're an Eagle Scout. You're an Eagle Scout. You don't do this stuff."

The Weirdness Virus had overtaken me, and I had to fight off the seething impulses motoring around in me. That's what I called the disease we all carried now.

When Max finished, with many corrections from Jon and a number of interruptions from Richie, I yelled in a roar I did not know I possessed, "I don't care what any of you do!" They were shocked. I was shocked at myself. I stormed out the glass front door and walked into the Flats.

Woodhaven Boulevard was filled with shoppers and people looking for scarce parking places so they could shop too.

A young man, perhaps in his twenties, had somehow managed to corner his car into a parking space and beat a forty-something rag bag of a woman to the spot. She was trying to argue him out of the space as I walked by.

"You took my parking spot. I was waiting here."

He was big, maybe six foot one, a solid block of fatness. He had on a loose black tee-shirt to try to cover up the jellies of fat rolling around his belly and chest. They say black is supposed to be slimming, but in this case, I didn't see how it helped. His black hair was long and insolent.

"Shut up!" he shouted at her.

"You took my space! You stole it!"

"Shut up! Shut the fuck up!"

This struck me as a great injustice. Instead of walking by, I tackled the guy into his own car.

"Wha?"

I pinned the block of fat on the hood of his car, and looked at him, ready for murder, my eyes streaming yellow goo.

"You shut the fuck up," I said. Then I hit him in the top of the mouth.

"Ow!"

I held both sides of his tee-shirt collar.

"This is a science experiment. I want to see if I can get my entire fist in your mouth."

"Fuck you."

I punched him in the stomach. The air went out of the big dumb balloon through his open mouth. I stuck my fist in between his teeth so he could choke on the knuckles. I could feel his tongue lolling around against my fingers.

He was too scared to try to bite. I took my hand out.

"You proved my hypothesis. Thanks for the help, fatty."

I ripped off his tee-shirt and walked away. So he could be embarrassed with his giant loose tits hanging out for everyone to see. The rag-bag of a lady looked pleased. She gave me a crumpled smile.

"Hey!" the fat kid shouted after me. I wheeled around.

"Want to try our experiment again?"

The fat boy backed away, eyes raised.

I threw the tee-shirt in a street garbage can and marched on.

A tree branch dipped low and I hit it with my head. I broke it off the tree with both hands. The cold autumn wood snapped easily and I threw it on the sidewalk. Shoppers looked at me uneasily.

A group of boys made a circle on the street. Some were wearing red football jerseys with big yellow numbers. Kids from the local high school.

"Kill 'em, Wayne!" somebody shouted.

Wayne was choking the crap out of a skinny kid with brown glasses. His books were splayed all over the sidewalk.

I ran straight into the group and bowled right over a few football player backs. Wayne was surprised enough to stop choking the nerd.

"Hey, Wayne. You like to choke people?"

Wayne looked around for help from his friends. None was forthcoming.

"Want to choke me?"

Wayne didn't respond.

"Want to try it, you little shit?"

Wayne got up. I wrapped one hand around his throat and tightened the grip.

"How do you like it, fuck-face?"

Wayne's eyes popped out a little. I smiled.

Down the boulevard, I saw a man with a trench coat and fedora walk down a side street.

I let go of Wayne, but not before telling him, "If I ever see you bother anybody on the street again, I'll kill you. Understand?"

He nodded, ticked-off and almost considering whether to fight me.

I got closer to him, so he could feel my breath, my fist held out about six inches from his eye. "Want to fight? I would love that."

Wayne took a look at my fist and my yellow river eyes, then his friends, surrounding him. The nerd gathered his books and sped off. He was embarrassed, but also scared enough to not do anything.

"Uh huh," is all he could manage.

"I would love to see your mouth smashed in, your nose broken and you breathing blood all over yourself."

"Let's go, Wayne," one of the other football players said. "This guy's nuts."

They walked off fast toward the north, the trees on the sidewalk covering their retreat.

I went south, looking for the man in the trench coat, but got distracted by another problem on the street. These are easy to find in the Flats.

The problem was a kid wearing black jeans and a black teeshirt, frayed at the collar, that said, "Queens—Where the Weak Are Killed And Eaten!" The tee-shirt had a smiling skull with blood streaming from its teeth and next to that a row of buildings in flames.

He wore a strict purple Mohawk, the hair sticking straight up with gel, and had a safety pin stuck through his nostrils, about six inches long, wider than his face. The safety pin kid was hassling a girl with white-blonde hair. She looked to be about 13, 14 years old and was wearing a Catholic school uniform with a long tartan skirt.

The boy, taller than the girl and with a lot of muscle packed on his frame, was cornering her into a brick wall between two stores. People walked by like they didn't see it. The boy was full of himself and the girl looked annoyed, but not extremely terrified.

"Come on, Marie. Give me a little kiss."

Marie put up her hands to ward off the boy. He leaned into her.

"Carl, cut it out!" the girl shouted.

"Yeah, Carl, cut it out."

He turned to me. "What's your problem?"

"You."

He stuck his finger in my chest. "I'll fucking kill you, old man."

I laughed. "I'll eat your bones for breakfast."

He took a swing, which I caught in mid-air with my palm. Carl looked astonished.

I grabbed his tee-shirt with the other hand and tore it in two, starting with the loosening collar. The bloody skull came next, along with the flaming buildings.

Carl looked as if I had cut off his bag of testicles. He was stunned and angry at the same time. There was a black Nazi insignia tattooed on one of his pectoral muscles.

That inflamed me even more.

"Oh, Carl, you've been a bad boy."

"You're dead meat, old man."

Marie backed off down the street and yelled at me, "I could have taken care of this, sir!"

Carl and I looked at her, not believing.

Then I rushed him and shoved him against the wall between the stores, making sure that the back of his head hit the brick, and closing my hands over his throat.

He grabbed my hands. I laughed. I kept one hand on his throat and closed the other on his safety pin, pulling it toward me.

"This is an interesting situation."

"Let go!"

I pulled the pin farther away from Carl's nose.

"Why don't you just do everybody a favor and go kill yourself?"

"What's wrong with your eyes? You're crazy, man!"

I got very close to him and whispered in his ear, one hand still on the safety pin.

Shoppers walked by us even faster now.

"Just remember, Carl, I'll be happy to kill you. Really happy."

He tried to push my hand off the pin, but I had the Weirdness Virus on my side.

"Go home now, Carl, and cry to your mommy."

I let go of the pin and he backed away, his naked chest looking smaller somehow. "I'll be looking for you, old man!"

"I hope you will, Carl. I hope you will. Because I'm going to carve that tattoo right out of your chest."

He turned and ran down the street. Women stopped in their tracks upon seeing the half-naked boy with the Nazi tattoo.

I wondered what to do next. Then I remembered the man in the trench coat. I walked in the direction of the side street he took.

I went down the street, quiet with houses and no pedestrians. There wasn't any sign of the man in the trench coat. I looked between houses, in back yards. I walked down several other streets, but I didn't see him.

I didn't know what to do with myself. So I walked over to the Woodhaven Lanes alley and went bowling.

After the third game of pretending the lead pin had Carl's and Wayne's heads attached to it, I sat down on one of the plastic seats. My scores for the three games were 229, 215, and 207. Apparently the Weirdness Virus had improved my bowling skills.

My wife sat down next to me, her hair swept back, long and soft and brown.

"I thought you might be here."

"Yeah," was all I could manage to say.

"The boys told me what you said."

"Yeah."

"Do you think it was a good idea to say that?"

"Don't talk to me like a school teacher, Helen."

She said nothing, looked ahead at the bowlers taking over my lane.

"I'm tired of the fighting," I said. "All the time."

"Me too. I heard you've been fighting too."

I didn't bother with any kind of denial. "How'd you hear about that?"

"Carol Rosenberg saw you on Woodhaven Boulevard. She called me. She said you threw a man on a car."

"Yeah, I did that."

Helen didn't know what to do with an upfront admission, so she just said, "Don't hit anybody anymore" in a quiet voice.

"I can't guarantee that."

That got her mind going. "You'll get arrested and then where will we be, Harold?"

"Surrounded by barbarians. Like we are now."

"I don't want to visit you at Rikers Island."

"OK." I surrendered for the moment.

"The doctor called."

"Yeah?"

"They don't know what the boys have."

"That's all he said?"

"It's not biological."

"What do you mean?"

"There's some kind of chemical mixture in the pus. It's artificial."

"Artificial."

"Some kind of synthetic compound."

"Where did it come from?"

"He doesn't know. They're going to do more analysis of the compound. It has to be sent to another lab. They have more sophisticated equipment there."

I absorbed this quietly. "It's poison."

"What?"

"Something is poisoning the boys. And now me."

Helen's face took a turn that reflected the special horror all mothers feel when their children are threatened.

"How?"

"I don't know, but I'm going to find out."

"How can you, Harold? You're not the police. You're just a home building contractor."

"I'll figure something out."

My wife looked at me with a certain sort of silent contempt. I knew I would never persuade her about my intent, so I said, simply, "You came over in the car?"

"Yes."

"Let's go home."

Our house in Ozone Park was the scene of a quiet dread. Whatever animal impulses the boys had to fight was stuffed by their new fear of me. It's not just what I said to them after I broke up their free-for-all. They had heard a few of the stories going around the Flats about me and what I did after Richie hog-tied the dog. Their friends on the block seemed to know all about what I had done. News travels fast, as they say. Some of the stories had been blown up like helium balloons, but people are like that. Somebody whispered to somebody else that I broke off several teeth from the guy who stole the parking space. I had only placed my fist in his mouth, an important distinction. The ripping off of the tee-shirts story was passed around too, except that they said I also made the boys strip to their underpants before running them off.

The next Sunday, Helen was at the hospital for her job again. The boys were mine. I thought about taking them to the beach. The weather was unusually warm for November—almost 70 degrees and dry. But I felt so damn tired. So after lunch I took a nap in the master bedroom. In retrospect, I should have taken the boys to the beach.

I was dreaming about being out on a motor boat, alone in the water of a bay, fog rolling in. Breaking glass blew open the dreamland I was in.

I ran to the front of the house. The glass door in the hallway had been shattered. Pieces of glass littered the hallway. I swung the door outward. Glass lay like pieces of a jigsaw puzzle thrown in the air.

Richie looked at me from the front lawn, about 12 feet away.

"He's in the bathroom, Dad!"

I didn't need to guess. It was almost certainly Max.

In the bathroom, Max was sitting on the closed toilet, his head lying on the water tank, the frontal lobes of his head awash with blood. His hands had some blood on them too, but they didn't look nearly as bad.

I ripped a white towel from the rack and pressed it onto his forehead. The little bubbles of cotton were made stiff by the drying blood. Max's eyes were percolating with little fountains of yellow pus, which mixed with blood from his wounds. I wasn't thinking that Max might be going into shock, so I calmly asked him what happened.

Dazed, he spoke to the ceiling. "Richie beat me up."

"That's all?"

Max's eyes, closed, then fluttered open and he spoke slowly like a 6-year-old learning to read new words. "He... wanted... my... basketball. He... stole... it. Ran... out ... the... house."

I could figure out the next things. Max ran after Richie. He was so angry he must have punched through the glass door Richie had just escaped.

Later Max told me that as he stood there, on the front steps, the blood splashing over his glasses, his brother yelled at him from the front lawn, "Get in the bathroom, you schmuck!" just to add a little dash of extra hostility to their battle.

Max slumped over the toilet. He had lost consciousness.

I carried him out of the house to the station wagon, passing Richie.

"Sweep up all the glass," I told him. "Use the big broom from the garage." He only nodded, his pus filled eyes cast downward like billiard balls with the numbers face down on the table. Even for our house, this was an escalation of violence for which we were not prepared.

I put Max in the back seat, and secured the towel to his bleeding head with a seat belt.

The hospital was only 10 minutes away. It was where Helen worked. The emergency room was busy. A 14-year-old boy had gotten shot in the arm while he walked out of a candy store in the Springfield Gardens neighborhood. A very large man was moaning on a gurney. Somebody had hit him in the back of the head with a baseball bat. A girl, about six or seven, was crying hysterically. Her orange hair was coated with blood along the exact line where she had parted it with a comb. Maybe she fell on the sidewalk?

Max was treated for shock in the triage unit. Once he was stabilized, we waited for a surgeon. The doctor sewed up the wounds, a line of jagged triangles straight across the forehead. He looked like a little Frankenstein.

"Your son has conjunctivitis," the surgeon, a guy named Detmer, told me when Max was resting.

"No, he doesn't. He's been tested."

"I think it's conjunctivitis," he pronounced, as if he were Moses bringing down the tablets from Sinai.

"It isn't. I just told you. He's been tested.

Detmer pointed at my eyes. "You have it too."

"And I'm telling you, he's already tested negative. It's something else, which we don't know what it is, and you better stop insisting on it."

The doctor backed away. He said in a high voice, "OK, Mr. Schreiber. I'll be going now."

I noticed that I had my right hand curled into a fist at about jaw level.

When we got home, Helen put Max in bed and I called a contractor I knew to put in a plexiglass fitting for the front door. As I waited in the living room for him to come, standing and looking out the picture window at the street, I noticed a man in a trench coat, fedora and black pants standing on the sidewalk in front of the house, staring at me.

Mark and Jon were sitting in the living room with me and they saw him too. They whispered to each other.

"What are you whispering about?" I demanded to know.

"Nuthin, Pop," Jon said.

I whipped out of the house to face him. He saw me coming out the door and ran off.

"Who the hell are you?" I shouted at him. He ran down the block. I chased him. He was very fast. The last thing I saw were his black pants flying off, which reminded me of that Dr. Seuss story about a pair of pants that ran around in the dark, scaring a little boy.

He turned the corner. I followed. The black pants were gone. The street was empty, like no one was ever there.

There was one other thing that was kind of weird. The guy was wearing sneakers, Converse high-tops, the kind of footwear a kid would run around in.

That night, Jon and Mark got into a fight after dinner. I was watching a war movie on TV and enjoying it. Max was resting in his room, drugged up on painkillers. Mark and Jon were in the living room, fighting over the dog.

I heard them and yelled: "Can't you just stop it! Can't you just cut it out for a minute!"

"No!" Jon shouted at me. "We can't just cut it out for a minute!"

I wanted to hit him. I did. I confess. But I held back. There was that old father-son bond putting a chain on my worst impulses. Yellow pus was streaming out of his eyes and mine too.

So I yelled at him instead, "Who was that man outside the house!"

"I can't tell you," Jon said.

"You can and you will!"

"He said we can't tell!"

"Or what?"

"He'll hurt us."

OK, this is a parent's worst nightmare and I felt terrible that we had so thoroughly blown the job of protecting them from a stranger. This wasn't some neighborhood eccentric.

So I bluffed. "I'll hurt you worse. Much worse."

Jon looked at me for a moment. He paused to consider whether I was telling the truth.

"I won't tell you."

I took my belt out of my pants, shaped it into a loop and stomped over to him.

"You tell me now or you're getting the belt!"

I have never actually put a belt to any of my kids. But the threat was my nuclear weapon.

Jon quivered. His eyes went wide.

"He said his name was Dr. Room!"

"How do you know him?"

"He said he was a detective!"

I was incredulous.

"He gave us candy on Halloween," Mark said. "And other days." Thank the Lord for my little truth-teller.

And I'm thinking, "Oh my God. The candy in the brown paper bags in the refrigerator. It's infecting us with the Weirdness Virus, over and over."

I marched into the kitchen, opened the refrigerator door.

"What are you doing?" Jon asked.

"You're not taking away our candy!" Mark said.

"That's exactly what I'm doing. This candy is making you sick. It's making us all sick."

There was something in the goddamn candy. I wondered how my wife and I had possibly missed preventing this most basic of all growing-up dangers. Don't talk to strangers. Don't take any-thing from strangers. We must be horrible parents.

I gathered up all four bags, still holding generous amounts of Milky Ways, Three Musketeers, Hershey's Kisses, Hershey's Bars, Starbursts, Sweet Tarts, Mounds, Almond Joys, Nestlé's Crunch, Gum Drops and other sugar carriers. I threw them in a plastic garbage bag and wrote on it: "Bad Candy—Do Not Touch." I walked out the door and put the goods in my car. At this point, I didn't know what I was going to do. I just wanted to get the candy out of the house.

As I put the bag in the back seat, I also realized that I didn't want to keep the candy in the car. I thought of a better place to take it. I drove to the doctor's office.

Of course Doctor Rivers wasn't there. I wrote him a note asking him to analyze a few pieces of the goodies inside and taped it to the giant bag of poison candy.

A new peace settled into the house. Max had been carried off the field of battle, so that was one less kid to worry about. With-out the rocket fuel of the candy, Richie was more subdued. I'd like to think he was upset about what happened to Max and his role in it, but we didn't really know what he was thinking. He just wasn't going to open up. Mark and Jon stayed away from each other. Jon, all of 8 years old, borrowed a kid's biography on the Buddha from the school library. He read it over and over again. His head seemed to be in the clouds, but Helen and I didn't question it. We were just happy that he wasn't warring with his younger brother.

A week later, Dr. Rivers called. Helen was on the phone in the kitchen and I took the other phone in the bedroom.

"There is a chemical in the candy that matches the pus com-ing out of the boys' eyes," he told us.

"What is it?" Helen asked.

"Well, it's not one thing. It's a combination of chemicals. It has amphetamine and something else. We're not exactly sure what that something else is."

"How can we find out?"

"I've sent a sample to a federal government laboratory, out here on the Island. They have the top state-of-the-art equipment to analyze what the chemical is."

"Why is the stuff coming out of their eyes?"

"I think that there's so much of it that your sons' bodies can't excrete all of it through the normal evacuation of bowels and urine. The body has to get rid of the waste somehow and the eyes seem the most convenient route. I'm just speculating, Mr. Schreiber. We won't really know until the federal lab spends the time studying the question. This is not my department. It could take several weeks of research. Unfortunately, you're going to have to wait. If you want results faster than the federal team can do, you could try a private lab, but I don't think you can afford it."

"You're right about that, Dr. Rivers."

"Thanks for your help," Helen said, and we hung up at the same time.

Somebody was feeding our kids amphetamines and some other creepy stuff, which was making them and me even more aggressive than usual. They had been turned into little fright machines of domestic destruction. The fear that hung over us was like a black shroud. Our house had been attacked by a little version of a plague.

That night, after dinner, Helen looked in on Max and made sure he was comfortable. He still had bandages over his forehead and the stitches were tightening as he healed.

Then she retreated to the bedroom. She wanted to watch TV to distract herself from our troubles. If she didn't do that, she would stare at the four walls and get really depressed about all the things that we had suffered recently. I knew my wife well enough to know how she operated.

She had her distractions. I had mine. I went bowling.

At Woodhaven, I bowled three lousy games. I couldn't concentrate. My form was off. The man in the trench coat and the fedora was all over my mind.

Afterward, I got in the station wagon and drove up Woodhaven Boulevard to Queens Boulevard. I felt like I needed to get out of the Flats.

I stopped in Forest Hills, near the Gardens. There's a little café there, right next to the train station. You can have a cup of coffee and feel like you're not in the city. The streets are cobblestone and there are a number of trees overhanging the streets. The houses are mostly Tudor, made of real stone, which you don't see a lot of anymore. It's quiet and pretty as hell.

As I drank the coffee, I looked out the window and considered the question of Dr. Room. Who was this guy? Why would he do this to my family? He had singled us out, no question about it. No one else in the neighborhood had this kind of trouble. We would have heard from the people next door or down the block.

The guy was still out there. He had hurt us plenty and could reach us again if he wanted, get through the defenses of our house, which had proved to be no more than flimsy tarpaper.

If I called the police, I didn't even know what I could say. They'd probably think I was nuts. I decided not to.

Thanksgiving passed without anybody in the house seeing the guy. Max started to feel better, and the stitches were taken out of his head. There were a few squabbles among the boys, but nothing on the scale of what we had during the Weirdness Virus time.

I decided to go looking for Dr. Room. After dinner, I started leaving the house, lying to Helen about checking on a job, which I could see she didn't really believe anyway. But she let me go.

The neighborhoods of southern Queens are very similar in many ways. You drive around and see lots of attached homes and the orange street lights illuminating the trees and storefronts. Many of the houses are made of brick and the storefronts too. Most of the buildings are low, not more than two or three stories high. In Forest Hills, you have some high-rise business buildings, but there aren't many.

Other than that, there wasn't a lot to see. There weren't a lot of men walking around Ozone Park trying to look like Sam Spade, but with sneakers. Dr. Room wasn't wandering around in plain sight. After several nights of nothing, I quit and wondered what to do.

An early December Sunday saw the Schreiber family visiting my parents at their house 10 minutes from ours. We all sat around Mom and Dad's living room staring at the grand piano, which nobody could play. My mother just liked having it around, because she thought it showed class and style.

Nobody talked much. My mother didn't really know how to ask the boys questions about their lives. They probably wouldn't have said much anyway.

Occasionally, Mom would say to one of the boys, "You're like a jewel. Seeing you is just joy."

Sometimes Mom might pop out with one of her aphorisms. "Life is what *you* make it," she intoned with gravity. We all looked at her. Then she would sit back in her great chair and look around at our faces to make sure we understood her words of wisdom. She wanted us to realize that she had just given us the Schreiber family equivalent of the Sermon on the Mount.

My kids didn't know how to respond to that. They nodded and smiled politely, squirming to get out of the house to play football or basketball.

Dad looked at the floor with vacant eyes, came up with an idea, then looked up and said, "You want a cruller?" That means doughnut in Old New York City-speak.

The boys all agreed on that. They ran to the kitchen, glad for any escape.

"Come back quickly!" Mom shouted after Dad. "They're here to visit their Grandma!"

After the crullers and milk, the boys dutifully returned to the living room. This was worse than sitting through a three-hour service at synagogue. In the pews at least you could leaf through a holy book filled with elaborate Hebrew letters you can't read, or failing that, torment your brother with a popped fist in the shoulder, or a deadleg punch in the thigh.

We sat around for a few more uncomfortable minutes. Dad said, "Ruth, let the boys play in the back yard."

The boys' eyes raced upward with hope.

"It's not right," she said. "A visit is a visit. They shouldn't use our house as a playground. It's only fair."

I couldn't take it anymore. "Boys, you can go play in the yard. There's a football in the car."

Mom gave me one of her dirtiest looks. She had hundreds of them. I didn't care and smiled at her like a Sunday school student.

Richie was on me like a hungry dog. He took the keys and the three younger boys followed him like they were all attached. I thought of the Marx Brothers.

This gave my father courage. "I'll go with you," Grandpa Abe said. Ruth gave him a nasty look too.

Helen ate a piece of hard candy from a dish and looked at the room, carpeted green (to represent plant life), the big 24-inch color television for watching *The Guiding Light* soap opera, a fleet of a half-dozen foot-high flower pots on tables, and long sofas and chairs with elaborately carved legs that looked like fake ivory. Oh, and there was a portrait above the mantelpiece, a painting of Abe and Ruth, young and tanned and fit, him in a suit, her in an elegant dress, smiling with triumph and ruling over the room.

"I like what you've done with the chairs," Helen said. The chairs hadn't been moved in 20 years.

"Thank you," my mom said gravely. At least one person understood her needs.

We sat in the living room for what seemed like hours but couldn't have been more than 15 or 20 minutes. I was reminded of what Einstein said and how time was relative. Time was going faster for my boys, slower for my wife and me.

Suddenly time speeded up faster than even I wanted. There was a giant yell from the back yard, seeming to come from all four boys at once, then a gunshot, then another collective yell.

Helen and I looked at each other. "Here we go again," is all I could think.

Helen moved out of her seat to go, but I was worried for her, so I shouted, "Wait here!" She actually listened to me.

I ran through the door to the yard. Mother stayed in her chair. She wasn't moving for any drama that didn't involve her.

Dr. Room was standing by a giant hedge, holding a gun, vapor from an escaped bullet leaking from the barrel. The football lay on the ground, deflated, dead and smoking. My sons looked at it sadly and then at the shooter.

I could imagine Richie heaving the football in the air, making a beautiful arc of the throw, Max and Jon running under it, stretching to catch it, and then the football, shot like a duck taking flight, suddenly stunned and bitten by lead, falling straight to the ground. I could see in my mind's eye all my sons looking at the deflated pigskin with wonderment and sadness as it settled to the ground, no longer a football, once one of the most magical of toys, but now just a piece of deformed leather.

After all this time, there he was in his fedora and trench coat and black pants and sneakers. He really looked more like a kid playing at being detective than a real detective, except for the thick scar on his nose he had given himself so many years ago, to escape Creedmoor.

The gun was a Walther P22. It doesn't have much recoil when it's fired. It is a good gun for training newcomers in gun use. The bullets still kill you dead, of course, but the gunman doesn't suffer from any unpleasantness like recoil.

"You've ruined all my fun, Harold, ruined all my fun, ruined all my fun."

"Hello, Derek," I said. I should have been more cautious, because he was clearly crazy, but my brotherly instincts to be sarcastic just took me over. "I don't see you for 20 years and the first thing you can think of to do is point a gun at my kids? We would have had you over for dinner."

"Cut the crap, Eagle Scout. I'm not a dinner kind of guy, Harold. Isn't this just like you, to visit your parents like a good little boy on a Sunday?"

"It's what I do. Why'd you poison my kids?"

"Oh, you have a perfect little set-up, don't you Harold? Working with Dad in the business, having a wife and children, building a little domestic heaven."

"If you knew anything about our house, you'd know it's not heaven, Derek. Far from it."

Max and Richie tried to back away in separate directions, toward the hedges on the borders of the property. Derek laughed at them and turned the gun in a 180-degree sweep, covering both of them.

"Come on, little boys. Let's not play games. You're not really good at this one."

They stood like statues.

My aged father scooped up Mark and Jon and tried to back them into the house behind him while Derek and I put the verbal moves on each other.

He whipped the pistol around much faster than I ever would have thought.

"Old man, I'll blow your head off right here if you move again. Don't you ruin my fun. You're always doing that."

The scars on my father's arms twitched.

"Why don't we go inside and talk about this?" I said stupidly. It was the only thing I knew what to say. The cops on TV always say, "Let's talk."

Derek leveled the gun at my nose and spoke slowly and carefully. It was a very humbling experience.

"I think it would be appropriate for all of us to be together in that house of horrors. I hate myself for agreeing with you, Harold."

We walked into my parents' house at gunpoint. The boys, who had been so alive moments before, were now scared and I felt a thought running through all our heads: "After all we've been through, what do we have to see now?"

My mother and wife were sitting in the living room, where we left them. Helen was looking at the back entrance to the house, anxious. Mom was staring at Helen, ignoring all the fuss around her, as if trying to drill thoughts into my wife's head, about cleaning, cooking, and gardening. Too bad she hadn't yet understood that my wife had a steel head and was therefore unable to receive her important life messages through telepathy.

When she saw Derek and the gun, Helen's head instantly rose up about three inches and I could hear the alarm inside her brain start blaring: "Warning! Children in danger!"

Mom said, "What's happening?"

"Hi, Mom," Derek said, pointing his gun at her, laughing bitterly. "So nice to see you again."

Helen moved to run over to her babies and hold herself over them, but Derek motioned at her with the gun.

"Harold's baby-machine, you don't get to save them. Stay in your chair."

We all settled on couches and chairs in front of the huge color TV, like we were going to watch a show, except this one was live and we were in it. It was a very odd feeling to sit on my parents' couch and have my brother wave a gun around at everybody. The Weirdness was coming on hard now. Reality was bending itself into something unrecognizable.

My father was halfway between anger and confusion. He didn't like having a gun in his face, but this was his son. Also, his age weighed him down. When you get older, you get more cautious. You know your body can't move the way it used to. Inaction becomes easier than action. So Dad's face was fairly tormented.

Mom was plain angry. She didn't understand the gun, or the circumstances, or chose not to. "Derek! I don't believe this. You haven't visited me in what is it—20 years? Don't bother coming to my funeral!"

Derek laughed, the big scar on his nose rippling like a snake, and pointed the gun at her. "I don't think that's going to be a problem, Ruthie."

"How dare you come into my house with a gun!"

Derek lowered his head as if he were composing a completely new face. When he came back up a few seconds later, there was no sick laughter in his mouth, just stiff sentences.

"You've got a lot to answer for, Ruthie. There's a real question of guilt on your head. So, if I shoot you, I can always plead that you drove me insane. I did escape from a mental hospital, after all. As I remember, you put me there."

Mom looked like she had been hit. She didn't know what to say. She decided to glare at Derek to make him go away.

Since this strategy was unsuccessful, Derek sat there and decided what to do next.

I glanced at my four sons. They were clearly frightened, even Rich.

I had another impulse to use the words I learned from the cops on TV to say things like, "Put the gun down, Derek. You're not a murderer. You may be a lot of things, but you're not that." But I stuffed the speech far down in my spine, because it didn't feel true and I didn't think it would do any good. I really did think Derek could kill everybody in the room and maybe himself.

There's a thing about brothers that nobody else can touch. They can be the greatest ally against the world, or your greatest enemy. There aren't a lot of in-between, lukewarm brotherly feelings. You may have a great relationship with your parents, but if things aren't right with your brother when you're young, the whole world isn't right. The Weirdness cleaves into the wedge between you and drives you together in a twisted dance of rivalry and menace and violence.

This was the only real psychological edge I had on Derek and I felt moved to play it. You can bring a guy back to his most vulnerable moments and he can be so shaken by the memory that it feels to him like he's reliving it.

"Dr. Room, you've really given yourself a clever name there. It's actually ridiculous, but you got my kids to swallow your crap. Room is the reverse of moor, as in Creedmoor. And D-R, that's short for Derek. Wow, did it take you a couple of days to figure that one out?"

"Harold, you don't want to antagonize me."

I stood up. "I do, Derek, I do."

He stood up too, to match me.

"And saying you're a detective to my boys. That was brilliant. Fake being an authority figure they'd trust."

"I am a detective," he said defensively, which surprised me. "I'm trying to ferret out the sickness in our family."

"No. You're just a little baby, shitting in your little diapers. Did they have you in a little diaper in your room at Creedmoor?"

He stomped over to me in a few angry steps, slipped the barrel into his palm and smashed the butt end of the gun into my chin. It told me something. He could have just as easily shot me, but he didn't. He first wanted to exact his revenge by toying with us, tormenting the family.

The blow staggered me badly. I fell against the keys on the grand piano and the notes that came up were like a kid raking the ivories for the chaos of it. I checked myself by shooting my hands out on the bench to catch my fall.

"Is that all you've got, diaper boy?"

He came up to me again and slammed the gun butt into my forehead. Stars exploded in my head, but I knew it was important to remain standing and talking, no matter how bad I felt.

I fell on the top of the piano, my backside hitting the keys with Weirdness notes. The force of the blow drove Derek into me and as I fell, he fell too. Despite the whipped pain in my head, I put my hands on his throat. His fedora fell backwards onto the floor.

Brother tried to rip my hands away, still holding the gun by the barrel. I choked him as hard as I could and little coughing noises came from his throat.

Something happened then that I did not expect. As Derek and I grappled on the piano, I saw Helen's face looming above him, her brown hair bouncing around in the air. One of my mother's ceramic flower pots was in her hands. She dashed it into the back of his brain.

Derek's head snapped back in reflex and his hands flew outward like a bird rising to take flight. I grabbed his gun hand and tried to twist it down into the floor. My arm couldn't hold onto the gun. Derek shot the television right in the face. The TV made a fizzing electronic sound as it died. I knew my mother would be pissed.

"Derek and Harold!" she screeched, like we were boys again, fighting in the living room over a little wooden train.

(Later, I wondered why Mom didn't run out of the room at the first shot. But this was her house, her exquisite living room chair, and she wasn't moving for anybody or anything, even a Walther P22. Besides, this was better than *Guiding Light*.)

Derek elbowed Helen in the jaw and she fell back. My father caught her in mid-air before she could hit the floor.

Brother's hand was now freely moving, so despite all the jumble in my head from the pistol I lurched and spread myself over him. We tumbled to the floor, the gun pointed at my mother's stocking legs. Unseeing, he pulled the trigger and blew out one of the fake ivory legs holding up Mother's chair. She fell off the throne and down onto the green carpet, screaming.

"Abe!" she called to her husband, scrambling desperately to get up and restore her dignity.

I pinned my legs over Derek's chest and tried to glue his hands on the floor with mine. He managed to fire the gun despite my best efforts. The bullet shot the TV again, but it was already dead. He shot another slug and this one blew off a piano leg. It fell like a great wounded dinosaur, smashing into the floor, bleeding keys all over the carpet.

"How can I end this thing?" I thought desperately.

I didn't realize it at the time, but the position I had over Derek was exactly what my sons did to each other during countless fights.

They knew what to do when you had a person in this position. You hold your brother down and yell, "Gee Gee Torture!" and the dog comes over and licks your face over and over and you can't do anything about it.

In this case, my sons threw themselves on the floor like they were skydiving and placed their bodies on my brother's arms and pushed them down with all their little kid might.

The gun was still out there, at the end of his hand. He got off one more shot, which took my breath. The bullet dug a hole through one of Mother's flower pots sitting on the mantel, below a portrait of her and Abe. The pot exploded, the pieces flying into the painted picture of Mom. It hit her portrait right in the heart.

My father was on Derek's wrist now, and he used what was left of his slaughterhouse arms to pry the gun out of Derek's hand. He limped off with it into the kitchen. Dad knew how to dispose of a gun. You pour Clorox into the barrel. If anyone tries to use it, the gun will explode in their hand.

Gun-less, Derek was enraged. He wrestled us all off him. I went flying backwards. My sons were tossed in random arrangements on the carpet.

He scrambled to his sneakered feet, his arms in wrestler's position, ready for attack. We didn't know quite what to do.

The police sirens flying outside the front yard were a wake-up call to everybody. Derek made a move to run out the back door. This was a position my boys understood. Here was a runner with a football trying to get through the defensive line. Richie jumped for my brother's waist. Max dove on a leg and bent the knee forward in the direction it was already going, heedless of his newly minted forehead scars. Jon and Mark took the other leg. I went for his neck.

We dragged him down as he pumped his legs furiously into the hallway. The Schreiber boys landed on top of their moving mass of uncle, who hit the white stones in the narrow space with an unforgiving thump.

He tried again to get up, rolling halfway onto his belly, but my sons were ready this time. Richie hit Derek in the stomach. Max and Jon punched their little fists on his shoulders. I was glad Jon had decided not to adhere to the Buddha's philosophy of non-violence, at least for the moment. Mark went at him from behind, trying to remove his head from his neck. I hit him square in the crotch, as hard as I could, just to make sure he stayed down.

He curled into a cat hairball and my boys got out of the way of his flailing arms and legs.

"Ohhh, you're a freaking Eagle Scout, you little bitch," he whispered. "How could you?"

We looked up to see the glass door fly open. Three police officers ran in and took over the wrestling job on Derek. I was never so glad to see New York's Finest. We cleared a space for them.

Derek was in no position to fight back. He went limp as the cops handcuffed him. When he was safely out of the house, my boys watched from the picture window as he was pushed into the back seat of a police car.

My wife stood behind us.

"Somebody had to call the police," Helen said.

We turned to see her with a broom in her hand.

"Harold, boys, help me clean up."

"Aww, Mom!"

"Them's the rules," she said.

"Where's Ruth?" I said.

"Abe's got her lying down in bed, telling her to rest. She's very upset about the living room."

The fact that somebody could have gotten killed didn't seem to be at the forefront of her mind.

As we carefully picked up the broken pieces of pottery and shattered chair legs, Richie muttered, "He killed my football."

"It was my football," Max said.

"Wrong! My football!" Jon yelled.

I shouted: "What difference does it make? The football is dead! Dead! Dead! Dead!"

That got everybody quiet, as the boys all mourned the loss of the dear departed football.

We were back to our usual domestic bliss and I was actually thankful.

Dr. Rivers called me a few weeks later, as Derek was back in Creedmoor. He explained that, according to the federal lab on Long Island, the solution Derek had injected into the candy was a combination of amphetamine and a synthetic form of adrenaline, the classic "fight or flight" hormone. In the case of my boys, they weren't going to run anywhere in a fight with their brothers. Their impulse was to punch. Derek must have spent a lot of time creeping around and spying on us to know that. He exploited this knowledge well.

Helen had to bring all the boys and me to a drug addiction center to have us examined and treated for any symptoms of withdrawal from the amphetamines we had been fed by my loving brother. That was a lot of fun.

We watched them carefully over the next weeks to see how they were doing with the withdrawal regimen. Aside from the usual arguments over a new football and who was cheating during any given game, the boys behaved pretty well. I like to think they understood the gravity of what had happened and were trying to be responsible. I like to think that. I always try to grasp onto the slim reed of hope, because without that I'm afraid I'd end up like Derek.

Also, I spent a lot of time thinking about Derek and why he had poisoned my kids with the Weirdness Virus. What kind of thinking does it take to devote your time to creating pain and suffering and injury in others, especially your own family? Terrorists have a similar mindset, but I still haven't figured them out either.

I got a call from Derek's new psychiatrist at Creedmoor, a Dr. Koblenz. She said Derek was flirting with her, and teasing her about where he had spent the last 19 years. I felt as if we had finally stuffed the Weirdness Virus into a bottle and corked it, but the blob was still pulsating with life, even in captivity.

So Helen and I took the boys to the beach. A lot.

FEET OF JELLY

The first things that got me were the heels. Red spikes hit the wood floor like bullets. Each step exploded in my ears.

Then there was a pause, a very short blessing. The heels had run up against a boundary, like a couch or a wall. The feet turned and the bullets rattled against my skull once more. My eyes locked on the heels with murder in mind.

Ah, yes, the eyes, those betrayers. For no sooner than my eyes have closed in on the heels like lasers, they could not stay there for more than a collection of seconds. Because the ankles, then the calves, and then the curve of the thighs invited my eyes ever upward. And I cursed myself because I knew what was coming next—The Weirdness was back.

The bikini was fire-engine red, to match the spiked heels. And it wasn't just any bikini. She was wearing just the barest snippet of cloth over her thighs and chest. The protrusions emanating from the chest were impossibly high for a woman of 45, almost even with the shoulders. The chest was somebody else's idea of pure sex. Hefner's, of course.

The trouble started with the stomach. It wasn't exactly flat. It bloomed out, to be kind. There was some flab there. I don't know much else besides construction, but I did know that bikini was all wrong for her.

Flabby stomach or no, I had been trapped by another tomato. My wife was going to kill her and me, I was pretty sure. I wasn't sure who would be first.

The name of the tomato was Jenna. For those who don't know me, I use the word "tomato" to describe women who are very good looking and yet have an obnoxious quality about them. Some people might call these women divas. Whatever name you want to use, they make you want to run for the hills.

Jenna wore her brown hair in a shag, coming to just above her green eyes. She laughed too loud and too much. The constant drink in her right hand gave away the reason for the laugh.

In the left hand, permanently attached, was an ice-black cell phone.

Jenna sold high-end real estate in the city. She spent most of the day stomping back and forth through the kitchen and the living room, trying to close deals and talking to her friends.

My wife and I took a share in a beach house on Fire Island so my four boys would have a fun summer. We bought the share in a town called Seaview. Boring name, I know. But we thought it would be safe for the boys—Richie, now 14 years old, Max, 12, Jon, 10 and Mark, 8.

The other towns on the island, like Ocean Beach and Ocean Bay Park, had too many bars and single twenty-somethings and drunks and who knows what else. We wanted the boys to have fun, not spend time with people and things they didn't understand.

So now here I had put our sons in a place they didn't understand. Weird.

My sons hated Jenna, but they couldn't stop staring, even Mark. My wife, Helen, hated her even more. We knew we would have to live with her and her friends for the rest of the summer. If Derek knew about this, he would be laughing.

Jenna first met my family and me at the house the afternoon of the first weekend of our rental, Fourth of July. I was hoping we could stay that whole week and just sit on the beach, watch a few sunsets, go swimming and take long walks. After that I wanted to let them stay and play at the beach during the week while I went to work in Queens. Then I would come see them on the weekends. I wanted nothing more ambitious than that.

"So, where do you people live?" Jenna asked.

"Queens."

"Queens. Yuck!" was what she said.

My first thought was to pop her in the mouth. She didn't understand me? Let her understand a fist. I've hit men for smaller insults.

But doing it to her would mean trouble. With cops, of course. But more so in my mind. I've never punched a lady. Never. And I had to reluctantly concede that I wasn't going to start now.

Then she turned everything around on me.

"You are kind of cute, in an ape-y sort of way. You have that puppy dog face. And those shoulders! Those arms!"

I just looked at her.

My wife, Helen, was in the kitchen, silently getting lunch ready for our family. Her face rose up from the cutting board. She had been chopping up iceberg lettuce for the boys' turkey sandwiches.

My wife is a tough lady in many ways. Her father was a cranky old guy. She put up with a lot from him, but she walked out on him when she was 19. Her dad wanted her to move from their home in South Carolina to Florida and run his new house for him. Her mom had died seven years before. But Helen wouldn't have it. She got into a college in the suburbs of New York City and ran off. That's where we met.

She told me that story on one of our first dates. I admired her for it. She's generally pretty quiet, but she's like a general with the boys and the house. This, however, was an entirely new situation. She wasn't sure what to do.

I could picture Helen, wearing her black cat's eye glasses, swiveling around and pointing the foot-long ax of a kitchen knife at Jenna and saying something really nasty. I saw it all happen, and then it vanished. Her tongue was about set to yell, but her innate quiet held her back. My wife kept her thoughts inside. She saved the anger, put it away in the bank for another time, probably keeping it for me.

I didn't breathe any kind of sigh of relief. The next time Helen heard something obnoxious from Jenna, her comeback might be much worse. And I would still be in the doghouse.

I rented the house over the phone at the last minute, with very little discussion. I talked to one of Jenna's boy assistants and closed the deal in about two minutes, tops. OK, I admit it—it was a bad move. But I wanted to get the boys to the beach for July and August.

The Queens streets are hot and angry in the summer. The Queens where I grew up and where I live is the kind of place where if you cough in the subway, somebody is very likely to say, "Cover your mouth and go back to your own country."

Queens means people throwing their plastic bags away by tossing them into the wind so they get caught in the branches of trees. Except for a few bumps in the road, the borough is one long flat plain extending to Kennedy Airport, and the streets bake under the sun. Drivers fly through stop signs and yellow lights, ignoring nervous old people who edge out to try to cross the street, then stumble back to the safety of the sidewalk as fast as they can. Some don't make it to the curb.

Women fight about who was first on line at the fruit stand. Bums on the street shout at pregnant women, "You're fat!" Junior high school girls try to stab each other in the neck with house keys.

Boys run after each other and beat their friends on the back with juvenile fists. High school kids walk the streets with baseball caps turned backwards, their pants hanging down below their hips, escorting pit bulls that look like their muscles have been pumped with steroids, to show they're tough. Minor-league drug dealers hang around the candy stores with a long stare that can freeze you cold.

Helen and I wanted to move, but we didn't have the cash to run to the suburbs. I was still in business with my dad, building houses and laying floors. But it's a tough life. The cash flow is uneven. My wife was still working at a part-time job at the local hospital to help pay the bills. Our four sons had large and growing appetites.

So the rental was an effort to help my family, to do my job as a protector. The beach helped calm down the boys and after Derek and the Weirdness Virus had hit us three years before, I tried to get them there as often as possible.

We had the money for it. I'd saved and squeezed where I could, because this was also a little gift for me. I didn't want to spend the summer at the counter at the T-Bone Diner, listening to this very loose-lipped doofus guy named Wolfson talk about what a great president George W. Bush was.

"Bush has a lot of guts. He's a real leader. He cut taxes. He beat the shit out of Saddam Hussein."

I nodded wearily, not wanting to get into it, to talk about politics in the hot weather. I just wanted to sit for a few minutes in a place where there was no danger of meeting the heat of the sun.

I would have gone to the movies, but they sucked. *Daddy Day Care? 2 Fast 2 Furious? Charlie's Angels: Full Throttle?* Are you serious?

Helen and I took Max, Jon, and Mark to see *Finding Nemo* (Richie refused to go, of course), but that only made me want to see the ocean even more.

The rental was sitting there in the newspaper, un-rented, and unloved, for months. It looked like a big, fat steak to me. And I wanted to eat.

"Schreiber, lunch is ready." She didn't call me "Harold" or "Daddy," her usual names for me. Now I knew I was dead meat as far as my wife was concerned. Whenever she called me by my last name, she was mad at me. I hated the name Schreiber, but I put up with it from my wife. She knew I hated it, but this was her way of punching at me. And she knew I wouldn't hit her back.

The Schreiber family ate quickly in silence, except for Mark, who said, "Mom, when are you going to make your special cookies?"

"They're in the fridge, sweetie."

My boys all smiled, temporarily relieving the tension. Helen makes cookies with nuts and chocolate chips melted and spread through a thick dough that's more like a brownie than a thin cookie. This is no mass-market cookie. It's a cookie that attracts my sons' friends from all over the neighborhood. People have asked my wife to sell the cookies, but she refuses.

"That would spoil things," she has said to these people.

After the quiet excitement of the cookies was over, my four sons took turns eating their turkey sandwiches, punching each other in the arm and calling each other names.

"Pong-head, pass the mustard," Richie said to Max.

"Pong-head yourself!" Maxie shouted back. But he passed the mustard. Jon laughed.

"You stink," Max said to Jon.

"You rot."

"Clown."

"Meatball."

"Creep-o-zoid."

"Freak!"

After a while it didn't matter who did the saying, just what was said. My sons were very witty.

My wife took turns staring at me, Jenna, and her plate. Jenna was on her cell, jabbering away about a real estate deal and drinking something pink from the widest martini glass I had ever seen.

"That's so dramastic! I'm majorly interested!" she said into the phone. I think she was trying to say "fantastic." Or maybe it was "dramatic." Anyway, it sounded weird.

Helen looked over at Jenna and mouthed the words: "Slut. Whore." I smiled, which was the wrong move. My wife turned to me and narrowed her brown eyes to slits.

I rushed the boys through lunch and had them run out to the beach. I jumped into the waves, violating all the rules about not swimming after eating. Richie, my oldest, stayed on our towel. At 14 years old, he was talking up every girl he saw and acting like he was far too cool to hang out with his family. Max, Jon, and Mark threw themselves into the water, paddling after me like little puppies.

Max got to me before the other boys. He liked to be first and he was desperate to be near me. His big brother had little interest in him, except as a target for sarcastic comments.

The boys and I floated along for a while on the salt water, the sun blazing away. We were very relaxed and happy.

Then Max and Jon decided to body surf and I let them go. Mark swam with me a few feet away.

A dark mass floated under Mark, just a few feet away. You have to be a father to understand the fear that ran through me. This thing looked to be about 10 feet long. I thought shark, but I was wrong.

Mark saw it too and started to cry.

"Don't move!" I yelled at him. I knifed through the water to him and held him near me.

The mass floated up and I could see it. It was purple with a huge pot-belly shape, a pulsating quiver of jellyfish.

I held Mark and kicked away from the pot-belly shape. Mark cried really hard. It was a monster to him. The tentacles floated out toward us. I kicked harder, but the tentacles kept extending. I held my precious son in front of me and away from the beast.

It kept coming. I found the sea bottom, and stood up with Mark's arms around me. Jon and Max saw us get out of the surf about 100 feet away and they swam toward our blanket.

I thought we were safe. Something touched my leg. There was a moment when the day seemed to freeze. Then it hit me. A sting like a knife through the Achilles tendon almost jolted me off my feet. I grunted. Mark screamed.

I couldn't move my leg.

"Mark, run for the beach! Find your mom!"

In a foot of surf, my 8-year-old boy did the right thing.

I fell down backwards in the water and nearly broke my spine on the hard surface of the beach. I got hit around the kidney with another lash. My nerves blew up.

By this time, Richie had seen me. He ran to the lifeguards and they ran over. Two boys, maybe 19, but almost as broad as me, dragged me out of the water.

A guy like me does not get helped out of the water. A guy like me does not need help from lifeguards. The physical pain ran deep. The humiliation ran deeper.

I remember my eyes shut tight against the sun. I heard lots of breathing around me.

"What's wrong with him?" somebody shouted.

"Jellyfish stings. Thing must have been big," somebody else said, close to me.

"Dad, are you OK?"

That was 12-year-old Max, crowding close to me. I could hear his voice coming like a hollow whine through the din of onlookers.

"Get back!" one of the boy lifeguards shouted.

"He's going into shock. We have to get him out of here," the lifeguard said to his buddy, from deep in a black hole in the sand.

"You look even cuter when you're so vulneripple."

"Vulnerable. I think the word is vulnerable," I said slowly. I felt like I was talking with gauze on my tongue. How was it that Jenna would be the first person I saw when I woke up?

"I said that."

"How did I get here?"

Jenna's enormous chest thrust forward.

"I asked the lifeguards to bring you in," she cooed. "I had the town doctor treat you. Your wife wants to take you to the hospital across the bay, but I think that's a bad idea."

"Where is my wife?"

"Right here, Schreiber."

Helen stood behind Jenna, hands on hips, and ready to kill.

Jenna turned around.

"I need to speak to my husband."

"I'm trying to help him."

"I need to speak to my husband. Alone." For my wife, that was restraint. She's full of iron but too polite to do what they do in the movies, where they say, "Get out" through clenched teeth.

Jenna looked at the ceiling fan. My wife stared at her with knives in her eyes.

"This is so flusterating!"

Jenna scooped up the remains of her pink martini glass and stomped out of the room on those red heels, shooting bullets in the wood, and yelling, "It's my house!"

Through the haze, I could see my wife approaching. Her hands were plastered with red sauce.

She saw me looking at them. "I was preparing dinner. Spaghetti with tomatoes and meatballs."

"Oh."

"Look, Harold, I know you're not feeling well. I think we should get out of here. This isn't a good situation and now you've been bitten by a jellyfish."

"Stung."

"You need to see a doctor."

Searching through my host of responses, I kept thinking of the money I had sunk into this house share. "I'll be OK."

"You're not OK now."

"I just need to rest."

"How am I going to handle the kids alone with you laid up? If we go back to Queens, I can get your parents to baby-sit the boys for a few days."

"I don't know if I should travel right now. And what about the share?"

"Forget the share. You think we're having a good time? Mark, Jon, and Max are terrified."

"What about Richie?"

"He's OK. He says he wants to fight the jellyfish."

I looked at her. The sun streamed through the bedroom window. Her brown eyes and brown hair looked like chocolate melting in a yellow wrapper. The silver spokes in her cat's eye glasses lit up like little stars. She was quite pretty. Angry, but pretty.

"Let's give it a few days. Then we'll see if we should stay or go."

A day later, I was feeling a lot better. I walked stiffly to the refrigerator looking for breakfast cereal. It was about five in the morning. I usually get up early. I've had trouble sleeping since we started having kids.

Sprawled unconscious on the couch next to the kitchen was an unfamiliar female, wearing tight jeans and a belly shirt, silver-sparkle high heels still attached to her feet.

I shook hard wheat flakes out of the box into a blue glass bowl. That woke up Silver Heels.

"Hello, sailor," floated up in a dreamy haze from the couch.

I looked over at the heels. They swung down, slow and shaky, to the target practice floor.

Her cheeks were puffy, the eyes barely open. Yet, despite all, they held a glint of mischief.

She had "tomato" written all over her.

I tried to head her off immediately.

"Listen, I'm sure you're a very nice person. But I'm a married man, with four boys."

She fell off the couch. The thud echoed through the main room.

And there she lay, not moving. I thought about trying to lift her back on the couch, a midnight-black leather job (totally inappropriate for a beach house, of course), then thought about how that would look to my wife. I let her stay there, watching the rise and fall of her back as she breathed deeply face-down into the wood planks of the living room.

The wheat cereal tasted especially good.

Jenna broke into the room a few moments later, wearing a pink silk nightie that ended just above her thighs. Just what I needed.

She shouted at me, "Harold, what's going on?"

I pointed at the tomato on the floor with my cereal spoon.

"Your friend is drunk. She fell off the couch."

"Why didn't you help her get up?" Jenna put her hands on her nightie hips and said, and I don't know if she was kidding, "You're not using the seven habits of highly effective people."

"What?"

"The seven habits of highly effective people. It's a book. You should read it. It's important."

"Right."

The Seven Habits of Highly Effective People was first published in 1989. It's a self-help book, written by Stephen R. Covey. It has sold more than 15 million copies in 38 languages since it was first published [source: Wikipedia].

I knew the book. My wife had recently gotten a free copy at work—managers were always on the game to raise staff productivity and get you to think positive and all that crap. My mother bought it for my dad and me to read. That really annoyed me. I wanted to throw the book in the garbage, but I didn't. I hid it in a drawer in the office somewhere, on the bottom of some old papers I hadn't organized.

"One of the habits is put first things first. Laura's need to be put back on the couch is greater than your need to eat your cereal."

"You've got to be kidding me. She's dead weight and she's a person who's not my wife."

"You're very flusterating, Harold. You're not the person I thought you were."

I continued to eat my cereal.

My 14-year-old, Richie, walked out the boys' bedroom at that moment and took a look at Laura.

"Ha, ha, ha!"

"You, what's your name?"

"Richie. I've told you like 800 times."

"Can you help me get Laura back on the couch? I can't do it by myself."

Rich looked at me. I looked at him. "OK," he told Jenna, "but this is going to cost you."

"What kind of kid are you?"

"The kind that wants money for helping you."

"You're in the wrong miasma here, Richie."

I piped up. "I think you mean 'milieu.'"

Jenna gestured for Richie to come over. They tried lifting Laura back on the couch, but she was way too heavy.

The body sank back down into the floor. Quickly exhausted, Jenna wiped her forehead and said, "Isn't milieu the French word for toilet?"

"Toilet means toilet," Richie said. "Milieu means environment, or setting."

"How did you know that, you little creep?"

"How do you know how to speak like an idiot?"

My 14-year-old son had defeated the woman who had humiliated me and fought off my wife in one-to-one combat.

"You should read *The Seven Habits of Highly Effective People*," Jenna said to him. "You're creating a lose-lose situation here. You need to focus more on the win-win. Help me try to lift up Laura again."

They tried. My other sons, Max, Jon, and Mark, hearing all the noise, scrambled out of the boys' bedroom in their little summer pajama shorts like clowns jumping out of a little clown car.

Jenna looked up and saw a win-win situation.

"You three little bozos. Come here. I need you."

Max looked hurt. I knew he would never forget the insult. He hangs on to everything. In fact, he wrote it down later in his black-and-white school composition notebook. He always writes as if the words really matter.

"Go bozo yourself," Jon told Jenna. Nevertheless, he tried to help.

Jenna grunted and whined. Max temporarily forgot the insult and the boys all laughed as they got to grab a grown-up woman's leg here or an arm there and tried to lift Laura back to the couch. It was great fun, but they got nowhere.

"All right now, I'll help," I said.

I asked Jenna to step aside. I took Laura's torso and told the boys to get an arm or a leg. We had a good hold of her now.

"Now you're using the seven habits, Harold," Jenna said approvingly. "You're being proactive."

We were in the middle of lifting our new houseguest onto the couch when my wife came out of the bedroom. My blood ran cold.

If Helen's eyes had been daggers I would have been gushing blood from the chest and shoulder.

"Hi, honey!" I said in my lightest voice.

"Schreiber, I need to speak with you right away." I let the "Schreiber" insult pass. I knew I was in the soup, big-time.

"She is just one bundle of bitch," Jenna said.

Richie, Jon, and Mark snickered. Max looked at Jenna, open-mouthed. In many ways he's the most innocent of all of them. He can't believe that people are capable of being so nasty.

My boys and I put Laura on the black-leather couch, as carefully as we could. I marched off to our bedroom. I wondered if my wife had built an electric-chair in there somewhere. Because if she had, I was going to sit in it, with the power turned on full blast.

Another habit of highly effective people is to seek first to understand, then be understood. The author of the book, Stephen Covey, says that you need to listen to a person and empathetically understand their situation before giving them advice.

If you don't listen empathetically, your advice may be rejected. Alas, I did not know this at the time. Otherwise, I could have avoided the prolonged miasma with my wife.

"Harold, this is getting out of control. I want to leave."

"I can handle it."

"You may be able to handle it. But the boys and I are not doing well."

"The boys are fine."

Helen stared at me for what seemed like several minutes.

"Schreiber, you're as stubbon as a mule. You don't know what you're doing."

In the end, we agreed to stay at the house. My wife agreed to stay mad at me.

That night the martinis flew out of glasses and into eager, parted lips. Jenna decided to have a small party. Laura lay prone on the couch for most of the day. She woke up in time to drink.

The party further endeared my wife to me. I wish I had listened to her. Our little family would have avoided a mountain of trouble if we had left when Helen asked to go.

A guy, about 25, walked in first. His dirty blond hair, parted in the middle, reached past his shoulders. He didn't have a shirt on.

Following the seven habits of highly effective people, he decided to be proactive. He hit the refrigerator first, took a cold light beer off the bottom shelf.

With the beer open, he looked around, as if for the first time. My sons looked at him as if he had arrived from outer space. He looked back, somewhat unbelieving at first.

"Hey, little dudes!" He saluted them. Then he saw me.

"Hi, Ace. These belong to you?"

"No, I rented them from the police."

He looked somewhat doubtful. Then he smiled. "Aw, you're messing with me, Ace. Four boys, man. I should bow down to you."

And he did just that. Shirtless got down on his hands and knees and bowed down to me four times. My boys snickered.

"You got a name?" I asked. That was a mistake.

"Cloud."

My three younger boys crowded around him, excited, bubbling about his name. For some reason, this made him their hero.

Only Richie held back, muttering, "Cloud, my ass."

Laura woke up out of her stupor and smiled. "Hey, Cloud. I missed you."

"I've been running around," he said.

"Yeah, I'll bet," Laura said. "How many beds have you been running in?"

"OK, OK, that's enough of that talk. This is a family show." I gestured at my sons.

Cloud tipped his beer at me. "Right, right, Ace!"

My wife entered the room at that moment. She decided to stay close to the enemy. I knew the tactic. Stay in sight and shoot threatening looks at everyone with the hope of dampening spirits so the party would break up early.

Jenna came in too, carrying vodka and rum bottles from the package store.

"Cloud, this so dramastic!"

"What does that mean?" Richie demanded of her.

"You'll learn when you're in the right metric."

"I may have to kill you," Richie said, "unless you learn how to speak English correctly."

Helen nodded approvingly. It was the happiest I saw her all night.

Jenna didn't take it well.

"You really hurt me. You don't know how fragile I am. I don't even know how fragile I am."

Another boy came in shortly after. He too was shirtless, but had short black hair and blue eyes. He was about 25 years old, I guessed. Richie's comment was soon forgotten.

"Hi, Bobby Black!" Laura and Jenna said at the same time. Bobby Black looked like a Ralph Lauren model—cool and deadly.

"Hey. Can I have a drink?" Bobby ignored my family and me. I respected his proactive, go-for-the-gold attitude. He had obviously read the seven principles.

Jenna poured drinks for Laura and the two man guests.

It was about eight-thirty. Helen and I tried to send the boys to bed. We wrestled with all of them to get them into their pajamas. They fought and shouted. Max, Jon, and Mark protested, but we got them into their bedroom.

Richie was the only one I couldn't muscle or convince. He stayed up, with the party. My wife decided to give me another slit-eyed look of hatred.

I couldn't get used to that. It hurt every time I saw it. I was beginning to see it a lot. I wondered how I could use the seven habits to help ease the situation. According to Jenna, visualization is an important part of the seven habits.

You must think about the end you want to achieve. Of course, she had a drink in her hand and she didn't say it that way.

She said this: "You gotta think about what you want, Harold. Then grab it by the nuts."

The party revved up. Jenna turned on the music—strictly club stuff—loud, with a strong electronic backbeat.

Cloud filed four drinks down his throat in 15 minutes. Cloud was definitely putting first things first. He decided to dance on the dining room table abutting the living room. Laura joined him, wearing a new belly shirt and those silver heels.

I'm pretty sure I looked at them both with my mouth open. My wife made an evil face and looked at me. She flew off to our bedroom.

Richie and I stared as Cloud and Laura went into a private rhythm only they seemed to understand. The table shook as they bounced up and down on it. I wondered if the beast would buckle.

Jenna and Bobby clapped along. I decided I needed a drink. I went to the bar and poured myself a vodka with purple Kool-Aid. I took a gulp, trying to forget what was going on behind me. Beside the welcome burn of the vodka in my throat, the Kool-Aid tasted too sweet, too much like candy. It hurt my teeth.

I put the drink down and turned around. My 14-year-old son was gone.

"Have you seen my son?" I asked Bobby, who was dancing with Jenna by this time.

"He went out the front door, Daddy," he said, mocking me without breaking a step with Jenna.

I made a mental note to punch him in the mouth later. I put first things first and decided to be proactive. So I ran out of the house looking for Richie in the midst of a Fire Island Saturday night.

The crowds on the walks were thick with kids. Seaview is between Ocean Beach and Ocean Bay Park. You can't drive a car on the island, so everybody walks everywhere. Twenty-something professionals from Manhattan get together in big groups and rent houses for the summer. They walk all night from town to town, looking for alcohol and hook-ups.

I found myself in the middle of several packs of people shuffling casually and slowly in the darkness, laughing, talking, planning the night out. The moon was the only significant light for me. Fire Island has no street lights outside of the main towns.

I tried running around them, but just off the three-foot-wide walks are strands of hedges, brush, sand, and poison ivy. There isn't much room to maneuver. I had to slow down to the kids' pace.

I called his name. Some kids in front of me said, "Yeah!" But they were just goofing around. I walked to Ocean Beach. I looked in the ice cream parlor. He wasn't there. I walked back to Ocean

Bay Park. I looked on the shoreline fronting the bay. Small boats hung on the beach, silent and dark.

I was forced to admit to myself that he might be in one of the bars. I started searching them. I went to Flynn's first, in Ocean Bay Park. It's on a point fronting the bay side of the island. The place was stacked wall to wall with hot, grasping, clumsy boys and girls eager to help them. It took me 20 minutes just to walk through them.

I tried the line of bars in Ocean Beach. I saw a boy, half in the tank, pour a drink all over his thigh to impress a girl. She wasn't. I saw another boy who had pinned a girl to the wall of the joint. She didn't seem to mind. I saw boys and girls playing drinking games at wooden tables. But I didn't find my son, my 14-year-old word warrior.

I walked back to our rental, then passed it. I decided to sit on the beach and think about how to find Richie. After about 20 minutes, I saw a mound lying near the dunes, packed with beach grass. I walked over. The hair was covering the eyes. I kneeled down and brushed the hair away. It was my son, sleeping. I picked him up. I'm used to hauling lumber, so his weight wasn't much of a problem.

As soon as I picked him up, he woke up, looked at me.

"Hi, Harold."

"Richie, why did you run off like that?"

"I didn't want to see anybody embarrass themselves. Even people I don't like."

I set him down. As soon as I did, I noticed another mound further on down the beach. Richie and I walked over to see what it was.

It's a funny thing about dead bodies. They're all jangled up. The elements have an immediate run at them. This one, at the water's edge, had wet sand all over it. The body was facing straight up, as if staring at the stars. The body had seaweed entwined around the soft belly, which was cold and bare.

It was a woman. I brushed the hair away from the face and I recognized her right off. The mouth was frozen forever in shock, like it couldn't believe what had happened. The eyes were still open and the face still beautiful.

It was Laura, Jenna's best friend.

"That must have been one hell of a party," Richie said.

I looked her over. Even in the dark, you could see that something was out of the ordinary. There were holes in both of her shoulders, about two inches wide. The skin was completely gone there. The muscle underneath poked out of the holes. I looked at her arms. They had similar holes with the flesh pulled up, both front and back.

I thought of my options at this point, none of them good.

I had to put first things first.

Richie and I walked to the police station in Ocean Beach and told the police what had happened.

At the moment, I still believed in straight-forward honesty. But I didn't have any reason to believe that any other course would have been the correct one. I was very wrong.

The station was a plywood shack. Two police officers were sitting behind a desk writing reports on drunken kids and someone who had been hit in the leg by a bicycle.

One cop looked up. "Hello. What can I do for you?" He looked tired, but friendly.

I wasn't used to politeness from cops. Fire Island isn't like Queens. I kept telling myself that.

I didn't know quite what to say. I was trying to turn all the thoughts over in my mind, thinking about how to frame a sentence that would mean something yet not sound too shocking.

"We found a dead body on the beach, in Seaview," Richie said.

"Really?" The other cop perked up. "You sure she's dead? Sometimes here people just get dead drunk and sleep on the beach. They're not actually dead."

"She's as dead as a whore at eight o'clock in the morning," Richie said.

"Where did you get that from?" I asked.

He shrugged. "I thought it up myself. I just wanted to try it out at the right time."

"This may not be the right time," I told him.

"OK, Dad."

The cops were impressed by Richie's description.

"Jack, why don't you go? I'll fill out the rest of the paperwork."

"You sure? Your shift is almost over."

"Don't sweat it. Go."

We went. Officer Jack took a flashlight. The walk was short. We marched like soldiers. The sand was cool through our sneakers.

I walked with Officer Jack over the rickety wooden steps above the dunes and through the waves of sand to the spot where Laura was. The officer flashed his light on the face, then saw the holes in the rest of the body.

"She's pretty dead," Officer Jack said.

"I've never heard of somebody who was pretty dead." Richie was about to say something else. I poked him in the ribs with my elbow. He shut up.

Officer Jack radioed in his location to his partner in the Ocean Beach shack, then called the Suffolk County Police.

We waited about 45 minutes for the Suffolk cops to arrive. They had to take a boat across the bay, then drive in a slow golf cart on the boardwalks to get to the beach.

After the crime scene people arrived with their little evidence-gathering tools and baggies and floodlights, Officer Jack asked us where we were staying. I gave him the address. The three of us walked back to the house.

When we came in, Officer Jack knocked on Jenna's door. She answered the knock by staying in bed and murmuring incoherently in that sullen, sleepy way we all have. Her boy Bobby was with her.

"Who is it, Jen?" he asked in a dream-time slur.

"Ocean Beach Police," Officer Jack said in a dull voice.

A blur called Bobby ran like a cannonball out of the bedroom. He knocked Officer Jack down and flew toward the door. I tackled him around his knees.

The noise woke up my wife and boys. The three younger ones came running out of their bedroom to see their father wrestling with a half-naked man in the living room.

Officer Jack was pretty mellow considering he had just been assaulted by a drunk in his underpants.

"Mr. Schreiber, let the young man go. Sit down on the couch, young man."

I let Bobby go. He tried to run out the door again. This opportunity was too great for my boys. They were raised playing football in the street. They yelled and ran and jumped on Bobby, gang-tackling the poor schmuck and punching him over and over again in the ribs. He looked like a deer trying to run away from a bunch of tigers. It was one of our happiest moments as a family that whole weekend.

Except for my wife, who killed me again with just a look.

"OK! Enough!" Officer Jack shouted. He had finally lost his cool, with good reason.

Bobby, chastised and beaten, sat down on the black leather couch. He looked as if he wanted to swim inside the beast.

Officer Jack composed himself. "Why did you try to run away?" Officer Jack said to Bobby.

He smiled weakly. "No reason."

"Well, we'll have to find out about that. The Suffolk County Police will do a search on you in their database when I call them."

That's when Jenna stumbled out of the bedroom, drunk.

"What's goin' on?"

"She's quoting Marvin Gaye songs," Richie pointed out helpfully.

"Hi, Jenna."

"Hi, Jack. What are you doing here?"

"She knows the cops and the lifeguards. This is great," Jon said.

"Your friend is dead," Officer Jack said, deciding to be pro-active, as Jenna lurched toward the couch where Bobby sat.

"Who?"

"Laura," I said, desperately trying to find the win-win scenario.

Jenna shook her head slowly as if trying to shake something loose. "Laura? How?"

"We don't know," Officer Jack said. "She may have been stabbed."

Jenna sat down on the couch next to Bobby and started to cry for several minutes. Bobby, in his underpants, hugged her.

Max brought our landlord a glass of water. He's always trying to help the mean ones.

We all stood there, embarrassed and feeling sorry for Jenna, until she turned on my wife.

Jenna pointed her very long index finger at Helen.

"She killed my best friend!"

My wife shot me a look that said death.

Fighting for her life, my wife's tongue unloosened.

"I had nothing to do with your friend. I didn't even want to be here. And we wouldn't be, if Schreiber had listened to me."

I was going to get mad about the Schreiber thing, despite the seriousness of the situation, but I got interrupted.

Jenna, using one of the first principles of highly effective people, took the proactive stance. She came at my wife, her finger and her chest marching as one unit, purple slip of a nightie thrusting forward, pushing slowly but inevitably across the living room floor at the midnight hour. She stopped just inches from Helen, who was wearing her cat's eye glasses and long white cotton pajamas, with placid yellow flowers on them.

"You took your big kitchen knife, and you stabbed Laura, over and over again."

My wife appraised Jenna coolly. She said nothing. She stared back.

Jenna repeated the accusation.

Helen stared at Jenna, her eyes squinting now behind the cat's eye glasses.

Jenna stared back, until she broke.

"Ahhhh! This is so flusterating!" Jenna yelled and walked away.

"This isn't helping your case, Mom," Maxie said, ever the serious, legalistic one in his little short pajamas with cowboy lassoes on them.

"I'd like to not visit you in jail, Helen," Richie said.

"We'll have to smuggle your kitchen knife into prison so you can still make your amazing cookies," Jon said. "But I wonder how we'll get the chocolate chips and flour inside. The guards would never go for that."

Mark looked up at the ceiling, as if to God, just like me. Not finding any answers, he stared at Jenna with quiet incomprehension.

I looked at them all, then Officer Jack. I had never been so depressed. And I don't get depressed easily. I wished I could go bowling. That always makes me feel better. I would have pretended Jenna's face was on the first pin.

"Where's the knife, Helen? Jack, that's the murder weapon!"

My wife looked at Jenna. Her cat's eye glasses fluttered very slightly.

"And Cloud is missing! She probably killed him too!"

Jack had no idea what was going on. He let the two women face off for a few tense moments.

"Jenna," he finally said gently, putting his hand on her bare shoulder, "we need evidence to charge anyone with a crime."

Then he turned to my wife. "Mrs. Schreiber, may I have the knife Jenna's talking about?"

Helen walked slowly to the kitchen sink. She silently dug into the silverware cabinet and withdrew the knife in question. It shone brightly in the yellow light of the house. Then Helen wrapped the blade in a yellow cloth towel so no one would get hurt.

She brought it over to Officer Jack as if she were carrying a wounded friend, holding it with the blade turned inward, even though it was covered in cloth.

My boys looked sad. This knife had cut and prepared thousands of meals and helped slice un-countable numbers of cookies.

Helen gave the knife to Officer Jack with the blade pointed down and away from him. He took the knife with what seemed to be great respect. Then he slipped it into a clear plastic half-gallon freezer bag he had taken from the kitchen, belonging to my wife, no doubt.

"Thank you, Mrs. Schreiber. We'll examine the knife as part of the investigation."

Her eyes, framed by her black glasses, were cast down to the floor. Helen asked, "Will I get it back?"

"If the investigation shows that the knife was not part of Laura's death, you will get your knife back."

Officer Jack turned quietly away toward the door. He walked a few steps with the freezer bag, then turned around toward us.

"Mrs. Schreiber, don't try to leave the island until we give you the say-so. Jenna, we'll check out the situation. We'll see what we turn up."

"You're majorly under-promiscuating!" she yelled at Jack.

"How does she sell so much real estate?" Max whispered to his brothers.

"Sex, you big pong-head," Richard whispered back.

"I think you mean under-promising," I said quietly to Jenna.

"We'll do what we can," the officer said. "In the meantime, you come with me."

He motioned to Bobby to get off the couch.

"Can I get dressed?"

"Sure. Jenna, bring this boy's clothes out from the bedroom so he can get dressed."

Jenna did so. When Bobby walked out the door with Officer Jack, she yelled at him, "Helen Schreiber should be under arrest, not Bobby! What an un-justice!"

No one tried to correct her.

In our bedroom, I tried to put my arms around Helen, to comfort her. She turned her back to face the wall.

When you get hit with the silent treatment, it sends a chill through you. It means the other person doesn't want to think of you as human at that moment.

I knew I had to do something. After I thought Helen was asleep, I got out of our bed and put my clothes on again. I walked out to the beach with a flashlight, to the spot where Richie and I had found Laura's body.

The crime scene people had gone. There was no police tape. The ocean doesn't understand crime. The waves just keep coming.

I sat down on the beach for a long time, about ten feet from the surf. I looked at the moonlight spraying over the mirror of water beyond the breakers.

Our Fourth of July weekend was a shambles. I had indirectly put my wife in legal trouble of the worst kind. My boys had been exposed to all sorts of adult issues. That just about covered things.

A fiery sting exploded in my foot, through my left shoe, up to my kneecap. I crab-walked backwards as fast as I could.

I felt like my leg had been lit up like a Vegas Strip casino at 6 pm. My leg vibrated from the pain. My head got jolted backwards into the sand, then sideways. I ate part of the beach and swallowed some sand. I started to choke. The sand turned into mud into my mouth. I tried to cough it out.

Something dragged me back toward the surf. Another sting filled my leg with dynamite.

The water soaked me through. I pushed down on the shore and tried to move back to the beach. The thing wrestled with my leg, got a good tight lash around it. The thing reminded me a little of my brother.

The black water and the dark night both got into my eyes. My heart exploded with panic. I felt two hands grab mine and pull. Whoever it was pulled hard against the beast holding on to my leg. I was being pulled in two different directions. It was tug of war with Harold as the rope.

I started kicking, blindly, at the thing dragging me into the water. I got a few good kicks in, and a few more stings too.

The person pulling my hands yelled with everything he had and jerked me hard backwards like he was running. This guy was pretty strong. The lash around my leg slipped off just enough.

I was being dragged again, as far away from the surf as possible, up near the dunes and beach grass. I wasn't in any position to complain. My leg felt as if it had been cut in two and my ribcage felt like it was trying to strangle my heart.

The guy put me down behind a dune. My breath came in short gulps, like a kid who's taken in too much seawater.

I vomited up some sand. I leaned sideways and just retched for what seemed like several minutes. My breath came in little stabs at the air.

I sat up.

"Ace, I thought you were gone."

I coughed some more. Wet sand came out of my nose and mouth.

"Cloud, Cloud," was all I could get out.

We sat there in silence for a few minutes. I breathed the air. The pain in my leg was a burning dead heat.

"Where did you go?"

He thought for a minute. "I couldn't save Laura," he said, sick with dread. "The thing got her. We never saw it."

"What happened?"

"Laura and I were making out on the beach. The water was coming up on us. Laura wanted it like that."

I stayed silent.

"She was on top of me one minute. Then she was just gone. I went in after her."

"I'm not feeling too great here. I don't understand."

I retched again, my hands planted on the beach for many minutes. Cloud sat next to me and watched.

When I recovered, Cloud said, "I grabbed her hand, but the jelly had her, man. I saw it take her in his arms and hug her tight. He stung her good. All over. Every sting looked like a little lightning bolt."

"Jesus."

"She was screaming and I tried to grab her. A wave hit me in the knees and I fell, man. I got stung too. That was it."

"What do you mean?"

"I tried to get her out, man, I tried." He started to cry. "It ate parts of her, man. It took chunks out of her with its arms."

I stared hard at a dune.

"Why did you run off?"

"I didn't know what to do, Ace. I didn't know what to do."

He put his head between his knees.

I looked hard at the ocean. The throbbing pain from the stings began to ease off a bit.

"I know what to do."

"What? What?" he cried.

"We have to catch that thing and kill it."

"You don't understand. The thing is huge. It's got tentacles and it's huge. You saw what it did to Laura."

"That's why we have to kill it."

Cloud didn't say anything for a while. I tried to get his spirits up about our mission.

"I'm in the United States Naval Reserve. That might help."

"How does it help?"

"I know how to swim really well."

"You fight in any wars?"

I had to be honest.

"I once sailed on a destroyer."

"Where?" he said, sniffling.

"We went to the Bahamas on a test run. Shake-down cruise."

Cloud started to cry again.

"We can't kill it, man. It's too big. It's too strong."

I looked at him with steel in my eyes. "Nobody steals our lunch money."

"What does that mean, Ace?"

"It's a Queens expression."

"Yeah?"

"Somebody takes something from you, you take it back. They punch you, you punch back. Harder. Much harder."

"You're crazy."

"I'm from Queens."

"What's the difference?"

"I don't know. But this thing is going down. Now, are you going to help me or not?"

He looked doubtful. "I guess."

"Don't talk to me like that, Cloud. I need muscle. Strength. Resolve. No doubts. Like Batman. Like Captain America."

He looked at the water and laughed grimly. "You're pretty nuts."

"Yes, absolutely. Are you going to help me?"

Cloud got quiet again. He wiped the tears from his cheeks. "Yeah."

"Good. Let's work on a plan."

Jenna moved out. She took a room in the Ocean Beach Hotel, over one of the big bars, called The Palm. My wife reported that Jenna said she did not want to live with "a murderer."

"We don't want to live with you either," Richie told her. "You murder the English language every day."

"Your odor permenates my nostrils. I can't stand you or your family."

"You mean permeate. If you're going to insult me, get your words straight."

Ah, my oldest son, ever the diplomat. Jenna stalked out on her red heels, tussling with one of those huge luggage carts on wheels you see in the airport.

Helen was just a little less tense after Jenna left. She had a less than credible murder charge hanging over her, but we're the type of people that don't like any uncertainty. As for me, I was more tense. Jenna said she was going to charge the Schreiber family for every day she was in the hotel. I had a beast to kill, and I didn't think I should have to pay for it.

During the day, the boys enjoyed themselves for a change. Officer Jack had closed the beach for several hours to see if there was anything else the Suffolk cops could find out about Laura's murder. I was glad. The jelly couldn't get anyone else, at least for another day.

So I kept the boys away from the beach and they didn't seem to mind. First, even though I was limping from the new jelly stings won the night before, I took the boys to play basketball at the village court. Then we went for a walk through a nature preserve. We walked on a boardwalk through trees and swampy water. There were lots of dragonflies. The boys were pretty interested in it, even Richie. He seemed to be calmer in a more natural setting than Queens.

After dinner, at sunset, the whole family went down to the beach. We built a huge sand castle and Helen watched the sun go down to the west. You can just barely see the tip of downtown Manhattan from the beach if you look really hard. Richie searched for driftwood.

I enjoyed it, but I knew there was a giant jellyfish out there lurking. I did a little reading about jellies in a science magazine at the tiny town library after I had talked to Cloud the night before. They can grow up to 300 pounds. They were increasing in number, possibly due to warming of the oceans. They don't have a brain. But this one certainly seemed to have something more going on in that mass of tissue.

As the sun went down in a shower of red, Officer Jack walked up to our blanket and sat down.

"Hey, you mind if I sit down?"

"Not at all, Officer."

My boys stayed cool and stared at the ocean. So did Helen, hiding behind her cat's eye glasses.

"That kid, Bobby, I found out why he tried to run off last night."

"Why's that?"

"He's wanted for penny stock fraud by the Manhattan prosecutor's office."

"Where is he now?"

"Sitting tight in the Suffolk County lock-up."

"Well, that takes care of one of your loose ends."

"Yeah, but the main question is who killed Laura?"

"Maybe the question isn't who, but what."

"I'm not sure what you mean by that."

I looked at the whitecaps. "It's not important."

Officer Jack, being Officer Jack, let another one slide by. He was one mellow cop. But then, he spent most of his days and nights patrolling a barrier beach with the summer wind at his back and his most serious problem public drunkenness. Even a murder didn't seem to pull much intensity out of him.

"We did some tests on your wife's knife."

"Did she kill a brownie by accident?" Jon asked. I was raising a brood of sarcastic children and I wasn't sure how I felt about that.

Officer Jack decided he didn't need to show respect to a 10-year-old wise guy by acknowledging the comment. He talked to me.

"There's nothing to indicate the knife was involved in the killing."

"Do you know what your next move is?"

"The Suffolk County Medical Examiner is going to take a look at the body and do an autopsy. We're going to wait for his investigation. That could take up to a week."

I thought to myself, "We don't have that much time."

On the blanket, my wife nudged me.

"Officer, my wife would like to know if she can have her knife back."

"Uh, I'm sorry, Mr. Schreiber, but the knife has been impounded. You'll need to fill out some paperwork to get it back, if you want it back."

"I don't understand."

Officer Jack took an apologetic tone. "Even though the knife is innocent, it's now in an evidence room in the Suffolk County police system."

Helen stared at the officer and grimaced like a man betrayed by his best friend. It was a difficult moment. My boys looked at the sand.

"How do you get a knife out of jail? Maxie, see if you can come up with a plan for that," Richie said.

Max, not getting the joke, wrote the idea down in his black and white notebook and said, "I'll see what I can do."

Helen smiled a little at that one.

"Officer, would you do our family a little favor?"

"What's that?"

"Would you please tell Jenna that my wife didn't kill her friend?"

Officer Jack wrote the request down in his book and said, "I'll see what I can do." Max nodded, approving of the officer's technique.

I didn't want Jenna to move back in. I just wanted her to ease up on my wife.

That didn't happen.

After dinner, we got a note from Jenna, delivered by a well-tanned man wearing a tee-shirt and the tightest little white bathing suit to enhance the contrast with his brown skin. I was embarrassed for him. The note was a bill for her stay at the hotel so far, about $300 for one day. She was being very proactive, but failing in the win-win principle. Nevertheless, she was a highly effective person, as seen in the effect the bill had on my wife.

"Harold, let's get out of here," Helen said to me. "There's no reason to stay now. We can go home."

"There are a couple more things I have to do," I said.

Helen looked as if she were going to choke me. "We're leaving tomorrow morning, Schreiber."

"Yes, dear."

After we had put the boys to bed, Helen went off to sleep. I begged off going to bed, saying I wanted to watch some TV. Then I sneaked out of the house to find Cloud.

In addition to their obese weight, jellies can grow tentacles up to 80 feet long. They drift through the ocean, picking up living or dead small fish, eggs and plankton with their tentacles.

Jellies are passive creatures. In contrast, the jelly that attacked Laura was very aggressive. It had apparently eaten some of Laura's flesh.

I knew I needed a lot of protection. Earlier in the day I looked in the kitchen for weapons I could use against the jelly. Helen had a toaster oven, a waffle iron, a frying pan, and several knives. I hadn't spent much time looking at my wife's kitchen utensils. It never seemed important before. I didn't think the toaster oven would do much. I considered the weight of the waffle iron and how I could swing it in the water. I held the frying pan. A frying pan might not hurt a jelly much. It didn't even have a head. I might have trouble with the knives. Helen was already mad about losing one knife. I couldn't risk losing another. I took the spatula.

I met Cloud at the cabana behind Jenna's house. He brought everything I asked for—fins, a thick rubber scuba suit for the body and the head, with a face mask so I could see clearly as possible in the dark water.

At the scuba shop, the sales clerk knew Cloud as Jenna's friend. So, at my suggestion, Cloud put the rental on her credit card.

Cloud also brought me two tasers, which he got across the bay at the gun shop in Bay Shore. I was suddenly grateful for gun dealers.

Cloud and I walked to the beach, carrying the gear and the spatula. The shore was dark, except for a swath of beach lighted by a three-story house with a deck facing the ocean.

On the beach, I dropped the spatula in the sand next to me. I got dressed in the scuba suit and fins. I tucked one of the tasers in my scuba belt and held on to the other. Then I kneeled down to pick up the spatula and put it in my scuba belt.

"How do I look?"

"Like a guy who doesn't know what he's doing."

"That's never stopped me before."

"Just because you're sarcastic doesn't make it any less true."

"That may be the most intelligent thing you've ever said. Wish me luck."

"Good luck."

"Stay here and spot me."

"What does that mean?"

"Call the cops if anything goes wrong."

"You're giving me a lot of room on this, Ace."

"You betcha." I patted him on the face, gently. "Use your best judgment."

I went down to the water's edge. The ocean lapped gently at my fins. I took off the mask to spit into the side facing my eyes. I don't know why I was supposed to do that, but I had seen divers do it on TV.

I was about to put the mask back on when a tentacle whipped around my leg and pulled me off my feet. The mask tumbled out of my hands.

The great beast took me on a roller-coaster ride out beyond the breakers for about 30 seconds. The tentacle stung, but the rubber suit shielded me from getting seriously hurt.

The ride put me into a kind of trance, though. When you're going fast in the water, it's really easy to get disoriented. That's what happens to body surfers who get pulled into the curl of a wave and smashed into the sand. You can't see very well and you're not sure where you are. Water is pouring into your mouth and the only thing you know is that you better close your throat fast.

I was being curled into the jelly's body. It got very quiet for a few seconds. I couldn't see very well under the water. My mask was missing. But I could appreciate the mass in front of me. The thing was very large. And it had no face. If the thing had a face I would have found some comfort.

The jelly's tentacles wrapped around me. I should have been dead from the stinging in a matter of moments. But the suit was thick and the beast didn't have the intelligence to find my un-masked face.

The grip got tighter. It seemed as if the jelly was a python and it thought I could be squeezed to death.

Water was flowing into my nostrils and mouth. I had no air. I tried pushing against the jelly, but the texture of its surface just gave way to my hands.

I didn't know what else to do, so I punched the jelly in what I imagined to be its face. I kept punching, punching, punching. It was very liberating.

My hand smashed through part of the jelly's mass. A drifting tentacle touched me delicately on the cheek. It felt like razor wire. The shock lit up my face like a heavyweight's punch. I hit the blob again and again.

Jellies have nerve receptors that can sense light and smells. Maybe they can feel pain too.

The next few seconds felt slow. I hated the slowness of time grinding forward. The seconds clicked off and I felt the tentacles release me. I pushed away and up as fast as I could.

I got up to the surface and sucked at the air, a blessed relief.

I was facing open water and turned around. The light from the big beach house oriented me. I was about 50 yards out. I swam back to shore. The sting on my face was starting to swell up.

As I walked out of the surf, I found my mask half-buried in sand. I brought the mask up to my chest and hugged it, as I sat down on the beach, the waves lapping at my fins.

Cloud wasn't there. The kid was always running off when there was trouble.

I breathed long and hard, and looked out at the ocean. I considered the options. One of the tasers was gone. I must have lost it on the ride with the jelly. I still had one left in my belt.

During these times, after a stressful event, some people may thank their own personal gods that they're still alive. I didn't. I was ticked off. The bastard was still out there and I hadn't done my job.

I cleaned the mask with sea water and spit. I placed it on my swollen face. I checked to make sure I still had the other taser. I put my hands around my scuba belt. My wife's spatula was still in place. I felt good about that.

The water was clean and cool. The sand slipped out from under me and gave way to the ocean and the soulless beast prowling around for something to eat.

I swam out about 50 yards. I was starting to feel stupid because it was dark and I had no real way to find a massive jelly except by dog paddling around and glancing down into the murk of the sea.

The Atlantic Ocean wasn't supposed to have jellies this size. The Pacific did, in increasing numbers. The Atlantic used to be a little more civilized, but after this, I thought, maybe all the oceans were turning into crappy neighborhoods with garbage animals like the jellyfish.

I heard someone shouting from the beach, but it sounded like a small voice. I tried to track it. The tentacles were around me then. The stings landed like bullets from a machine gun, but were dulled by the suit.

I'd had enough. I took out the taser and jammed into it the blob's body, blasting away. The jelly lit up with sparks. It looked confused. The tentacles drooped a little. I took the taser to it, but I ran out of juice fast.

The tentacles rose up. I had nothing left. So I stabbed the jelly with the spatula. This little kitchen implement is really handy when it comes to attacking giant jelly fish.

Two tentacles lashed me in my rubber-covered head. That just made me mad. I plunged the spatula into its mass again and again.

One time when I had pulled the spatula back, a tentacle tried to sting it. A little flick of fire came down my arm. The spatula dropped into the deep, forever lost.

So I took my other arm and dug into the jelly, grabbing hunks out of its body. The frenzy was in me now and I just clutched at it over and over. I was in a fever to kill.

As I was fighting the blob I was vaguely aware of other voices, excited voices, shouting from the beach.

"Are you all right, sir?"

A Suffolk County cop was shouting at me through a bullhorn from a police boat about five feet away.

Gasping, I squeezed out, "Just killing a large jellyfish!"

"I'm not sure you can do that!" he yelled.

"Right, right, but this thing killed a girl!"

"How do you know that?" he shouted at me. The bow of the boat was almost on top of me.

I was about to answer something incoherent when a nest of tentacles snapped out of the water and stung the cop. He dropped his bullhorn into the water and fell backwards into the boat.

Another cop pulled a gun to shoot the jelly.

"Get out of the way!" he ordered.

I didn't listen. I thought I was spent, but I just dug in and started scratching out its jelly flesh. The tentacles flew at me. Massive stings bounced off the rubber suit.

I got inside the blob's skin. The thing had no spine, no brain. I just kept ripping away at jelly matter. The cop continued to yell.

"Get away from the fish!" he yelled from the bow of the boat.

"He's not a fish!" I yelled back.

Perhaps it wasn't the right time for a science lesson. A tentacle whipped out of the sea and burned the officer in the neck. He fell into the water, gurgling in pain.

I ripped out more pieces of jelly flesh. Then I remembered the cop. He had fallen on the other side of the jelly, and he had been stung badly. I got around the back of him, clasped my arms around his chest and started pulling him toward the shoreline.

A tentacle grabbed my leg and started to sting. I felt a burn, but kept going. The cops on the boat put a wide yellow light on the jelly and shot. The stinging tentacle let go of me. The cops' bullets sounded like little puckers in the water. At first I thought a submachine might help speed up the process of killing the beast, but then I figured it might not.

I dragged the officer out of the surf and laid him down at the water's edge, then ripped off my mask. The officer wasn't breathing. I slammed my fists down on his chest. Nothing. I pushed seawater out of his lungs. I gave him mouth to mouth resuscitation. Nothing. His mustache bothered me. I pushed more seawater out of his lungs.

People had surrounded us in the dark. Among the voices shouting with excitement and fear were all of my sons. The loud drama of the police activity on the beach was far too much for them to resist.

"Dad! Dad! Dad!" Mark, the little one, was shouting. "Breathe harder!"

My breath flew into his mouth, heap upon heap of oxygen. I flailed at his lungs, fighting against time and brain death.

"Get back, pong heads!" That could only be Richie, yelling at the crowd.

I punched the cop's chest as hard as I could. One cough came out.

I breathed into his mouth again. He turned himself over and spit out what seemed like a gallon of seawater. Breath came and went from him in quick jabs. His neck was bulging out and bleeding where the jelly had struck him.

"We gotta get this man to a hospital," I said, more quietly than I wanted. One of the island cops called in the emergency number on his walkie-talkie. Now we would have a spectacle.

My own cheek started to burn. I took off my scuba glove and felt blood mixed with the salty sea water.

Officer Jack leaned into me. "You OK, Harold?"

"Yeah, I think so."

"You should have told me about this."

My cheek throbbed. "You wouldn't have let me go."

"Damn right," he said, half-smiling. "This was a really crazy, dumb thing to do."

"Yeah, Ace. Yeah, Ace. I ran and told the cops," Cloud said, crowding in, shaking my hand. "But what you did was cool enough."

My sons gathered around me, edging Cloud out, and they gave me a hug. Except for Richie, of course. He hung back, seeing that I was OK and giving his younger brothers the chance to show emotion. Hugs are not usually within the spectrum of a 14-year-old boy's behavior.

My wife watched from the perimeter of the crowd, nodding. I looked at her, tried to hug her with my eyes. The cat's eye glasses were hard to see in the dark, so I never did see what she was feeling.

"How are they doing out there?" I asked Officer Jack.

"They're still shooting at the jelly."

The hospital in Bay Shore treated my facial wound and drained the toxin out of the cheek. My boys insisted on coming with me across the bay, so of course Helen escorted all of us there and back to Fire Island on the water taxi for one last night to sleep in Jenna's house.

Before we left the next day, I begged my wife for a couple of hours to clean up some business. I checked in with Officer Jack. My sons came with me while Helen cleaned up the kitchen and packed. The cop I had pulled out of the surf was doing OK. He'd been flown to the County Medical Center by helicopter. The cop, name of Young, was in guarded condition, but breathing on his own.

Maxie wrote down Young's name and badge number to send him a get-well card. He seemed to be getting a little smarter about whom to treat nicely.

"The Suffolk County cops dragged your little friend in from the water," Officer Jack said, not quite believing it.

"What little friend?"

"The jelly."

"Yeah?"

"He's sitting on the beach now. They netted him and dragged him onto the sand and shot him hundreds of times."

"Oh my God."

"They were never really sure he was dead. It can be hard to tell with a jelly. And they were pretty upset about the jelly stinging one of their men."

"I guess this means it was OK with the Suffolk Police for me to go after him."

Jack waved me off. "Nobody mentioned that to me. It's not like you were trying to kill a bald eagle."

"Dad, can we go see him?"

"I don't know, Mark, I don't know."

"Dad, come on! We want to see him!"

My cheek burned.

"Let's go, let's go!"

Jon ran out the door first and Maxie and Mark followed. I walked with Richie and Officer Jack over the sandy sidewalks to the little wood steps moaning in the wind over the dune. And there, plopped on the first slope on the beach, was the beast I had fought the night before. A few dozen kids and adults were staring at it.

"Don't get too close," I shouted at the boys. "The tentacles can still sting."

He was about the size of a small car and must have weighed 500 pounds. The size of the thing can throw off your sense that we're the kings of the planet.

"This is a Nomura Jellyfish," Officer Jack explained. "They're found in the Sea of Japan."

"Wow. How did this guy get so far away from home?"

"Don't know. Maybe some jellyfish eggs hitch-hiked on a freighter coming into New York. We called the Marine Biology guys at Stony Brook University to come down here to take a look."

The beast was sliced up with hundreds of bullets, which you could see through its translucent flesh. You could also see dozens of the hunks I had torn out of the thing.

"Their stings don't usually inflict so much harm. This one seems to have evolved in a different direction."

"No kidding," Richie said. "It eats human flesh."

"Well, we're not sure of that," Officer Jack said. "The Stony Brook people will help figure out the biology of the jelly."

(I got a call from Officer Jack several weeks later. He said the Stony Brook team, working with the Suffolk County Police, had confirmed that the jelly did in fact kill Laura. Some of the tentacles on the Nomura had hooks that could slice and sink into flesh. Nobody had ever seen a jelly that could do that before. Pieces of human skin and muscle fibers had been found in the jelly's stomach. Laura's DNA matched up to the contents they found inside the jelly's digestive system. Even though there was never another sighting of a Nomura Jellyfish there, we never went swimming at Fire Island again.)

"Hey, there's Mom," Mark said.

Helen marched down the wooden beach stairs and waved her largest kitchen knife at us.

"Schreiber, I told you, we're leaving."

"We are."

"This isn't leaving. This is lingering."

Helen got very close to me, close enough to hold my hand. Underneath the cat's eye glasses, there seemed to be something resembling anger. My wife raised the knife to about the level of my chest. Officer Jack, my sons, the rest of the crowd all looked stunned.

The knife went higher in the air, as if it would be launched like a javelin. It came down in a perfect arc and landed solidly in the flesh of the jelly, in the farthest part of the body from the tentacles.

"You lost my best knife. You lost my spatula."

"How did you know about that?"

"I couldn't find it when I was packing up. I can only imagine what you did with it."

"Mom, the spatula sleeps with the fishes," Richie said.

"You had to fight a giant jellyfish to prove you're a man?"

"Aw, Mom, lighten up. You can always get another knife set," Jon said.

"Yeah, I think Target's holding a special knife sale just for you, Helen," Richie said, snickering.

My wife took the knife out of the jelly and waved it at all of us.

"I'm not going to Target. I'm going to Fortunoff's. No, no. Williams-Sonoma. I want a deluxe set."

"OK, Mom," Maxie said.

"Schreiber, you're paying." I winced at the name. Helen waved the knife in another arc at my sons and me. "And you all are coming."

"Aw, no, Mom," all the boys said at the same time.

She plunged the knife into another part of the jelly.

"Oh, yes, you are, all of you. And I don't want to hear it. Now we're leaving."

Helen looked as satisfied as I had ever seen her. The crowd around us applauded Helen's little show of steel as the Schreiber men bowed their heads and shuffled off the beach.

We packed quickly and quietly. The boys walked with their backpacks stuffed with toys, softballs, mitts, and games. Maxie carried his notebook and a basketball. Richie carried a jelly jar and a piece of driftwood he had found on the beach. Jon held a book of Buddhist philosophy and Mark a science fiction book and his CD music case.

On the walk to the ferry, we ran into Jenna. Officer Jack had alerted her that we were leaving.

Over her bathing suit, she was wearing a black tee-shirt with the name of a punk rock band I had never heard of. I was relieved she had dressed more modestly.

I wanted to be civil, and yet, not. But I didn't get the chance.

"So the evil doers are going."

"We are," Jon said.

"I heard you cut off some animal's testicles because you thought it killed Laura."

The three younger boys all giggled.

"I can't take any more of this," Richie said.

"I know she did it," Jenna said, pointing at my wife.

Maxie looked in his notebook. "It was a jellyfish. A jellyfish has tentacles, not testicles."

"Your summer rental's been evoked," Jenna said.

"That's revoked. Your summer rental's been revoked!" Jon yelled.

"How would you know, you little tweezer?" Jenna said.

"I'm a Buddhist. I never miss a thing."

"Tweetie, did she say tweetie?" Maxie said.

All the boys huddled together.

"Tweetum?" Jon asked.

"Twit?" Mark said.

"She said tweezer," Richie decided. "You meant to say tweener, pong-head. And Jon is no tweener. Maxie is."

"Whatever," Jenna said in a huff.

"You're not using any of the seven principles here," Maxie said quietly.

"Oh, yes I am," Jenna said insistently. "I'm sharpening the saw."

"Yes," Richard said, "but sharpening the saw is supposed to be about balanced self-satisfaction. And there's nothing balanced about you."

"You are all so self-involved. You don't know anything about the principles. Besides, I'm dispensing with you all. I'm getting rid of you and you're paying for the whole summer's rental."

Maxie mumbled something. Nobody heard him.

"What did you say, you little tweezer?"

Maxie searched through his notebook, leafing quickly through the pages, talking to himself, eyes wide with panic when he couldn't find what he was looking for. He settled on one page and smiled.

"Umm, actually, you can't. That's a breach of contract."

"What?" Jenna screamed.

"If you want us out, you have to refund my dad's money."

"This is ridiculous."

"It's in the contract. You signed it," Maxie said in a low voice, never looking up from his notebook.

"I don't accept what you're saying," Jenna said, cocking one hand on her ample hip.

"You're a stinky-head," Mark said to Jenna.

"A clownie," Jon told her.

"A meatball," Maxie joined in.

"You're done. Face it," Richard said, glaring at Jenna.

My wife smiled quietly behind her cat's eye glasses.

"This isn't over," Jenna said.

"You're right. It's not," I said. "My lawyers are going to look into your business relationships with your boyfriend Bobby Black. I believe he's been arrested for penny-stock manipulation. The Manhattan District Attorney will be very interested in your friendship."

"This is so flusterating. I'm not wasting any more time on you," Jenna said, sticking her nose in the air. She stomped off to her house.

And there it was, our golden moment as a family—exactly what I had hoped would happen on our vacation. The Schreibers had realized one of the seven principles. We had just engaged in a carefully selected recreational activity together—insulting our landlord.

"What can we do to her?" Jon asked.

"Dad, her house would burn down in a matter of minutes," Richie said. "A few vodka bottles and matches are all we need and the house is history."

"Yeah, let's burn her house down!" the three younger boys all shouted.

I laughed and said, "While that would be lots of fun for all of us, it's not what we do."

"Aww," the boys all said together in a fake moan.

Some monsters you can kill. Others you have to let walk around in red heels.

But you can sue them.

ON THE ROAD RAGE

The SUV was going about 60 miles an hour. It blew past a yellow light just turning red and hit the old guy head-on. He flew like paper in the wind.

The SUV kept going, sprinting east on the boulevard. The old guy crashed onto the hood of a parked car in front of the Nosh Diner coffee shop I was sitting in with two of my sons.

Next to me, Larry Hapgood laughed about it. "Did you see the way that guy flew through the air?" he said to me. "What a crazy street. Crazy!"

My sons, Maxie, 14, and Mark, 10, and I looked at Larry like he was totally nuts. Maybe he was. Derek, shut up in Creedmoor, would have liked him a lot.

When you meet somebody like this, you hope they get help. You hope they get better. But what happened to Larry just made him worse. The Weirdness had leaned in hard on Larry, and when that happens, you just hope the guy knows how to stay cool.

Larry was one of my new plywood suppliers. I didn't know him well, which was why I wanted to see him. I thought bringing some of my boys along might help warm up our relationship, and help me get a better price for my plywood.

I didn't realize that we were all about to get to know Larry much better.

"Hey, Harold, can you pay for the lunch? Can you pay? You'll pay, right?"

The fact that an old man was lying on a car hood, probably dead, didn't seem to bother him much.

I stood up.

"I'll pay, after we help the guy on the car."

"Oh, sure, right. Right, right, right. Yes."

I called the police on my cell phone. I told Maxie and Mark to stay in the coffee shop, by the window, where I could see them. I walked through the door.

The old man's eyes were crushed shut. Blood was leaking out of his bald head. The legs were twisted, broken. The hands were whiter than white. One finger on the right hand pointed out toward the window of the coffee shop, an accusation.

I didn't go any closer. The cops in Queens don't like it when you try to help. They're very jealous about their corpses.

I looked east on the boulevard, to try to see the SUV that killed the old man, but it was well down the road and over a slight rise, already about 100 yards away and moving fast.

Larry ran out of the shop, a tall cup of coffee in his hand, the contents spilling onto the sidewalk, like blood.

"Wow, this guy is dead! Dead, can you imagine, Harold? Really, really dead."

The sirens started pounding about two blocks away. I wanted to punch Larry in the head. If he were a regular guy on the street, I would have. But he was a supplier, a business person I needed to deal with, no matter how obnoxious. I forced myself to be polite and clenched my teeth.

"There's no getting around it, Larry."

When the two blue supermen swooped in 20 seconds later, I gave them everything I knew, which wasn't much. My sons were plastered to the window of the coffee shop. Larry kept staring at the corpse.

After the cops called in the boys with the body bags, they blocked off the street where we thought the point of impact was. Managers and owners came out of their shops with a weary curiosity. The air was complete with sadness.

We had all seen this too many times. The boulevard takes people away with great regularity. Giant yellow warning signs the size of your body are posted all over the crossing strips.

"A person was killed crossing this street. Walk with care!"

Walk with care. If only the drivers were as attentive.

"You gonna pay the check, Harold? You gonna pay the check? The waiter. The waiter's waiting. Waiting."

"I got it, Larry."

"You know how it is, Harold. I gotta go. Gotta fly. Gotta go."

I was so absorbed by the old man's death that I didn't ask Larry about the next plywood delivery. I just stared at him. My very precocious 12-year-old, Jon, a philosopher from the birth canal forward, would have said I was truly living at that moment, that I had lost my sense of self in devotion to the greater world. It didn't feel that way.

Larry shook my stunned hand, made the universal sign for a phone next to his ear and walked backwards a few steps. His car was at a meter on the service road.

"Call me, Harold. Call me."

He took off.

The handshake was quick but incredibly hard. I'm not tall, but I've got lots of muscle in my arms and shoulders. Hauling plywood will do that for you. Larry's handshake was like a python. My hand had been strangled.

I paid the bill, left a tip. The boys and I piled into our station wagon, with a fog over us from the accident. I still preferred the station wagon to a van or an SUV. You can stack a lot of plywood in a station wagon. And the kids had room to play in the back when I wasn't carrying anything from work and we were going on a trip.

Larry drove an original Humvee, just like the Army had in Iraq. Gets about 8 miles to the gallon. It squats on the road and takes up the whole lane. I call it "the beast." Despite its bulk, the beast can go really fast. It must have cost Larry quite a bit of money to buy.

"Dad, Mr. Hapgood's car is really cool!" Maxie had said the first time he had seen the Humvee.

"Do you think he'll give us a ride?" Mark asked that time.

I answered Max, but not Mark. "Yeah, it's cool, all right. Like a tank."

"Hulk would drive that car!" Mark said.

Max agreed. "It's the only car the Hulk *could* drive!"

Now there was only silence. My sons had seen a dead man for the first time and there was no wondering about it, only the black shroud of mortality.

The newspaper the next day said the dead guy's name was David Jacobshvili. His address was in the paper. I decided to make a condolence call on the family.

I thought about whether I should take the boys with me. They were a little too young to have seen death. Yet they had.

I thought a condolence call on the man's family might help the man's kinfolk feel better. Then I decided against it. It felt too much like dragging the boys through mud.

Also, my wife, Helen, would probably want to kill me. I get enough grief from her over going bowling. I didn't need to get in trouble over something like this.

As we were cleaning up dinner, I told the family, around our round kitchen table, that I was headed out, to go over to Jacobshvili's house. It was about two miles from our house, in a section of the city called Rego Park. We live in Ozone Park. Even though we live in Queens, the real estate people think if you call a place a park, people will want to live there. They're mostly right.

"I'm going out," I said quietly to Helen.

Her cat's eye glasses perked up.

"Where?"

"I'm paying a condolence call on the Jacobshvili family."

The boys heard even though I tried to be quiet. You can't keep many secrets in our family. Elliot Spitzer would have been kicked out immediately.

"The guy who got killed yesterday?" Jon, the philosopher son, asked.

My 16-year-old, Richie, said, "Why would you want to do *that?*"

The philosopher son, all of 12 years, came up to me, pulled my shoulders down, and kissed me on the top of my balding head.

My wife's silence meant assent. I was walking out the door when I heard the general whine of an immature 14-year-old's request.

"Dad, can we go with you?"

That would be Maxie. And he was including 10-year-old Mark in the request.

Helen gave me a sharp look.

"Let's ask your mother."

"Boys, it's not appropriate to go," Helen said.

"Awwww," Max said. "Come on, Mom." He was in full annoying mode now and he knew it.

"You could have just walked out of here without saying anything," Helen said to me. "Now we have a situation."

"You asked me where I was going."

"That's true, Schreiber, but you could have explained it to me later."

"Yes, but you would have been mad. And one of my main goals in life is trying to avoid getting you angry." Such conversations are the very lifeblood of romance novels.

"Why didn't you pull me aside when the boys were doing the dishes?"

"Too suspicious. The boys would have thought something was up."

"I certainly want to hear all these witty exchanges between you two," Richie said. "Can't you just wear microphones all the time so I can capture every incredible insight when I'm not in the room?"

Helen and I just looked at him.

Maxie, afraid of losing the focus on the original question, broke in.

"Mom, come on."

"Don't you have homework to do, boys?"

"Yeah, but..."

"Do your homework first and then you can go. I don't agree with this in the slightest. It's not right. But your father has given me no choice."

So I had to wait for Mark and Max to finish their homework. Man of action defeated again.

When you have children, you wait around a lot for other people.

We headed out to Jacobshvili's house about 7:30 pm. The nights were coming on earlier now that it was late October. The leaves were starting to go brown and getting ready to die off the branch.

The house was down a side road a block away from the Boulevard of Death, as the local news reporters and some residents called it. It was part of a row of attached houses.

My sons made frequent visits to the table of crackers and cheese and cookies. Max and Mark looked with great curiosity at the table of goat meat and caviar and vodka. Their spirits were high. On one hand, I was glad that they didn't connect this event to the death the day before. On the other hand, I was upset that they didn't connect this event to the death the day before.

Black drapes hung over the mirrors. A portrait of Jacobshvili was placed over a mantelpiece. The living room was small and filled with people milling around talking fast in Russian.

I looked around the room, feeling a little lost. At least when I focused on Max and Mark, I had something to do.

My family came from Russia to the United States more than 100 years ago, but those roots seemed far away. I loved basketball and bowling, hamburgers and fried chicken, politics and newspapers, the Fourth of July, weekends at the beach, and driving.

Oh yeah, and I loved movies. I had recently seen *Sin City* and *Crash*. The names alone reminded me a little of my own neighborhood—I don't know why.

Whatever Russia did to my family had been washed out of me. We were from the city of Minsk. Family legend has it that my grandfather was an officer in the Czar's Army. The deep roar of winter, the chill of the Czar's police breathing down your neck, my grandfather's Army service were all just stories to me. I didn't feel them. I knew three words of Russian, not much to brag about.

I was American and happy about it.

At the Jacobshvilis' house, I was so obviously an outsider I didn't even realize the men were talking about me. One of them was deputized to come up to me.

"You knew David?" he said in very twisted English.

"In a sense. I was sitting in a coffee shop with my sons. We saw him get hit on the street."

"Excuse me."

The deputy went back to the crowd of men. They began talking fast and heatedly. One of them gestured violently in my direction. This made me nervous. I thought for a minute I might get surrounded by an angry group of mourners. I could only wonder what my wife would think then. I should have brought my best friend Al Manning to this soiree. He could have helped.

After a few minutes of arguing, the pitch of the men's discussion grew to a shout. Someone tried to shush them. A few of the women started to weep. I walked quickly up to my boys to tell them we were leaving.

A second man came up to me, old, age patches on his bald head, large stomach and badly-fitting suit, but rushed and fevered. He backed me up against the mantelpiece. I didn't like this.

"What's your name?" he demanded.

"Harold. Harold Schreiber." I fingered my cell phone at the end of my right hand, digits ready to dial 911.

"Welcome, Harold. We are grateful for you to come. You have respect. My brother was a good man."

"I'm sorry. I didn't know him. I just saw him…"

"We know who you are now. One of our friends saw you with him."

"At the car accident?"

"From across the street. At the time he didn't know it was David who got hurt."

These guys are everywhere. The Russians, like many immigrant groups, have tight networks of friends and family from the old towns and villages. They've transported them en masse to Queens.

"My name is Moses Hartun Jacobshvili. You tried to help."

"It wasn't much, I'm afraid."

"No, this world, it's too cold. You did what you could."

"I tried."

He drew himself up, white hair, sagging stomach and cheap jacket, and pulled himself into a tight statue of fury.

"This crime, it must not go unpunished."

I made the mistake of trying to be reasonable.

"I don't see how you can find the killer. He was out of sight in seconds. The police will do what they can, but—"

"Harold, do not misunderstand. We will find this man."

"How do you know it's a man?"

"It's a man, trust me. Stop interrupting."

"OK."

A man behind Moses recited some words in Russian over and over again—an incantation, I thought. It seemed like some kind of religious devotion.

Then Moses said, "We will find this man. He has committed a great sin. He has taken my brother from me. He has taken a husband from his wife, a father from his children and grandchildren, a revered man from his family."

Moses had been jabbing the air while he said this. He reminded me a little of my father. Then he did something my father would have done exactly.

The jabbing finger disappeared into Moses's hand and the hand clenched into a fist in front of my face.

"My brother will have his revenge."

After the condolence call, I took the boys to the accident scene by the coffee shop. We walked. It was just around the corner from the Jacobshvilis' house.

"Dad, can we go to the coffee shop?" Max asked.

"Why?"

"We want chocolate cake."

"Yeah, cake," Mark agreed.

"You guys just stuffed your faces. No way."

"Awww. Come on, Dad," Max pleaded.

"No. Nice try though."

Max opened his mouth, ready to commence a new assault, but he saw me crouch down under the police tape at the scene. The bright yellow tape was attached to the meters on the service road. Max desperately wanted a piece of cake, but here was death. And that beats dessert every time.

I don't know what I expected to find. The car David Jacobshvili had landed on was gone, impounded as evidence. Glass fragments from its windshield, split into fine cubes, still splattered the asphalt. The gutter was filled with grease and candy wrapper trash. An empty can of Red Bull, streaked with dirt, was nestled next to the curb.

The service road was relatively empty and quiet. Drivers can only go 35 mph there. It runs next to the coffee shops and beauty parlors, discount stores and bakeries, newsstands and Russian restaurants. A metal railing separates it from the main road. There are a lot of reasons to go slow.

The boulevard is a different story. The road looks like a giant bowling alley for the gods. Cars and trucks barrel down the boulevard, gathering speed every second, blazing through yellow and red lights like quicksilver. It's a place on fire with SUVs, diesel trucks, sedans, and sports cars moving like whippets over the asphalt. And Larry's Hummer too.

In the darkness, it would be hard to see an old man dressed in a gray-black suit crossing the street. But the accident had happened during the afternoon. The light had still been pretty good.

I thought about Moses's threat, decided it was just anger talking, and turned away. There would be no way to find the driver. Another person had gotten away with murder. He was lost to history.

The next week, Larry invited me to the gym for a meeting. I wanted to talk about plywood. He wanted to talk about his forearms.

"Harold, you're boring me. All you ever talk about is plywood. Spot me on this lift."

Larry wore one of those tee-shirts that wasn't really a shirt at all. It was more like a cloth poster for your muscles. The neck was covered, and the belly. The chest was exposed for all the world to see.

We were in a place called the Black Hammer Club, on the boulevard, about a half-mile from the coffee bar where we met.

Larry grunted with the lift. Then he got up off the bench, took a deep breath and looked around.

"You like this club?"

"It's OK. How about we go bowling next time? The Woodhaven Lanes are just two miles away."

"I hate bowling. Bowling is boring and stupid. Stupid. Makes me wonder about you. Yeah, I wonder things about you. You like the chicks here?' God, I love chicks."

"They're OK. I'm married."

"That doesn't matter. I bet I could get one of these girls to go to bed with me right now.

"Hey!" he yelled at the club. "I'm Larry Hapgood and I am freaking ripped!"

Even though I was embarrassed, I had to admit that Larry was very ripped. His arms exploded out of his shoulders. I have seen a lot of cannons in my family, but this guy had cables of muscle on muscle.

One of the managers from the club walked over.

"Hey, Mr. Larry. We love you very much. But you must keep it down," he said in a perfect, flat American accent with none of the obviously shattered grammar of a recent immigrant to the neighborhood. There were thousands of Russians and Russian Jews who had bolted here after 1991.

"OK, Yuri. Sure. I can be good. I can be cool. Just watch me."

As soon as Yuri turned away, Larry walked up to a trim, brown-haired girl wearing a jet-black top trimmed with lace around the neck and shoulders.

I tried to do some curls, but I couldn't take my eyes off the little drama by the mats next to the mirror.

I thought he would try a little sweet talk, but his line was perhaps the most annoying in the history of gym pick-ups.

Larry pointed to his muscles.

"You like these? You like these? I pop. I rock. I've got energy to burn. Know what I mean?"

The girl flipped her eyelids.

"I'm meeting a friend."

"You can't be serious," he said. He flexed for her.

The girl's face started to dash around Larry's massive chest, looking for somebody to save her.

"I have to go," the girl said, a little scared.

"Hey, don't be like that," Larry shouted. Then he grabbed her by the shoulder.

"Don't touch me!" the girl shrieked.

Larry slapped the girl hard on the face.

The manager ran over, with two assistants/bodyguards. I came too, even though it was completely unnecessary. Instinct, I guess.

"Out, Larry. Out now!' the manager yelled.

Larry took a step back. The girl fled, crying, screaming about suing.

The manager put a finger in Larry's chest and said, firmly, "You are out of control. Calm down."

Then my plywood supplier hit the manager right on the cheek. I thought I heard the bone pop under the eye.

The two assistants jumped on Larry with some kind of Russian military fighting moves. They buried his face in a mat, but not before he yelled, "Harold! Help me!"

I wanted to run out the glass double doors onto the street without getting back into my street clothes.

But I threw my hands up and shouted.

"Hey! Let's take it down a notch, boys."

One of the assistants punched Larry in the eye. I knew how the Russian felt.

"Ow! You son of a Russian bitch!" Larry shouted. The other guy kicked him in the ribs.

I kept coming at them. "Let's all calm down," I said, with my hands raised. The bulldogs were ready to beat the hell out of Larry, and possibly me. But my tactic confused them. They stopped for a minute.

"Let's just mellow out," I said. "It's all OK."

One of the assistants asked, "What does mellow mean?" I knew I had them.

"It means, 'Let's all be cool.'"

"Get him out of here," Yuri the manager said.

"I will. I promise. Can somebody get our clothes? Here are the locker keys."

Larry was silent. His eye was angry with purple and black spots, but he had shut up.

Once outside the club, we put our street clothes on over our shorts. An old lady with a shopping cart full of laundry walked by and looked at us like we were space aliens.

"You want me to take you to a doctor?"

He looked me up and down. Larry thought about it.

"I don't know. I think I'll go home and just put a piece of cold meat on the eye."

"OK."

"You'll call me about the plywood delivery?"

"Sure."

I didn't call. I decided to go with Harry Greenbaum instead, even though his price was higher.

The coffee shop is nothing special. The food is OK. Desserts are pretty good, and the coffee passable. The main attraction of the place is its great location. It's near a lot of my construction jobs. The other thing that makes it a draw for people are the shop's floor-to-ceiling windows. You can see all the drama on the sidewalk. An unintended feature is the fact that you can see the boulevard of death quite well. But when the shop was built in the 1930s, nobody thought the boulevard would become a demolition derby.

The laws of unintended consequences played out in front of me again in late November. The post-Thanksgiving weather had turned cold fast. A torrential rain in the morning became snow in the afternoon. I told my carpenters to go home early. We were doing inside work on a house in Elmhurst. The roads had turned into ski runs. They would have a long commute home wherever they lived.

We knocked off at 2 pm. My station wagon slid on and off the road. I drove slowly east to my home in Ozone Park, but the car kept fishtailing on me. I leaned into the skids, and came out OK. But I felt lucky and I don't trust luck. If you have to rely on luck, you've already lost control.

Then I had to get on the boulevard. It's the main east-west road in Queens. This road may have been a good development originally, but it didn't feel that way as I was trapped in ultra-slow traffic. There were so many cars on the road trying to escape the city that everybody crawled over the packed snow and ice. The flakes were thick and visibility was about five feet, with my lights on.

After two miles, the long parade ground to a halt. I cursed and hit the steering wheel. We sat for 15, 30 minutes. The parade resumed, rolling at about two to five miles an hour. It was ugly. I turned on the radio. The news radio station's traffic watch said there had been a bad accident on Queens Boulevard. Duh.

I reached it in another hour, right near the coffee shop, almost exactly where Jacobshvili had been killed. The cops were there, of course, with emergency vehicles, an ambulance, and tow trucks.

An enormous SUV was a smoking ruin. It seemed like the height of two full-size cars. The frame was black. The wheels had popped from the heat and the vehicle was sitting on the road, black ash tailing off the frame and mixing with the white snow.

Piled into the passenger side, right into the gas tank, coming off the service road onto the main boulevard was a Humvee. The Hummer had caught fire as well. The driver's side was a blackened shell. Derek would have loved this.

I wondered and feared the driver was Larry Hapgood. If it was Larry, he must have had the raw instinct to try to shoot off the service road and merge onto the boulevard in the face of an angry snowstorm. The only question in my mind was how he had been allowed to work up his engine to such a great speed. The service road must have been pretty quiet. The driver probably figured he could intimidate anybody driving by and get them to back off. He either didn't count on the intensity of the snow or the idiocy of the other driver. One thing he did count on was his own luck. I thought about Larry. Goodbye, control.

As I drew slowly next to the accident, I could see into the Hummer. A body slumped in the front seat, charred. The skeleton's foot was still punched way down on the accelerator, one hand raised in a crumbling salutation, like he was waving hello to somebody. The other hand had an unshakeable grip on the wheel, in a textbook stance at ten o'clock.

You have to respect death. Because it doesn't respect you.

The *Post* had the story on Page 3 the next day, with color pictures of the fire-blown vehicles in the white snow, with the four-word headline "SNOW CRASH SMASH BLAST!"

The sub-headline said: "Blvd. of Death Claims Two More Lives." My eyes ran over the story for Larry's name. It wasn't there. A line in the story said the driver was an unidentified male.

My theory about the driver was only half-right. The driver had sped up on the service road and the Hummer slid on the ice where the road merged with the boulevard, colliding with the SUV's gas tank just hard enough to ignite the contents.

The coffee shop was quiet that day. Even though the sun had come out, a lot of people stayed home. The snow was piled high on the side of the boulevard. The plows were pushing the snow and salting the asphalt, but there were still plenty of bad patches on the road. People were afraid of getting stuck, of not being able to move. I didn't know if my carpenters would show up on the job. Sometimes it's easy to hate my work. I don't like relying on other people to help me do my job, even though it's inescapable.

In the coffee shop I got a call on my cell phone. I was expecting Harry Greenbaum.

"Harold Schreiber?"

"Yeah?"

"Lieutenant Paradiso, 612th Precinct."

This couldn't be good. Here was my old friend, who had arrested me outside Creedmoor, complete with a black eye punch, way back when I was 14 years old, when Derek went missing from that old goony place. I wondered if he would remember me.

"Did you know Larry Hapgood?"

"Yeah."

"He had your business card—it says here Queens Flooring."

"That's me. How did my business card survive that crash?"

"It didn't. We searched Larry's house, with permission from his mother. We found the card in his Rolodex."

"Whoa, let's take a step backwards. How did you guys find out the driver was Larry?"

"The back license plate's numbers on the vehicle were still visible, more or less."

"OK, so why did you search his house? Isn't this case closed?"

"I'm afraid it's not that simple," Lt. Paradiso explained. "Come in so we can talk about this."

"What time?"

"Now."

"I'll be there in 15 minutes."

I hadn't even had time for a cup of coffee. The precinct was just a few blocks from the coffee shop. But I didn't like the cop's tone, so I ordered a coffee and drank it, slowly.

As I drove over to the station, I ached to go bowling. I could see the pins in front of me, shining in the fluorescent alley light, beckoning. But I never met them that day.

A patrolman with huge arms and a gut to match ushered me into Paradiso's office. I resented the patrolman immediately and wondered what would happen if I got into a fight with the guy. I thought I could take him. It would have been an interesting match.

Lt. Paradiso had deep pockets under his eyes. Purple crescent streaks like parentheses underlined the pockets. The brown hair was going silver. He looked too young to be so exhausted.

The officer went through a file with Larry Hapgood's name written in thick black ink and didn't look up when I came in. He didn't seem to recognize me at all and I was thankful for that little piece of grace.

"You went to the gym with Larry Hapgood a few weeks before he died."

"It was more like a month."

Paradiso wasn't going to give me an ounce of courtesy, so I didn't give him any either.

"You also had lunch with him a few times at the Nosh Diner."

"What do you care?"

Paradiso pulled out a pair of eyeglasses from his inside coat pocket and put them on. He turned over several more pages of the file.

"Mr. Schreiber, did you ever sell steroids to Larry Hapgood?"

"Excuse me?"

"Steroids. Juice."

"I know what they are."

"You're pretty built yourself, so maybe you're taking the stuff and selling it too to cut down on your costs."

"Joking, right?

"No joke."

"Get outta town."

Paradiso took off his glasses. "I have no intention of getting out of town, Schreiber. You selling steroids?"

The lieutenant put his glasses back on.

The guy had no sense of humor. He should meet my wife. I would have to play it straight.

"No, I don't sell steroids, Lieutenant. I don't take them either."

"I've looked at your file. You're in the United States Naval Reserve. This kind of activity could get you thrown out of the service. You might even lose your business."

I couldn't take his act.

"Don't you have better things to do, Paradiso?"

He looked at the file again.

"I see here I arrested you when you were just 14 years old."

Oh, hell.

"You really embarrassed me."

"I didn't do anything wrong. I was looking for my brother."

"You were trespassing at Creedmoor."

"And you punched me in the face."

"I really enjoyed that."

"I'm glad I could help you out there."

Paradiso smirked. I would have been happy to take a machine gun to that smirk.

"Back to the current business, slimeball. Do you sell steroids?"

A deep, heavy sigh escaped me. I couldn't help it. "What is this about, really?"

Paradiso shot me a deadly look. I had scored with just the sigh.

"Schreiber, do you know what steroidal intoxication is?"

"No, not really."

"Your good friend Larry Hapgood was so loaded up with steroids that he fired up his Hummer to 70 miles an hour on the Boulevard of Death in the middle of a freak snowstorm."

"He wasn't a friend. But, yeah, he did good work with that Hummer."

"Hapgood had so much juice in him that we found it in his bones."

I spent a few minutes digesting this and swore at myself for not seeing it before—the fast talking, easy boredom, nervousness and aggression. It all added up to steroid addiction.

Lt. Paradiso took off his glasses again for dramatic effect.

"So, how'd you do it?"

"Do what?"

"You got the juice from a local lab and sold it to Hapgood and other clients."

I pointed at the detective and yelled as loud as I could, "That never happened!"

This had no effect, which surprised me. "You selling dope to little kids too?"

"You're pretty nuts."

I stood up.

"I'm leaving now."

"Running guns for the Russians?"

"Goodbye, Lieutenant Paradiso."

"Laundering money for Uzbeki terrorists?"

I wanted to slam the door, but I didn't think having a squad room of cops descend on me, nightsticks ablaze, would have been a good idea for my face.

On the drive home, I wondered about the trouble Lt. Paradiso could cause me. My former plywood supplier was a steroid addict, if the possibly delusional police lieutenant was to be believed.

On the boulevard, through the snowdrifts piled on the sides of the road, I saw a skinny young kid, about 13 or 14 years old, with his thumb stuck out to get a ride.

As I got closer, I saw it was my son Max.

There is no shoulder on the boulevard. So I put on my warning lights and stopped the station wagon in the right lane of traffic. I got cheered by several SUVs behind me, with multiple honks and curses. I stuck my middle finger out the driver's side.

Max dove in the passenger side.

Other men might take the time to yell, "Are you crazy? Why are you hitchhiking on one of the most dangerous roads in the city?" I tried to be sensitive.

"Where are you headed, son?"

"I missed the school bus going home."

"You could have called."

"I forgot."

I tensed up and dropped the sensitive parenting approach.

"You'd forget your head if it wasn't attached."

Max looked moodily out the windshield, with his brown eyes crowned by thick black plastic glasses typical for 1965. Unfortunately, this was 2005.

"Dad, I'm sorry, but—"

He didn't get to finish the sentence. My ample forehead got thrown into the steering wheel. Max, who hadn't yet buckled in, hit the windshield with his face.

My head came back up and we got rammed again. A piece of loose plywood in the back seat came rocketing through the car and hit Maxie square in the back of the skull.

I swung the car onto the sidewalk and almost killed an old woman wearing a red kerchief on her hair.

"You stinking bastard!" she screamed at me.

I wouldn't care much about this sort of thing under any circumstances, but with my son bleeding from the face, I was especially incensed. I made a mental note to kill her later.

The SUV that hit us was the immediate focus of my hatred. The front end of the vehicle was crumpled, despite a grille that would put a tank to shame. Max pulled me out of my desire to beat the living crap out of the SUV's driver.

"Dad."

"Max!"

"Dad, I can't feel my lip!"

"Max!"

"Dad, where's my lip?"

I pulled a towel from the back seat and pressed it onto Maxie's mouth. Blood was squirting from his forehead and mouth and I was completely panicked about it. I held the rag on his face and made myself feel sad because it was so dirty from being wrapped around plywood.

"Maxie, hold on to this."

I thought about calling for an ambulance with my cell phone. I decided it would take too long. There was no time for getting the other guy's license number and insurance card.

I buckled my wounded son in, swerved the wagon back onto the boulevard and threw the car across three lanes of traffic, cleaned mostly of snow. The Parkway Hospital's emergency room was five minutes away. The guy in the SUV stared at me, mouth open. I wished I could have shoved my fist into it repeatedly.

The wagon roared into the hospital's driveway and braked hard. I ran with Max in my arms through the double doors and yelled loud enough to pierce through the racket of aches and pains resounding through the triage room.

It was only when I passed my son like a football into the arms of a concerned-looking nurse that I had a painful realization. Our car had been hit in the same place on the road where David Jacobshvili and Larry Hapgood had been killed.

We spent five hours waiting for a surgeon to arrive to stitch my son's face back together. He had an inch-long cut on the forehead and three-quarters of his lip was cut through to the gum. He had a concussion too.

The kid was always getting hurt. Years before he'd taken several huge cuts in his forehead from running through a glass door, courtesy of the Weirdness Virus that had infected us—Derek's handiwork that time.

My wife stayed at home with the boys. She was tense with me on the phone. What happened to Max was my fault. Helen didn't say that; she didn't need to.

I sat next to Max while he lay on a gurney, a towel pressed to his lip. I held the towel. We talked so he would stay awake and not lose consciousness.

"Dad, can we go bowling when I'm better?"

"Sure, Max."

"How about the Mets?"

"We'll go in the springtime, April, I promise."

"What's it like in the Navy?"

"I'm not really in the Navy. It's the Naval Reserve."

"But you get to go on Navy ships."

"That's part of the training. You have to be ready to serve if there's an emergency."

"Too bad there's no Dad Reserve."

"What do you mean?"

"They can't train you to be a dad."

"No, but there are plenty of books. And there's your mother."

"I'm not sure I can be a dad."

"You don't have to worry about that now, Max."

"OK, Dad."

In the dead light of the hospital's overhead lamps, I saw Paradiso and another cop walk up to me. Max got quiet.

"Now you're molesting little boys," Paradiso said.

"This is my son."

"You left the scene of an accident."

I appraised Paradiso in the frozen light. Without his glasses he had a solid American face—strong jaw, straight nose, white teeth, flat stomach. His shoulders were wide enough to give anybody trouble.

The eyes gave him away, though. They were the soft eyes of a poet. Underneath all that bluster and insult, he was sensitive and he could be hurt.

"Let me ask you a question, Lieutenant. Do you have any children?"

This threw him off a little. "I'm not married."

"I didn't think so. You don't have children, so you don't know how wide open a father feels when his kids walk out the door in the morning. Sometimes you have to fight the whole world so your kids can survive."

"You fought an SUV and lost."

"I didn't fight anybody. The guy hit me from behind."

"Your karma's all wrong," the other cop said to me.

Paradiso and I looked at the partner. He was quite odd. His clothes were rumpled. He wore a thick, frizzy beard. His cheeks popped out like he was hiding nuts.

"What's your name?" I demanded.

"Marx."

"Groucho or Harpo?"

"Carlo."

"What planet did you blast out of?"

"You can't talk to me that way. You broke the law. That makes you a criminal."

"And you're a wacko."

"I'll take you down so far, Schreiber, you won't know which end is up," Paradiso said.

"Give it a try, buddy. You'll be coming with me."

On the gurney, Maxie groaned. That didn't stop Paradiso.

"I'm going to be looking at you, Schreiber. All this stuff is connected through you—the steroids, the Uzbeki terrorist money, the gun business with the Russians. Now this accident."

It was Marx's turn to look at his partner like he was an idiot.

"You're kidding me, right?" I turned to Marx. "Tell me he's kidding."

"There's bad karma all around," he said.

I looked at Paradiso.

"Can't somebody turn you off?"

"I'm like TV—I'm never off."

"If you actually had any evidence, you would have booked me already. You came here because you're fishing and you're coming up with zero."

"I think you mixed a metaphor there," Marx said.

"I did not mix any metaphors," I snapped.

From under his towel, Max said something nobody could hear.

"What's that?" Paradiso asked.

"Eagle Scout."

"What?"

"My dad's an Eagle Scout," Maxie said, drowsy with pain. "He'll always be an Eagle Scout."

Max took twenty stitches in his lip and an icepack home from the hospital the next night. His brothers were merciless.

"Did you cut yourself shaving?" Jon said, losing his usual philosophical detachment to become a 12-year-old boy again.

"Kissed a truck going 80?" said Richie, the clever one.

Max just looked at me, helpless and hurt in the face of the onslaught. Even if he could have talked back, I'm not sure he would have. He gets flustered easily when his brothers insult him.

My wife and I got Max to bed. Helen was cross with me. I sat around for 15 minutes and considered my options. I thought it would be best to go bowling.

I took Mark, the quiet one, to Woodhaven Lanes, along with my 16-pound ball. Mark bowled a 78, not bad for a young kid. My score was 214. I would have done even better, but I missed a split on the last pin.

There were only seven other bowlers, it being a weeknight. The lanes had a certain quiet majesty. The wood alleys were polished and bright, like a new parquet floor.

When we finished, we passed by Dino, the alley maintenance man. He was wearing a blue sweatshirt, greasy jeans, and sneakers. His brown hair was greasy too, but he was an honorable man, and that counts for something.

"Hey, Harold."

"Hey, Dino. How's it going?"

He smiled a little smile. "I get by. You?"

"Getting by."

I had known him for years, but we knew each other in the way private men usually do. We talk in nods and shrugs and index finger salutes starting at the forehead and ending about a foot away.

The smell of freshly-tapped beer, one of the sweetest smells I have ever known, was oozing through the back steps of the alley. The restaurant was serving cheeseburgers and fries with cola. After we bowled, Mark and I ate in silence.

A sign said the place was closing soon. Dino didn't say anything about it, but it's not his nature to bring up anything, serious or otherwise.

I got upset about the closing. I wondered what would happen to league night.

A couple in a Ford Expedition was killed on the boulevard the next night. The driver had collided with an Escalade and the Expedition flipped over.

Two nights later, five people in a Land Cruiser and a Dodge Ram were killed, and three injured, when the Ram pushed through the wrong end of a yellow light and crashed into the driver's side of the Land Cruiser full-on.

The next week a Lexus SUV piled into a dump truck and exploded on contact. Three nights after that, a half-dozen teenagers in a Chevy Dakota rammed a Volkswagen and rolled over. The driver in the Volkswagen survived somehow. The six teens did not.

Every accident happened in the same place where David Jacobshvili was killed. The *Post* was splattered with red.

I thought about revenge. David's brother had made a vow of revenge. Was David taking on the SUVs of the world?

I thought about Derek, too. These types of crimes were something he would be very interested in doing. I called Creedmoor, just to make sure he hadn't gotten out again somehow. Nope. Still there.

I decided to look into it myself. After dinner, about an hour before league night, I sneaked out of the house. Off the kitchen there's a patio area that we never used. Three little concrete steps lead from the kitchen to this little patio strip, which is no wider than five feet. We put three walls around it, and built a screen door.

The screen door leads you to the side yard, about two feet wide, abutting a neighbor's hedge. You can quietly slide through the path and get to the street.

I drove to the Nosh Diner and had a cup of coffee. From the window of the shop, the road is flat for several hundred yards. Then there is a slight descent and a rise, a small hill. I thought of the gently rolling hills of the place where I had gone to commuter college for a while. There was nothing gentle about this place.

The original intention for the boulevard was to imitate the boulevards of Paris, with two slow-moving lanes of traffic and lots of trees and flowers and elegant shops on the sidewalk. As with so much in New York, this plan quickly fell by the wayside. The city fathers decided that Queens had room for lots of factories and warehouses. The small street was ditched for six lanes of traffic, essentially an expressway to connect Manhattan to Queens and the suburbs beyond the city on Long Island.

After the coffee, I walked across the service road, stood on the median strip and studied the area where all the accidents had roughly taken place. The boulevard is not a quiet place. Trucks, cars, SUVs, Hummers, city buses shoot over the road like pinballs. The vehicles cut through the wind like knives. A plane coming into LaGuardia Airport every 10 minutes roars like a Tyrannosaurus rex overhead. A freight train wouldn't be out of place here.

Despite all the noise, I heard something different. The sound was low, but distinct from the cars and trucks. It touched my mind first, then my ear.

I winced from the pain of it. The sensation reached right inside me, grabbed my heart in a death grip and twisted. I fell back a few steps and stumbled on the median strip.

At first I didn't believe what I was hearing. I crouched down on the median strip again, the closest safe place to the site of all the accidents, and examined the road to make sure I understood the sound completely. And yes, it was true.

The asphalt was screaming.

The Jacobshvilis' house seemed empty, despite repeated rings and knocks on the front door. After 15 minutes of getting no result, I sat on the front door step and thought about what to do.

Moses walked up to the concrete steps about a half-hour later. His black fedora threw a shadow over his face. Smoke laced the man's jaw in the orange light of the street.

"Harold, I didn't expect you."

"Moses, I need to know what that guy said the night I met you, on the condolence call."

His face pulled back and he appraised me closely.

"Come inside. Let's talk."

Moses made strong coffee. We sat in the living room and drank silently.

"You once told me about revenge. And this is good coffee."

"Thank you. Let's not talk about revenge. I was angry."

"When you were talking to me that night, a man behind you was saying something in Russian."

"It's not important. You want a cookie?"

"A cookie would be great. Can you tell me what the man said?"

"He's my cousin. Would you like a chocolate-covered fudge cookie or a vanilla mousse cookie?"

"Chocolate covered fudge."

"You're from Russia?"

"No. My grandfather was, but I was born in Queens."

A thin smile formed on Moses's lips. "You look Russian."

"I'm not. Good cookie. Can you tell me what your cousin said?"

Moses looked away, at the mantelpiece.

"We could use a fire."

The conversation was going nowhere. We needed a radical change. So I threw the half-eaten cookie at Moses's head and hit him square on the cheekbone.

"Hey!"

"Are you going to tell me what your cousin said?"

He rubbed the chocolate fudge off his cheekbone with a handkerchief for a few seconds.

"I could have you killed, just for that. Killed for a cookie. How would your little sons like that?"

"Moses, I don't know if you read the papers, but people are getting killed out there on Queens Boulevard, in the exact same place where your brother was hit. Now, you swore revenge for your brother's death. And you're getting it."

"You're right. You're not Russian. You'd never understand."

"What the hell is going on out there?"

Moses lit a cigarette and studied me.

I reached down for the plate of cookies and picked one up.

"You want another cookie in the face?"

He put the cigarette in an ashtray and let it smoke. He appraised me with a hard squint.

"Are you familiar with dybbuks?"

"No."

"They're the wandering souls of dead people."

"That's all Old World crap."

"Dybbuks enter the body of a living person and control their behavior."

"But there's no person involved. I think the boulevard is possessed."

"Now who sounds like they're full of crap? It is very unusual, but possible for a dybbuk to find an inanimate place and stay there."

"What did your cousin say that night?"

"He pronounced the road a shonda—a disgrace. He wished for Gehenna to visit the Earth in the place where Jacob was killed."

"What's Gehenna?"

"You should be ashamed of yourself. You've completely given up your roots."

"What's Gehenna?"

"Hell."

The snow fell as thick as butter shavings on our heads. Moses stood like a statue, letting the snow slide down his cheeks and nose. Next to him there was a rabbi in a black rain coat.

"This is Rabbi Benishtik," Moses explained. "He's the spiritual leader for our community."

"Shalom," the rabbi said. "Let's say a little prayer that we've met, even under these circumstances."

I nodded, skeptical of all this religious hoo-hah.

We three stood on the median strip between the service road and the boulevard. It was about the width of two trucks. The Nosh Diner was behind us. The rabbi said his prayer.

It was a minor sort of miracle that I had gotten this meeting together. Just an hour earlier I had been sitting with my family in our house. We sat at our round wooden kitchen table after dinner on Saturday night. Max, Mark, and Jon cleared the dishes. Richie disappeared into his room to get ready for a movie with a girl. Jon went to the living room to wait for a friend to arrive for a sleepover.

"I have to do something."

Before the words to explain the lie I had planned, Max and Mark were all over me.

"Dad, can we go? Can we? Can we? Can we?"

I looked at them. "No."

"Come on, Dad. Come on."

Helen sat next to me, her eyes condensing into a severe frown behind the cat's eye glasses she had worn since our wedding so many years ago.

Picking up the cue from the wife, I said, "No."

"We want to go," Max said.

"We want to go," Mark repeated.

This sort of thing could go on for a half-hour. They knew how to wear me down, until I was so sick of hearing them that I would say yes. Except this time I couldn't.

"No. Go to bed. Do your homework. Watch TV. Read comic books. Run around in a cape. Do whatever you do this time of night."

Maxie walked off sulking, hands on hip, Mark behind him.

"I'm on strike!" Max yelled.

I was happy to have gotten rid of them, but now I was alone with my wife, a very dangerous place to be.

"I really do have something to do," I said weakly.

Helen shot me a look that said, "I don't believe you." But she said nothing. On such silent tensions a solid marriage is built.

"Where is the place?" Moses said to me.

"I'll walk you to it."

The three of us walked single-file several feet along the median strip dividing the service road and the boulevard. It should have been easy to hear the curdling sound I had heard coming from the road a few days before. The boulevard was pretty quiet. The snow was like a wall. Cars and trucks and the ubiquitous SUVs rolled slowly over the road, being made over as a fragile path. They emerged through the fog like ghosts straining against a plastic shower curtain.

Then I realized the snow, that great insulator, must be muffling the sound. When a parade of cars had trundled past and it was safe, I kneeled down and scraped the snow off the road next to the median strip. I felt Moses's and the rabbi's eyes plunge through my coat. They must have thought I was a little touched in the head.

There was no sound. The rabbi sighed.

"I was having a very nice dinner with my wife at Gan Eden, Moses. And you pull me out here for this?"

He had gone from Man of God to Man of Queens in record time. Thirty seconds ago he was saying a prayer. Now he was just another ticked off guy ready to start an argument.

"It's his fault. I'm going to have the dybbuk kill him," Moses said with the loveliest of smiles.

I felt a slight thrum in my chest, then the physical sensation of the blood tightening in the artery leading to my heart. Acid was flowing through me, I was sure of it.

I stepped back. Moses had fallen down and was staring at the white sky, clutching his chest. The rabbi was holding his face in his hands, so he couldn't see, like he was afraid to see.

At that moment Max and Mark arrived.

I felt the screaming road inside me, as I tried to warn my sons away. But no words came out.

The boys, concerned, crossed the service road in the snow, against the light. I put my hand out in a stop motion. They kept coming.

Max reached us first. He hugged me around the waist, his lip still thick from post-surgery healing. Mark came next.

"Get back!" I whispered.

Too late. A thin line of blood ran down Mark's nostril, then another came from the other nostril. Max's healing lip swelled up and he started to bleed as well, in a crescent from nose to mouth.

I grabbed them, one in each arm, my heart stabbing at me. I dragged all three of us across the road to the Nosh Diner corner.

"How did you get here?" I yelled at them.

A great non-answer came from Max. "Dad, we're bleeding!"

Mark's nose was bruised and he vomited all over the white snow.

I kneeled down. It looked like his nose was broken.

I held them by their shoulders and we sat down on the side-walk to get a breath.

Rabbi Benishtik peeled his hands from his face and crawled to the spot of the screaming. He looked onto the road. The rabbi's hat blew off, from the wind or the scream, I couldn't tell.

He put his hand on the road. Chunks of asphalt blew upward into Rabbi Benishtik's face. He fell over onto the road.

"Stay here!" I yelled at the boys. They weren't in much of a state to protest. Max's wound had opened up again, like a split seam, and Mark's nose was swelling up.

I propped them up against the diner's wall and ran for the rabbi.

A Nissan Pathfinder was rolling toward Rabbi Benishtik in the snow. "The Pathfinder can't see him," I thought.

I ran on the road, whipping my arms as fast as I could. The Pathfinder braked, then slid on the snow.

The rabbi was lying face-down on the road. I picked him up by the chest and dragged him onto the median strip. The Pathfinder kept sliding toward us. I put my body over the rabbi's back.

The Pathfinder rolled as I tried to pull the rabbi's unconscious heap in inches across the median strip and onto the service road, doing anything to get out of its way.

A crunching sound stopped the rolling. The Pathfinder had managed to stop on Rabbi Benishtik's ankle. He woke up and yelled like a wounded ram.

"Is he OK?" Moses said, on his knees. He was drenched and pale and scared.

"I think his foot is broken."

"We have to get him to a hospital."

The rabbi moaned.

"No kidding."

"Let me call a friend," Moses said.

He rang up a number on his phone and said in a hushed voice: "The rabbi is hurt, maybe badly. Come quickly."

He got a private ambulance, colored lime green and red, which pulled up in five minutes, faster than the regular hospital jobs, even with the snow. The Russians even have their own emergency vehicle network. How's that for assimilation?

The ambulance men, efficient and mindful of hierarchy, came for the rabbi, checked his vitals. The snow fell in clumps around us. Then the men loaded the rabbi on a gurney and popped him into the back of the ambulance like he was a delicate loaf of bread. I brought my sons over from the corner. Mark could barely walk, so I just picked him up and carried him to the emergency vehicle. Maxie stumbled along beside us, bleeding and frightened.

Before I got in the back with Moses, the rabbi and the boys, several more chunks of asphalt blew in the air, hitting one of the brake lights of the ambulance. Out of the hole came a roar that was full of venom, a hungry, vicious sound.

"Let's get the hell out of here!" I shouted to the driver.

"Da."

An hour later, we sat at the same old hospital, with the same dead light.

Mark had a broken nose. He had gotten it set and dressed. Maxie got a few new stitches in his lip.

Mark slept for a couple hours after the operation. Maxie, miserable because his face was once again blooming with fresh scars, was placed beside me after the little work he had received.

"How did you guys get out of the house?"

Maxie stared straight ahead and answered me in a flat voice, drained of emotion. He mumbled a little because of the puffed-up flesh on his wounded lip.

"We sneaked out through the patio screen door after you left."

"Where did you learn that?"

"From you, Dad. We've been doing it for years."

"Oh."

The rabbi's ankle was broken and his face was cut up pretty good where the asphalt chunks had risen up against him. A bruise colored his cheek.

The rabbi's wife had come. We saw her run through the emergency room to her husband's bed. She looked afraid and stricken. You could tell she really loved him.

Moses had a heart scare, but he was OK. The ER doctor discharged him and he sat next to Max and me in the waiting room.

"The only people for you are the mad ones, eh, Schreiber?"

My eyes rose up to meet Paradiso. Then I looked at my companions. Max looked like a boxer who'd lost a fight and under the harsh light Moses had the face of a washed-out bum who needed a bottle.

"At least they're not you."

"He talks like this to everybody," Moses, the angel, said.

The lieutenant smiled. Marx was with Paradiso again. Marx shook his head.

"You two need to get your attitudes in rhythm. You know, like two jazz musicians."

Paradiso stepped up to me and stood over me. "We're going to get our attitudes in rhythm, Schreiber. You're going to tell me all about how this accident is keyed in with your steroids business. Then I want to know about your connections with the Russians and the narcotics and the guns and the prostitutes, the Kazakh connection, how the Uzbeks tie in. You're the center of this whole thing, I'm sure of it. We're going to spend a lot of time together."

I blew the cop a kiss.

"I'm looking forward to it, sweetie. It's been a long time between drinks, Lieutenant."

"You're going to take us to the scene of this so-called accident. I want to see it."

"I don't think you do."

"Don't tell me what I want."

"I think you'd rather spend some time in the desert at noon."

"You guys need to get in tune. In tune, man. In tune," Marx said. He described a circle with his hands.

"Let's go," Paradiso snarled.

"My sons are here."

"Call your wife. She can take care of them."

"I called her. She's already not talking to me."

Paradiso gestured at Moses. "What about this guy? He can watch them."

"He's not a family member."

"Why don't you let the guy get the kids discharged? Then Schreiber can take us to the accident scene," Marx said to Paradiso.

"Why are you being so nice?" I asked Marx.

"It's my nature. I love mankind. I'm a Buddhist."

"You're not from Queens."

"Brooklyn."

"Oh, that explains it."

My mind was twisted around about twelve different ways. How could a Buddhist be a cop? Nothing about Marx made sense, although he would make an excellent mentor for my son Jon. I wanted to invite Marx over for dinner, so he could meet Jon, but I could also see my wife's cat's eye glasses shooting laser-beams at my head for having a cop in the house.

"No guns in the house, Schreiber," she would say. "That's the rule. I don't care if it's a cop or President Bush."

The discharge process took about a half-hour. Mark was awake now and miserable. I desperately wished for some way to make him happy and whole again.

As we were about to walk out, Moses asked to come with us. The cops followed.

"Don't leave yet!" the rabbi's wife shouted at us from across the emergency room. Several doctors tried to freeze her with their eyes, but she didn't care.

The wife ran up to us, a little breathless.

"He wants to talk to you, Mr. Schreiber. Please come quickly."

"I'm walking with you," Paradiso said. "You're a little robot, with a little man in you who tells you to run away."

"If I didn't know any better, I'd say you were schizo."

"And I'd say you were ready for a pop in the mouth."

"Please, Mr. Schreiber!"

"OK, Mrs. Benishtik. Let's go."

She led us quickly to the bed. The rabbi was pretty out of it. His foot was in a cast. There were painful rips across his nose and cheeks and forehead, from the asphalt explosion.

Mrs. Benishtik pulled me to the rabbi's pillow. He gasped.

"What's that?" I asked.

"The dybbuk," he said, labored and slow.

"Yeah, it's a dybbuk. I got that."

"The dybbuk is…"

"Right. A dybbuk."

"The dybbuk is not…"

"Is not?"

The rabbi looked at me like I was an idiot and that whatever he was going to say would completely change me into a smarter person.

He breathed in and gathered his strength.

"The dybbuk is not David Jacobshvili."

"What do you mean?"

"It's not David. When I went to talk to the dybbuk, he told me he wasn't David. He got mad."

"He told you this?"

The rabbi struggled with his breath. "He told me in my mind."

"It's not David," I said, trying to sound rational even though we were talking about a possessed piece of road.

"He got mad because we thought he was David. That's why he lost his temper."

"He lost his temper? That's what that was?"

"You need to rest now, honey," the rabbi's wife said. "Let's not talk anymore."

I had to ask one more question. "If it's not David, who the hell is it?"

The rabbi collected himself again. "He wouldn't say. He said we were stupid, stupid, stupid, and we should know who he is."

Paradiso looked over the snow-covered median strip with his flashlight, Marx trailing him. Marx made sure I stayed next to him. Although I wasn't under arrest, I was a person of interest, as they say.

"Are you sure you want to come here?" I asked helpfully.

"What is this?"

Lt. Paradiso leaned into the hole the dybbuk had blown up through the asphalt. It was about the size of the rabbi's face and cordoned off with police tape. I love police tape. It's so official.

The road wasn't screaming for a change. I wondered why.

The edges of the hole were red and glowing, like a volcano. I thought about somebody with a bad temper. If you were a road and you were in a bad mood, perhaps you'd color yourself with red flame.

I envisioned a meaty hand thrusting itself upward out of the hole, grabbing Paradiso and dragging him down into the abyss. Unfortunately, no such thing happened.

I wished I didn't have to be there. I thought about bowling again. The alley at Woodhaven Lanes was out there, waiting, but not for long. The lanes were closing and I would be losing my bowling escape.

Paradiso stared into the hole for several seconds. Snow swirled around. We heard a sloppy wet sound. An invisible rope tugged Paradiso's neck into the hole, and then it bounced back.

He stared into the road and the scream started. Marx tried to pull him away, but Paradiso seemed stuck in place. He was seeing something he had never seen before. His mind was being filled with something that was breaking him, to tell from the look in his eyes.

I looked on, and I realized quickly that I would have to do something to help. I hated that. But I ran as fast as I could in the snow and tackled Paradiso with my shoulder as low as I could, knocking into him at the ankles. The cop felt like a rock, but he fell on his behind with a great thump. Paradiso looked at me with surprise. Then his face changed into something else.

He pointed at me.

"You're a robot, sent to poison the water supply. You and the Russians are trying to kill me, with air conditioning. And you," he said, pointing at Marx, "want to start a movement of evil with Schreiber."

"Your karma is a little off, my old friend," Marx said.

Paradiso stood up, dusted the snow off his backside. He looked at Marx, then me. The Glock was out of the lieutenant's holster very fast and the gun was aimed at my chest.

"You're the demon from the underworld, a freak, a stinkpot of flesh."

I thought about putting my hands up and decided it wouldn't do any good. I didn't think it would do any good to speak either. I simply wished I could make the flesh on Paradiso's gun hand melt.

He clicked the Glock's safety off. I knew what was coming next. The impact alone would push me back several feet and onto the median strip, where I would come to rest on my back, bleeding quickly.

Marx's radio crackled.

"Anybody there?" said the voice on the other end.

Paradiso pointed the gun at Marx. "More robots. More robots," he said in a dead voice.

I scooped up a handful of snow and threw it in Paradiso's face. He waved it off quickly, but I had a snowball ready. I aced him on the bridge of his nose. His head went to one side, then came back like a bobble head doll.

He aimed again, but a shot from Marx plugged him in the kneecap.

Paradiso fell backwards in the snow into a sitting position. He looked only mildly surprised at being shot.

I threw several snowballs in his face, like this—one, two, three, four, five!

Paradiso aimed the Glock at me, but missed, firing wildly into the air. He hit the hood of a Ford Explorer rolling toward us heavily through the packed snow on the road. The bullet penetrated to the engine and started a small fire. The Explorer rolled slowly on, flames trailing out of the hood. The driver jumped out and let the vehicle slide to a stop into the metal railing beyond our little piece of median strip. The dybbuk's curse was still hard at work.

Marx hit Paradiso in the shoulder. The cop looked like a broken toy. He tried to aim the Glock again, but the blood gushing out of the hole in his shoulder told him he wouldn't accomplish it.

I threw a snowball in the lieutenant's face again. He fell over. Paradiso's head hit the median strip with a soft plop. The snow helped cushion the blow.

"Was that really necessary?" Marx howled at me.

"I thought so. Obviously."

"Give the man his dignity!"

"I didn't think he had any left."

In the ambulance, with Paradiso mumbling about robots and nuclear weapons the size of toy cars, Marx talked to himself, not really thinking I was listening. As a "person of interest," I was still in a loose form of custody by Marx.

"How am I going to beat this thing?"

"We need the rabbi."

The cop looked up, as if he was surprised to see me there. "The rabbi's pretty messed up."

"So's your friend."

"Alcohol took him away from us. The hole in the road didn't send him over the edge. He was already running to it."

"He's probably schizophrenic, too. You must have noticed."

"I tried not to think about it."

"Why didn't you get him some help?"

"I tried. It wasn't in his heart to take help. When he gets healed up, I'll send him home to his mother."

I was disgusted. "Let's not talk about it."

We rode in silence until the hospital. Before we loaded out with Paradiso, Marx turned to me and said, "You better be right about this, Schreiber. Get the rabbi."

In one of those bizarre weather changes that seem to happen in New York with great regularity these years, the next week turned sunny and unseasonably warm. It was 60 degrees during the day and 40 at night.

All the snow melted before Christmas, much to the disappointment of my sons.

Marx and I had met with Rabbi Benishtik at the Gan Eden restaurant to ask him for help. Gan Eden means Garden of Eden, or Paradise.

It didn't feel like paradise to me. Russians eating swatches of lamb squinted at Marx and me with great suspicion.

The rabbi limped into the restaurant with a cane, his broken ankle wrapped in a soft cast. He sat down with us and we exchanged quick hellos.

"Getting rid of a dybbuk is tricky business," the rabbi said.

I looked at his face, with all the cuts from the asphalt chunks that had flown in his direction.

"What you did was very brave," I said. "But we still have a problem."

"You do. I don't have a problem."

"Can you help us?" Marx asked.

The rabbi chewed on a carrot set at the cold vegetable plate on the table and looked away as if he were thinking hard. Then he turned back to the cop and me.

"I already risked a great deal the first time. I did it for Jacob and for Moses. But now, I think this is a thing I will not do."

"Where is your sense of justice?" Marx demanded, a little too loudly. The diners stared at him and me with red cigarette eyes.

"I have a terrific sense of justice. I also have a sense of self-preservation. I don't want to get killed."

"A lot more people could get killed," I said. "As a rabbi, you know what that means."

"Oh, don't bring that up," the rabbi said. "You have no idea what the concept really is. You're a business man, no better than a street punk in terms of your knowledge of religion."

"The tension in here is getting pretty thick," Marx said. "Maybe we should leave, let this whole thing cool down."

"When you kill a person, you destroy a universe," I said to the rabbi. "That's your creed."

"Who says I have to live it every day? I'm a rabbi. I deal with spiritual matters. I'm no action hero. That's your job."

"What are you talking about?"

The rabbi chewed on some celery, loudly. "Hey!" he shouted to the waiters. "Can't we get somebody to take our order?'

Two waiters lounged against a wall by the kitchen and looked at the rabbi with disdain. I knew why. He had brought strangers into their home and they didn't like us at all.

"I heard what you did to the police lieutenant," he said to me. "You have a little reputation, Mr. Schreiber."

"You're being a jerk."

"And you're being a nopocehok."

"What does that mean?" Marx asked.

"It's Russian," I said. "One of the few words I know. I learned it from my wife. He just said I'm a pig."

"Let's stop this. We're not in harmony," the policeman said. "This was a bad idea."

"You have kids?" I asked the rabbi.

He stopped chewing the celery and looked at me as if I was going to make a threat. "Two boys. Why?"

"How old are they?"

"Twelve and fifteen. Why?

"Do they like basketball?"

"Yes, very much. Why?"

"I know your house. You live over by the Grand Central Parkway."

"So?"

"You have a big yard in the back. I have a buddy in the concrete business. We can build you a basketball court, for your sons."

"You think I'll risk my life for a basketball court?"

"No, but you might to make your sons happy."

"You I don't like," the rabbi said. He began chewing celery again. Marx looked at me, worried and beginning to draw away. He studied his cell phone messages.

"How do we get rid of the dybbuk? At least give us some advice."

The rabbi yelled across the room and pointed his finger at one of the waiters. "You—come here now. I know your mother, Gisele Feinstein."

Exposed, the little Feinstein boy slinked over to the rabbi and meekly took his order.

After the waiter left, Marx said, "This is no day at the park, Schreiber. It's all very uncool. Let's melt out of here."

The rabbi picked up several cucumber slices in a stack and shoved them into his mouth. We waited a few minutes for him to finish.

"First, you have to say some prayers to weaken his resistance and ask to send his soul back to Gehenna," the rabbi said slowly. "Then you have to annoy him."

"I can annoy him. Will you say the prayers?"

"You're very good at annoying people," the rabbi said. He waved his hand in the air as if to dismiss us. "I'll say the prayers.

"Now leave. You two are ruining my reputation in the community here."

The Woodhaven Lanes closed down. My sons and I were sad. There would be no bowling alleys within five miles of our house anymore.

"Now where am I going to go to get a beer?" That was Richie, the 16-year-old wit.

"I don't believe it," Maxie said, always so serious.

"Economics, man," said Jon, our 12-year-old Buddhist philosopher. "Bucks. It's bucks that did them in."

"This is depressing," Mark, my 10-year-old jewel with a diamond of a broken nose said.

My wife, on hearing the news, smiled a little smile.

"You're happy about this?" I asked her.

"No, Schreiber. (That name again!) You've lost league night. You need an outlet for your anger. Where are you going to find that? You can't throw snowballs at cops anymore." She smiled again, politely and falsely.

"I can't believe you're happy about this."

"Now you have one less excuse for sneaking out of the house."

So how was I going to tell my wife that I was sneaking out of the house yet again to help rid Queens Boulevard of a wandering demon soul from the underworld?

And how was I going to figure out how to annoy this demon enough to get rid of him?

"I hate to break this to you, but I have to go out."

"What is it this time? Have to meet a new supplier at the strip club?"

From the depths of his depression, Mark rose up and shouted: "Dad has to find a new bowling alley!"

Mark's comment knocked me backwards a few steps. I knew what I would have to do.

"You just gave me a great idea," I told him.

"What did I say?" he said.

"I'll tell you later."

My wife remained unimpressed. "Where are you going?"

I waved to my wounded wife and sons, grabbed my ball bag in the closet and ran out the front door, shouting, "I'm going bowling!"

I leaned my face down into the red-caked hole where the dybbuk was. Rabbi Benishtik and Marx the cop were behind me. Also there was the alley man from the Woodhaven Lanes, Dino, clad in his usual blue sweatshirt.

The screaming had begun as we approached the hole. We told ourselves to ignore it, to press on. There was no choice. It was either that or let a demon terrorize and destroy dozens of lives traveling on the boulevard.

My nose started to bleed. My chest felt tight, like I had a clogged artery. The rabbi held his hands to his ears. Marx the cop put gun fingers on his forehead as if he had a profound migraine. Dino smoked a cigarette and looked bored.

I stuck my face right into the screaming.

"Hello, Larry."

"Go to freaking hell, Harold!" Larry screamed in my mind.

"I'm already there, buddy."

"I never liked you!"

"Back atcha, buddy."

My chest tightened. Two hands gripped my heart. It was a crushing blow.

I took a breath.

The rabbi started to say a prayer using a book with a black cover.

"Want to go bowling, Larry?"

"You know I hate bowling, Harold."

"I'm going to go bowling right on your face, Larry."

"What are you talking about?"

Amidst the screaming, which grew louder, I turned and asked Dino, "Can I have the pins?"

Cigarette in his mouth, the alley rat handed me a bag.

I unzipped the bag and set up the pins in the triangle pattern in front of the screaming hole. The rabbi continued to mumble prayers into Larry's giant scream. The rabbi's ears were bleeding.

The alley rat continued to look bored, until the cigarette exploded in his hand.

"Son of a bitch," he said quietly, looking at his burnt fingers.

He got another one out of the pack and lit it.

"How's it look, Dino?"

"Not bad, Harold. Let me fix two in the back row."

The screaming reached an even higher pitch. It was like getting zapped with a live wire.

I yelled at Dino. "How come you're not affected by this?"

He smiled like it was a little joke. "My kids are much worse."

Rabbi Benishtik fell over and the book dropped onto the median strip. Marx and I rushed to him.

"I'm OK, I'm OK," he said. He got up, brushed the dirt off his back. "This dybbuk is very tough."

"It's the steroids, I bet," I said. "He's super-charged and angry."

The rabbi picked up the book, kissed it and started to bow and pray again.

The standard length of a bowling alley is 60 feet from the foul line to the head pin. Dino calculated that 40 feet would be best for maximum impact on the pins. Marx had the right lane of the road cordoned off on both sides with orange cones and police sawhorses. I was starting to appreciate cops more.

Out of the darkness appeared about one hundred men from Rabbi Benishtik's congregation. I saw Moses. He nodded at me. The men lined up on both sides of the orange tape. I wished I had that kind of muscle in my business, but I like to be alone too much to enlist this kind of organization.

Dino drew a foul line with chalk. I held the ball in front of me, leaned down and studied the alley. The road wasn't exactly straight. It dipped to the right and down at the shoulder. I would have to take that into account.

Larry screamed so hard he upset the pins all by himself.

"You're going to have to bowl a lot faster if we're going to do this!" Dino yelled.

He set up the pins again. The rabbi continued to pray, the blood flowing down his ear in a little stream.

I threw the ball down the road as fast and as hard as I could.

Boom! I got eight pins and Larry blew out the spare with a scream.

Dino bowled the ball back to me and set up the pins again. They were shaking from Larry's screams. But he wasn't able to knock them down. Maybe the rabbi's prayers were having some effect.

My ears were pretty rattled, but I got off a toss. The ball landed on the left side of the pins, taking half. It wasn't a good roll and I was mad at myself. But I didn't have time to really punish myself.

We set up again, this time with Marx helping. Larry shot sparks out of his hole. I tried to make this one count.

The ball hit the first pin head-on and blew back on the others. They made a good rattle. Larry threw flames out of the hole.

Dino set it up a fourth time and I just jammed the ball the wrong way. It hit one pin and the rest were left standing. The one pin I hit fell into Larry's hole.

Dino went to look at the hole. He backed off quickly. The pin came flying out of the crater on fire, like a rocket. We saw it shoot into the air and fall on top of a parked Nissan Armada's roof.

Dino threw the ball back and I stopped caring about form. I flung the ball as hard as I could down the road and the nine pins smashed together.

We did it again and again. The scene was wild to me, but I felt wild too, with the rabbi standing on the median strip praying, the hundred silent men watching us, the front end of the Nissan Armada now on fire, the alley of cones and sawhorses and my alley guy running to the pins and setting them up as fast as he could, then throwing me the ball, and me throwing it back as hard and quick as I could, the demon Larry's screams vomiting out of the hole, then bending backwards and down into the road.

The rabbi, swaying and praying, fell down for the last time. Marx went to him and cradled the rabbi's head in his Buddhist cop arms. Drenched in sweat, my right arm about to fall off, I threw the ball like a fist into the pins. The ball swept through the pins and scattered them. The ball knocked down into Larry's hole as if drawn by a magnet.

The ball shot back out of the hole, a molten mass of plastic, flaming and stinking, demon cannon fire. It fell down onto the boulevard, bubbling and spitting superheated gloss, my favorite bowling ball, a casualty of war. Dino looked at the mess as if it were a corpse. For the first time, Marx looked scared. The rabbi was a spent force, but his hundred followers didn't move.

"That's it!" I yelled. "Nobody kills my bowling ball!"

I ran as fast as I could. The screaming rose and rose in my ears, but I didn't care. I dove into the hole.

When we wrestle with ghosts, usually nobody ends up losing but you. I was determined not to let that happen.

Yet I found myself falling farther than I thought possible. It was about 20 feet down. I landed on my non-bowling arm. I felt good about that, but little else.

I suddenly understood what Gehenna was. In a city as dense as New York, I was stuck in a hole about six feet wide on each side. Warm air blasted over me from a subway vent. Who knew there was a subway vent underneath this part of the boulevard?

Things got worse from there.

Larry was there with me. He wasn't exactly a physical presence, unlike the usual dybbuk inhabiting a body, but I felt him around me. And he couldn't stop talking.

Not literally, like a real voice, but more inside my head.

"Let's lighten the mood a little," he said. "Lighten everything up. Light. I love light. I miss light. Give us light."

The hole burned yellow and orange, hopeful like the morning sun. But there was nothing hopeful about what I saw.

On the walls, or I should say in the walls, were the faces of the lost and wounded, the broken souls who had been killed on the boulevard in recent months. I saw David Jacobshvili, the couple in the Ford Expedition, the five people in the Land Cruiser and Dodge Ram, the pair from the Lexus SUV, and the six teenagers in the Dakota.

Stalin said the death of one person is a tragedy, but the death of multitudes is a statistic. You read about people dying in the newspaper, from cyclones and earthquakes and suicide bombings. And it may never really hit you that we are talking about human beings.

Even for me, reading the stories in the paper, the deaths of these people hadn't been vividly real. David Jacobshvili's death had been real to me. I had seen him get killed. As for the rest, though, I hadn't understood their pain, until that moment.

But now, the dead were brought horribly to life for me, their faces frozen in horror, screaming a silent scream, raging against the injustice of the boulevard and their discontents.

I wondered how fast Lieutenant Paradiso's mind would have melted down in this little subway vent wax museum.

"That's my trophy wall," Larry said.

"What?"

"They're my little pets."

"You own their souls somehow."

"Harold, you've always been smart when it's too late."

"I think that's the definition of tragedy."

"This is no tragedy. It's a laugh and a half."

"The rabbi and I couldn't get rid of you because you're using the energy of these poor people to stay here on the boulevard."

"I came close to getting your sons, Harold, very close— Maxie and Mark, right?"

I winced hard at that news.

"I'm surprised you don't have a nose and an upper lip hanging from your wall, Larry, where you got them hurt."

He laughed. "I'll try that some other time. But now that you've unexpectedly dropped in, I don't have to stay here."

"What does that mean?"

"I can get inside you. Walk around inside you. Become you."

I winced hard again.

"Not me. You'd have my body. But that's about it. You're exactly the opposite of me. You're a first-class creep from the word go."

Another laugh came inside my mind, like liquid trash.

Larry's image formed in front of me, the pale shell of his muscles, massive hands, and square head.

"I have to get a little organic to start the merger, pal. Then your brain will be a little piece of dust inside me."

I was about to say something sarcastic, but a bowling ball dropped on Larry's head.

It was purple and white and glossy and beautiful.

The shot smashed Larry's demon head into his neck, then disappeared and reappeared after ripping a bowling ball sized hole in his crotch.

Larry and David and the rest of the broken souls cried out in protest against the incursion.

"Son of a bitch!" Larry yelled.

Larry lay on the floor of the vent like a deflated blimp. I stared at him, a mistake.

"This is a minor inconvenience, Harold."

I watched as he reconstituted his body. It was like watching soldier ants build a colony at super-speed.

I wasn't totally stupid. I picked up the bowling ball and silently thanked Dino for bringing an extra.

"You think that bowling ball's going to help you? You're just a human being."

My wife thinks I'm angry. I thought this would be a good time to find out how angry.

Larry took a step forward. We were standing nose to nose. The stink of his becoming organic was like getting hit by the smell of a city landfill, rotting fruit and diapers, decaying hamburger meat and fungal bread all thrown together.

I hit the walking landfill in the stomach with the ball. He laughed. I took a shot at his head. It bounced off the wall and came back like a rubber band.

I'm an Eagle Scout for life, it's true, as my son says. But I had to fight dirty. I wound up my arm, brought it forward and crushed Larry's groin with 16 pounds of molded plastic.

He staggered backwards, fell into the faces on the wall for a few seconds.

He looked up, really angry. Larry grabbed my throat and rushed me against the wall.

"You're dead meat."

I tried to say something clever. Nothing but bubbles came out of my throat.

I understood that maybe anger wasn't going to win this fight. Maybe Larry was right. I'm always too late with realizations.

So I let him in, invited him into my mind. I slumped down and he came with me, hugging me close. I felt like a grasshopper infested with baby wasp parasites. The smell was so intense, it filled me with nausea.

Then Larry was there, with me, in my brain. He was happy as hell.

Now my hard work would really have to begin.

I thought of Rabbi Benishtik and how he read his chanting book with such intensity, crowding out everything else and focusing on the task right in front of him.

Larry's thoughts came careening through. There was the Hummer going fast through the snow, Larry talking fast and angry on his cell phone. Then the fast, too fast slide into the SUV, the metal looming up. The explosion, big and hot. Burning, panic, everything happening quickly.

The fire burned so hot, Larry's cell phone got welded into his ear. He screamed. I vomited.

Other Larry thoughts percolated around. We were in a bar, talking to a girl, then another, taking somebody home. Strip joints, an abundance of female flesh gyrating on a raised stage, many shots of whiskey, alone in sad red lights. Meeting steroid dealers in gym locker rooms, a booth in the T-Bone Diner on the boulevard. Shooting the stuff into the gluteus maximus. More drinking alone, in the living room, watching late night television with all the lights out.

Yelling at his mother. Throwing chairs in her house. Sleeping with girls. Punching one in the jaw while in bed. Slapping another hard on the cheek. The girls crying. An apology, not enough to stop the girls from running out of the house, half clothed, not caring, just wanting to get away.

High school images now. Rolling dice in the back of the school during classes. Challenging the results of throws, saying the dice are loaded. Beating up a kid who stood up to him. Taking his money.

Inheriting a plywood business from his father, like I did. Shorting a buyer on a delivery. Yelling at the guy on the phone when he found out. Shouting, "You're a liar! You're a liar! You're a liar!" in a sing-song voice like a little schoolgirl. Slamming down the phone and smiling.

Afternoons at the Mets game with Dad, Dad drinking too much at the game and in the living room. The NFL on Sundays in October, the NBA on CBS in February, the pale Queens light fading out of the room early. Mom fading into the fabric of the curtains with every pull Dad takes on the bottle. Larry watching it all, taking it in.

Larry stood up and he was taking me with him.

"Hey!" he shouted up to the street. "Can somebody help me?"

Marx and Dino looked down into the hole.

"Schreiber, you all right?" Marx yelled.

"Yeah. Can you get me out of here?" Larry said in a voice that didn't sound like me at all. I hoped someone would notice, but 20 feet above a subway vent, who might notice that Schreiber didn't sound like Schreiber?

"We called the fire department to come get you out. Where's the demon?"

"Gone, man, gone."

"Hey, that's great," Marx said. "Just take it easy for a few minutes. The guys will be here soon."

I noticed that the faces on the wall had faded out. The subway vent wall had gone back to being a wall. Larry must have released them. He didn't need them anymore. He had me. But I wasn't ready to give up the ghost.

Here was a chance and I took it.

I forced images of my four sons into what was left of my mind. Pictures of the boys running around the house, jumping off couches, goofing around on the floor.

Larry staggered a little.

Then more pictures. Sitting around our kitchen table, the boys ranking on each other, Richie winning most of these battles. Then they're playing football on their knees in the living room, fighting over what they would watch on television, breaking the wooden coffee table. Maxie crying. Jon crying. Maxie hitting Jon in the shoulders and arms. Richie sitting on Maxie's chest. Mark threatening to kill Richie.

Larry stood up. He smiled. The boys hurting each other appealed to his mind. I would have to change the picture show fast.

There I was walking with my wife on quiet streets when we were engaged. Going to the movies. My wife walked down the aisle toward me, with a white covering on her head, her lips ruby red. Dancing at the wedding. The honeymoon in Florida. Helen's cat's eye glasses. Beautiful white sand, blue water lapping at the shore. The beach at sunrise. My wife cooking lamb. Dipping it into mint jelly.

Larry felt a little sick.

I flooded more images into the theatre of our shared mind. Here I was finding 5-year-old Richie and 3-year-old Max sleeping together on the floor of the bedroom, their heads touching. Me trying to hide behind 2-year-old Max on our little lawn as Helen takes a picture of us. Maxie holding Mark's hand when we go to an amusement park. Max and Jon playing goofball detectives to copy the show they see on TV. Richie riding a cheap old bicycle for the first time on the sidewalk in front of the house. Mark kicking a goal in the midget soccer game. Jon reading a philosophy book way too advanced for him.

Then I hit Larry with the nuclear bomb of my mind's eye. I sent pictures in this bomb, pictures of me paying the mortgage on the house, the bills for the electricity, cable, and Internet, the monthly lease on the station wagon, balancing the checkbook, walking a construction site and worrying over whether the carpenters would show up that day, hitting baseballs in the street to my sons' eager mitts, buying winter clothes with Helen and the boys at Modell's.

The Modell's movie was like a solid punch to Larry's stomach. Next I hit him with a right hook to the jaw.

Helen stood before me in our kitchen, a chocolate linoleum floor beneath us and a Felix the Cat clock above (for the boys, of course), pointing a butcher knife in the air as if it were an extension of her finger, saying:

"Schreiber, I love you, but you're extremely mentally ill."

My life isn't like that television show *Seventh Heaven*, not even close. But thinking about all the details required in maintaining a family were enough to blow through Larry's steroid-addled soul.

I saw Larry's mind collide with mine. We fell on the cold concrete floor. We started banging our head on the wall of the vent. We drew blood out of the forehead.

Still, I couldn't get him out of my mind. My best chance to evict him was gone. I had blown it. I wasn't strong enough.

A wide yellow light shone on us from the street.

"Mr. Schreiber, we're going to get you out of there. Hold on," said a Fire Department voice.

A relieved and sick laugh came from us. It wasn't mine, but Larry's. As a ladder slid down to the floor of the vent, someone yelled, "Wait!"

Rabbi Benishtik, sick with fever, but leaning over the edge, was shouting. "That man is not who he says he is!"

The ladder banged on the concrete. We started to climb, the demented laugh coming through me like a bad taste of whiskey, leaving the purple bowling ball behind. I would never have abandoned a beauty like that.

"Wait!" the rabbi shouted again. But it was too late. Larry and I were climbing up and up.

We heard lots of shouts and fast talking. As we climbed up the ladder, Marx appeared. He aimed his Glock at us and a crazy laugh echoed off the walls of the vent.

The Buddhist bullet sliced through our left shoulder and there was still enough of me left to thank Marx for not hitting me in the bowling arm.

Solid hot lead poured through the wound, tearing muscle and snapping bone. Burning, burning, burning.

We fell down the ladder like a kid taking a backwards flop on a water slide. The impact on the floor seemed to fold our knees in half.

We spit up blood lying on the cold concrete. Marx was a true artist, a poet of pain.

He was poised now on the top of the ladder, facing away from its solid cylinder steps, the Glock out and ready to sketch a new picture. A bullet hit the bottom and dug up a piece of concrete the size of a quarter. The chunk hit us in the eye.

Another bullet described a straight line as efficiently as a geometry whiz kid's pencil mark and blew out the elbow of the left arm. Amazing, I thought. He's trying to save my bowling arm. Here was the portrait of the cop as a truly sensitive man.

With two bullets in us, we were pinned to the bottom of the hole.

"The cop is going to kill us," I whispered to Larry.

"Not me, man. Not me!"

"The cop is going to kill us."

"No. No. No," he whined.

"Go ahead, scream like a little baby. It doesn't matter anymore."

"This can't be the end."

"It is the end. There's nothing worse than a ticked-off Buddhist cop. They're very directed."

Silence from the Larry part of my mind.

"He has a goal. He'll keep shooting until we're dead. Dead. No more pretty girls. No more Hummers. No more whiskey. No more nothing."

A wisp of fire speared through our left thigh. Marx had hit us again.

"That was the big one, Larry. The cop hit an artery. We're going to bleed out in a matter of minutes now."

The dybbuk made a run for it out of the tunnels of my brain and I let him go. Extracting himself from me was as nauseating as the merger. His screaming felt like a sonic cannon.

I hadn't realized my eyes were closed shut. As the smell of landfill hit my nose I opened them. The demon was out of me, next to my head in the subway vent, more of a bubbling brown and green mass now than a half-formed man.

He was losing energy, and time. I wished I had a portable, battery-operated vacuum cleaner like my wife had.

The purple and white bowling ball was on the other side of me, by my right arm. I picked it up, fingered the grips. Shot up with more holes than a doughnut, I still loved the feel of the cold plastic on my hand.

Without a vacuum, I raised the purple and white ball over my head and made my own invisible painting of an arc, bringing the globe down on the stinking mass formerly known as Larry.

I rolled over with the ball still in my hand and swept over Larry the Landfill, flattening him against the floor, unintentionally mixing him with my flowing blood.

I wiped him everywhere I could—the subway vent, the walls, the corners of the hole. It was like trying to paint applesauce on a house with a fork.

But it worked. Little pieces of him pulsed and bubbled. Some of Larry got into the holes of the bowling ball and I plunged him down even further with my fingers. There was a tingling sensation in them, which quickly died.

My thigh and shoulder were numb. I was starting to drift away. The funeral home director would have a hell of a time peeling my rigor mortis fingers out of the bowling ball. It wasn't a bad way to go, but I thought of my sons and my wife. I saw them at the funeral. Helen was crying. My sons looked bleak.

Now it was my turn to say, "No" in a quiet voice, with the subway vent as my only audience.

A shot bounced off a wall and hit the goo that was Larry by my feet.

"Hey, goddamn it, Marx! Stop shooting! It's Schreiber!"

Several men shouted at each other. I heard the rabbi yell something at Marx.

Marx slid down the ladder with an EMT man behind him.

"Where's the dybbuk?" he shouted, all heat, with a spark I had never seen before.

"Dead. You killed him. This bowling ball helped a little."

"Don't move, Schreiber."

"I can't. You hit an artery, pal."

The EMT man wrapped my thigh and shoulder and elbow tight with tape. He removed my fingers from the bowling ball. Then the guy whipped me over his back like I was no big deal and started to climb the ladder. Marx followed.

"I thought Buddhists considered all living things sacred," I whispered in a haze.

"Yeah, well, Buddha didn't have to deal with any demons from the underworld."

"Don't leave the bowling ball in the vent," I rasped to Marx.

The lights went out.

A week at Parkway Hospital felt like a year. I had the sensation of being pinned to the bed. There was an IV in my arm and a plastic clothespin attached to my index finger to check my pulse. The clock on the wall made a loud tick with each second. The TV spewed out game shows and reality shows with rich, snotty-looking people with names like Audrina. What kind of name is that? It sounds like something you use to clean out your sink.

In between all the pap, a local news show at seven o'clock did a feature on a screaming subway vent on Queens Boulevard. A reporter noted that on the road above the vent there were a number of fatal accidents in recent weeks. The accidents had stopped, at least temporarily. But the screams unnerved people walking by with their dogs and children and groceries.

An investigation by the police department found nothing in the vent that would cause the screams. They did find a 16-pound purple and white bowling ball, which was promptly claimed and returned to a former alley maintenance worker at Woodhaven Lanes. The subway authority spokesperson said the trains could make sounds like screams when they lean into a curve.

A doctor arrived and, impressed with himself, talked in surgical language I didn't understand. When I asked him to explain it, he said it wasn't important for me to get it.

"Just do what I tell you," he said.

"I'd punch you if I could get out of this bed," I whispered to the guy, named Dr. Leifstadt. Unfortunately, I don't think he heard me.

Leifstadt let me out on a Saturday morning. I was so sorry to miss the cartoons on TV.

Marx drove me home.

I rolled down the window and put my head out to feel the fresh winter air on me. We were both quiet for a few minutes.

"I'm going to leave the force."

"I'm sorry. What'd you say?"

"I'm done. I quit."

I made a sour face. "Why are you doing that?"

"Paradiso, and shooting you three times."

"Those aren't real reasons. You did what you had to do."

"I think I'm more of a poet than a cop."

"Yeah, but poetry doesn't pay nearly as well."

"True. But I'll figure it out somehow."

"I hope you do."

He let me out by the front door. I walked up the steps in my coat, which hid most of the bandages. I was limping and cranky with pain.

Then I opened the door to the foyer. Max, Jon, and Mark, eating breakfast, ran to me. That's one of the greatest feelings in the world.

Richie hung back, as usual, but there was an actual smile in his eyes.

Behind him, my wife appeared, with a spatula in her hand.

"Schreiber, you want some French toast?"

"Sure, that'd be great."

"After breakfast you can do the dishes."

"Would that make you happy?" I asked.

"That would make me happy," she said.

I did the dishes.

SUBWAY TROOPERS

"You want me to come over your house? You owe me money, you little fuck. Yes, you do. I can be there in 10 minutes. I don't have to sit here being nice and polite on the phone. I can be at your front door, banging away."

I was sitting in Happy Cimongila's back yard, in wealthy Forest Hills, on the north side of the 67th Avenue subway station, on an early June evening. Black flies were landing on the table in ones and twos, crawling up our arms. I waved them away. I hate flies. They thrive on crawling around on top of excrement. These guys live for only 24 hours and they have to pack as much shit into their day as possible. I wondered what possible purpose they could serve in nature. I'd have to look that up. I briefly wondered about destroying every single fly on the planet. Too big a job and nobody would pay me for it, like this guy.

Happy owed me $10,000. He looked like a turtle. His cheeks sunk in toward his mouth like they were trying to mate. His nose was a large piece of fish fin, maybe shark. His eyes were small and narrow in a way I didn't trust.

I should have known better than to work with him. But jobs were getting scarce for the moment and Happy offered me top-line parquet flooring work on a new McMansion he was building up north of Queens Boulevard, near his own house. The economy was caving in all around us, but some guy out there had enough money to act like a corporate titan. I wanted to meet him, to ask how he had gotten all that cash.

I did the job and then Happy said he couldn't pay me. Instead, he asked me to come over to his house.

"Listen, Harold. This guy, Steve Malinka, he owes me money. A lot of money. That's why I can't pay you. Once I get the money from Malinka, I can pay you."

Now I was involved in business with two very tough immigrant Russians. The vast majority of Russian immigrants in the neighborhood are of course quite civilized and pleasant, but in construction, it's often ugly. There's a lot of threatening and posturing and if that doesn't work, somebody may get shot.

I was over at Happy's house because he wanted me to listen to the phone call. That way I could really understand why Happy couldn't pay me the thousands of dollars he owed me. We sat among his children's toys. His sons were 5 and 7.

One of the toys was a plastic model of an Escalade SUV, which a 5-year-old can sit in. The Escalade is three feet long and battery-powered. It can go about three or four miles an hour. The ultimate toy for that SUV driver in training, it must cost at least a thousand dollars. I saw Happy's kid happily drive it through a local playground, scattering kids everywhere. I had taken Mark there, under his extreme protests, which is how I was privileged to see this.

Mark, now 13 years old, clearly didn't want to be there. I think he was embarrassed to be seen with me, and angry about it. Then the Escalade appeared. My kid was fascinated by the battery-powered mini-SUV, and he followed it around the playground. Mark said, "I want one!" (It didn't matter to my kid that he was too big too sit in the thing.)

Aside from the toy truck, the boy didn't seem too interested in anything else within the sweep of his eyeballs. He was growing older and bored with playgrounds. I made a mental note to look for new entertainments for my boys which could involve me. They're far more interested in riding their bikes and watching MTV and playing video games than spending time with their father.

Bowling was still OK for them. I took them to a place up in Flushing, since Woodhaven Lanes had closed. The boys had invented a game called Speed Bowling, which required the bowler to pick up the ball and fling it down the lane as fast as possible, with no set-up, no concentration, no strategizing. To a purist like me, it was painful to watch, but at least I could get them all together to have something resembling fun.

The boys were eating a lot more too. I really needed the money from Happy. His kids get thousand-dollar toys. Mine don't. They need calories.

I had other worries as well. Derek had escaped from Creedmoor a few months before. They had held him for six years this time. He had gotten himself a volunteer job in the hospital's kitchen and slipped out of one of the truck bays in a food delivery van. The cops were doing their usual bang-up job in looking for him. He was out there somewhere, a little low-rent terrorist warring on the Schreiber family. I was hoping he might lay low and leave us alone.

When Happy hung up the phone, we looked at each other.

"Harold, you don't need to be involved in this. I'm going over to that fat fuck's house right now. I'm going to get you your money."

I was looking at Happy's massive tank of a house, which was built out to take up the whole property, as any good McMansion would. It looked as big as a Wal-Mart to me. I was thinking, "You've involved me. I'm involved. Can't you just sell the kid's Escalade and some of the other expensive toys I see in the living room and give me some of the money?"

I held my tongue. You have to be careful around some of these guys. "OK, Happy. Let me know what you can do."

"Thanks for the confidence, Harold. You're a good guy. I don't care what anybody else says about you."

I looked at him.

"Ha, I was just kidding! Making a joke!"

I nodded, not smiling. "Right."

I got up to leave. Happy stood up too. He took my arm, which I didn't like. He looked me in the eye.

"We're going to take care of this."

"OK."

It was dinner time. The heat was oppressive. The boys still had school, but most schools in the city aren't air-conditioned. I could easily imagine how my kids would make it through the day. Either they might fall asleep in class, or simply cut out and go to the beach with their friends.

I walked out of Happy's air-conditioned door into the heat to get to my station wagon, through a sea of toys. There were Harry Potter action figures, tin robots, and foot-high versions of Superman and Batman. An army of G.I. Joes had been positioned for battle by the carpeted spiral staircase.

I walked into my house in the Ozone Park Flats. Helen had purchased KFC fried chicken for dinner. It wasn't nearly as good as hers, but she had less time to cook these days. She had taken a full-time job as a dietitian at the hospital. We needed the money.

Nobody rushed to the door to greet me anymore. The boys were old enough to be totally absorbed in their efforts to talk to girls, hang out with their friends, play sports, read books, or listen to new and weird music, like hip-hop, which I'll never understand.

Richie was now 19. His blond hair was parted in the middle with two wings reaching down toward his shoulders. Despite an illustrious high-school career spent playing soccer, lacrosse, and basketball, picking up girls who were enchanted with his sarcastic wit, and working on being a happy kid/man, he had gotten into college at the state college at Brockport, near Rochester. He had just finished his freshman year and the tuition bills were killing us. It was late June, he was home from Brockport. My supply of beer in the refrigerator was totaled virtually every night. Richie was going to work at a summer camp in the Catskills starting July 1st, and my beer was grateful.

Max would be going to college the following year. It would have to be a state school—we couldn't afford anything else and we would be stretched even further.

Max, at 17, with long, stringy hair, sporting prominent scars on his forehead and lip, looked much tougher than he actually was. His outward shell was that of a quiet, sensitive boy, but if he felt threatened, he could get a little crazy. You could punch him, or insult him for weeks, or even months, and he would just take it. But there was an invisible line he had somewhere in that unknowable head of his, and when somebody crossed it, he would go totally nuts on them. He would keep punching, or snarl constant insults to pound the other person into submission. He would not stop. At those times, he reminded me of Derek.

Max divided his time with basketball and reading and trying to ignore as many people as possible, even kids trying to be friends with him. He was finishing up his junior year of high school and he wasn't even excited about it. Instead, he was very keyed up about taking the state Regents exams in English, Social Studies, Earth Science, and Algebra. They count as 20 percent of your grade and he cared about his tests, which struck his older brother as an odd affectation.

"You're just going to plod along through life, aren't you?" he told Max. "Settle in to a life of quiet desperation, working in a faceless cubicle at some giant corporation, anxious about making the mortgage every month. Be a drone."

Max looked stunned and hurt and surprised, even though Richie spent much of his free time pounding away at his younger brother's psyche. When he was around. Most of the time he was out with a girl or his friends, drinking and doing things I wouldn't be comfortable admitting to myself.

Jon, at 15, also long-haired, was into philosophy and Buddhism. He spent a lot of his time reading and finding friends who had somewhat odd and suspect last names, like Ahini, Siegfried, and Finkler. He'd also taken up cigarettes, which didn't seem to fit comfortably with any Buddhist philosophy I was aware of, but I'm not entirely up on these things. Jon was smoking at school quite a bit, in the alcoves and even the back of the cafeteria, which had gotten him suspended a few times. He enjoyed the defiance part of it. It was a game to him.

Mark, 13, had proved himself a really good soccer player with lots of promise, despite the hair that fell in his eyes at every opportunity. (My hair was cut to about a half-inch off my balding skull. I hated all this long hair on my kids, but they were all teens at the time and of course I was powerless to do anything about it.)

Mark read a lot too, started showing an interest in electronics, and hung out with a kid named Howie, who lived down the block and who seemed mostly devoted to spending as much time in our house as possible, taking bagels and cream cheese out of the refrigerator, as well as consuming the boys' critical supplies of orange juice and milk.

Despite their busy schedules, the boys all seemed to find a lot of time to watch awe-inspiring amounts of television.

To try to cut into the TV time, I paved the back yard with asphalt and put up a basketball hoop with a wooden post so the boys could play basketball and not have to go anywhere, just like I had promised Rabbi Benishtik once.

The boys started to come home after school and eat half a box of Oreos, then play basketball for three hours before dinner.

Helen yelled at the boys to come to dinner, the KFC chicken bucket in the middle of our round wood kitchen table. It took several minutes of good old-fashioned yelling to get them all to come to the kitchen.

The first cockroach crawled onto Max's plate. He hadn't seen it because the kitchen table is a deep, dark brown, matching the roach's shell. When he saw the thing, a mid-sized block of insect, slip onto his plate, he screamed and squashed his hand down on it, squeezing its body into the smallest possible space between his palm and the ceramic.

"You killed it!" Jon yelled, protesting.

"You're kidding, right?" Richie said. "You want to build a shrine for the thing?"

Helen was upset.

"Give me your plate, Max."

He did, his eyes wide with hate for the roach, and Helen wiped his two drumsticks and mashed potatoes into the garbage can, set the plate into the sink, and ran water and soap over the remains.

Then she brought Max a new plate and he reached into the bucket and brought out a new drum stick, coated with crispy fried skin.

A roach launched itself onto Mark's plate. He jumped back and tried to slap it, but it spread its wings and flew upwards.

We were all stunned. We didn't know roaches could fly. I rose up and centered the bug flying around the middle of the kitchen. Then I slapped my hands together and crushed the roach inside them. I used to kill roaches using a piece of tissue or toilet paper, but after a while I realized you don't have the luxury of time with roaches. So I just started killing them with my hands. The boys followed my lead.

I went to wash my hands at the kitchen sink, using the dish soap to clean them.

"Schreiber!" My wife was yelling very loudly. I crunched my teeth together when she called me that. But her panic meant something really bad. I turned around to see a dozen roaches attacking our dinner table. Richie, Max, and Mark stood up and started bashing them wherever they saw something crawl.

Jon got up too, and shouted, "You shouldn't kill them!"

Richie killed three roaches with several swift slaps. Slightly out of breath, he shouted at Jon, "We should take them to see the Mets?"

A number of roaches were dispatched. A few managed to fly or run off and were lost to us. Roaches are really fast runners.

After that, nobody felt hungry. The boys helped their mother clean up dinner and I called the exterminator.

What I really should have done was call a Weirdness Exorcist.

Roaches are so ingrained in New York City that nobody questions whatever stories you tell about them. Except if they fly. The exterminator, with the very ordinary yet somehow odd name of John Jones, didn't believe me when I told him over the phone about the flying bugs.

"It's very rare to find roaches that fly, Mr. Schreiber. Not in New York, anyway."

"I know that. But these did."

"I mean, the roaches in Florida fly. They're called Palmetto Bugs."

"Whatever they are, they need to be killed. Can you come over?"

Mr. Jones came over. He found a few small bugs partying in the kitchen. He used a thin hose to spray poison in the cracks between the cabinets and the refrigerator and some of the walls. Our house is more than 60 years old, so there are plenty of cracks as the place has settled. Max and Mark watched Jones work, fascinated. To them, the exterminator was a warrior fighting for the family.

Jon heard the exterminator come in, but wouldn't watch. His Buddhism was reaching new heights of transcendence and he said he couldn't look at lives being taken, even roach lives. We all nodded our heads, trying to look like we accepted what he said. He went to the room he shared with Max and smoked a cigarette. I could smell it coming from under the door.

Things went back to normal for a few days. Mark and Jon were delighted that school was ending soon, talking about it and laughing, loose, knowing they'd be having a good summer simply because they wouldn't be trapped in a room doused in olive green paint while a teacher lectured them in Spanish, Math, or Science. Max was sweating about his Regents exams.

Richie got his grades in the mail from Brockport. He decided to celebrate his barely successful completion of freshman year by sneaking even more beer out of the refrigerator every chance he could. Happy still owed me money and I wondered how I was going to get it. I needed cash for college tuition and the economy was sliding thoroughly.

After watching some Leno on the TV in our bedroom, we fell asleep. About 1 in the morning, Helen got up.

"What's wrong?" I said sleepily.

"You're sweating again, Schreiber. I'm going to sleep in the chair."

The chair is next to the bed and reclines.

It was better this way. As my business was getting increasingly precarious, I was having a tough time relaxing after work. Just like when I was a kid, I started to sweat in my sleep. It seemed that every pore of my skin was flushing moisture out of me. In the morning, you could see an outline in water of how I slept. There was no reason Helen should have to suffer with the tension I was extruding.

Later in the night, maybe about 3, I felt something crawling on my head. I slapped at it, but it flew away. Helen screamed.

I turned on the light. She was up out of the reclining chair, shaking a dozen roaches out of her light blanket. They fell to the floor and scurried away, under the bed.

I got up and saw what looked like hundreds of roaches on the floor. They were coming in through the bedroom door. Helen and I just started stomping on whatever moved.

We heard two screams.

"Oh my God, the boys!"

Helen and I ran from our room to Max and Jon's room. They were slapping roaches dead with their hands. They stepped on roaches with their bare feet. They were hard at war. Apparently, Jon had lost his Buddhist inhibitions when directly attacked.

We checked on Mark. The dog had been sleeping with him in his room. Mark was killing cockroaches, dozens of them swarming all over the place. Gee Gee was snapping at the little bugs and eating quite a few of them. This couldn't be a good thing. I was afraid she would get sick.

Helen stayed with Mark and worked on the killing operation there.

I checked on the den room, where Rich slept. There were several roaches there, but nothing like what the rest of the house had. He was using a lacrosse stick to kill the bugs, which didn't seem particularly effective. One flew at him and he netted it, then curled his stick and hurled the bug like a lacrosse ball into the closet door. It made a very satisfying splat.

After a half-hour of a Schreiber killing frenzy, the combined efforts of our family seemed to have thinned out the attack. Most of the roaches were gone, either run off or dead. Much of the floor of the house crunched under our feet.

Helen directed us to all take showers. "They're filthy and they cause disease." The general had spoken and we obeyed her orders.

Once we took our showers, Helen asked me to call my parents to see if we could stay over at their place for the night. Dad said yes.

Everybody got into the car, including Gee Gee. On the short drive over, Helen looked really upset.

"How could this happen, Schreiber?"

"I don't know."

"I keep a very clean house."

It was true. My wife is a fanatic about scrubbing. And we're very careful about food. Bread goes in the freezer, opened cereal in the refrigerator. We provide very few opportunities for roaches.

"It's like they're being driven by something else," I said. "Why would they come to the bedroom? There's not much food there."

"They can eat wallpaper and glue," Jon said.

"And our house is a goldmine of that stuff," Rich said. "I'm not buying that."

We were quiet for a minute. Then Richie, his mind turning, said to Jon, "I thought you didn't believe in killing anything. I heard you were quite the killer back there."

"Buddhists believe life is suffering. Let the roaches suffer a little too."

"So, you were giving them a religious experience by killing them?"

"Exactly," Jon said.

Helen and I talked over our situation in the kitchen at Mom and Dad's house.

"I don't want to go back there, Harold."

"You want to live here at my parents' house?" I could think of worse nightmares, but not many.

She shook her head as if she thought I was being ridiculous.

"Let's call John Jones again."

Before she could finish, Max, who was sitting close by, as were all the boys, shouted out, excited, "J'onn J'onzz, that's the Martian Manhunter!"

We all looked at him.

"Well he is, in the comics."

Ah, yes, the green-skinned dynamo from Mars, a minor strongman character from the DC Comics line-up.

"We're talking about the exterminator, you pong-head," Richie said. "Not some idiot superhero."

"He's from Mars," Max said, lamely.

"Can you call him to help us out?" Richie shouted. "Otherwise, I don't want to hear about it."

Max was stricken with embarrassment.

Now commanding silence, Helen resumed. "I want him to bomb the house."

A pesticide bomb. It could destroy any living, breathing bug even thinking of setting up shop in our little home.

That would make the place uninhabitable for three days. That meant we would either have to live in a hotel or my parents' place.

"I'll ask Grandpa if we can stay at his house," was all I said.

The boys looked worried, but I knew it was the right thing to do. Nature makes me nervous. And these roaches were nature run amok. I called Jones and we set the date.

The two middle boys grumbled about the situation. Staying with their grandparents really threw them off.

Max said he couldn't find a quiet place to study. Jon asked, "Where am I going to smoke?"

"You shouldn't be smoking at all. You're 15 years old!" Helen yelled.

"It's a dirty habit," I told him.

"I'll leave the clean living to Superman," Jon said.

I gave up. I knew we wouldn't get anywhere with him in this state, which could take about four or five years before it died out.

Mark was OK—he watched television with our dog.

Spending three days in my parents' house, I started to really notice things I missed on a typical one-hour visit. Like how my mother was increasingly declaiming, "Life is what you make it!" while sitting in her favorite chair, or turning over the blanket on top of her legs over and over, in some kind of obsessive compulsive disorder. Or how my father's skin had turned to parchment and got bruised or cut with the slightest touch against the doorway.

"They're getting old," Richie said to me.

"I know," I said grimly.

Dad walked up to us, his once impregnable arms turning into thin sticks, "You want a cruller?"

"Sure, Dad."

Richie, Dad, and I sat and ate his chocolate doughnuts around the kitchen table and I almost found myself tearing up looking at my old man. I'd been afraid of him for so long when I was a kid and now I was thinking he might be my best friend. He had something that I had always aspired to—honor. I don't think he even knew he had it. He may not have been a soldier in a war, or ever rescued somebody from a burning tower, but he had done the best he could.

He had fought his way out of a stink-hole New York City ghetto and become a successful businessman. He had done what he was capable of to perform his duties as a husband and a father. He was not a perfect man, but who is? He had told me a few times he regretted how he had made so many mistakes in raising Derek, and that was to his credit. Dad's past was already written in stone, but he was picking up the rocks labeled "errors" and studying them, writing notes to himself, trying to learn, even though it was too late.

After three days, we drove back to our house. The boys were very excited. As soon as I braked the car, they were out the doors and running to the steps, our little black dachshund following.

I opened the storm door and put the key in the lock to the main one. Helen, the boys, and the dog followed.

The air in the house had a sharp industrial chemical accent.

"Uggh!" Jon said and he spoke for all of us.

Jones had left a note on the kitchen table. "I left you a can of stuff in the closet, if you need it again. It will be added to your bill."

I checked the closet. There was a metal can, with a metal top, about a foot high, clearly labeled and with the traditional skull and bones decorating both sides.

We opened every window in the house. Then Helen and I inspected each room for cockroaches. We swept each room with our eyes. We looked under beds. We checked the wood moldings hugging the floors. I looked over the basement with a flashlight, with my four boys trailing me. We checked behind the boiler, the washing machine and dryer, the cedar closet.

There were about a half-dozen dead roaches of medium to large size, several daddy longlegs spiders and a water bug that had once been living behind the sink next to the washing machine. I went into the crawlspace behind the basement wall and found nothing.

For a few days, everything went back to normal again. As normal as can be in our house, anyway. The major drama had to do with the dog. Gee Gee started licking the walls in the kitchen. It took me a couple of days to figure out what she was doing. She was eating the pesticide residue the bomb had left.

I grabbed her up, held her in my arms and yelled, "Stop it!"

She looked at me with uncomprehending eyes. "That's poison!" She promptly vomited on my shirt.

Max, Jon, Mark, and I took her to the vet.

Kleinfeld, the vet, said, "She's a strong dog. Stupid, but strong. She ate a lot of pesticide. I fed her a mixture to wash it out of her system. Please try to make sure she doesn't eat any more of that stuff."

We took the dog home and waited for her to be OK. She was, but the house wasn't.

In the night, as everyone settled down to bed and I put on Leno, Helen said, "Did you hear that?"

"No."

"It sounded like water."

"Maybe the neighbors are playing their TV too loud or something."

"I'm going to see."

I sighed. "Why can't you just relax?"

"Because you're too relaxed, Schreiber."

"Well," I wanted to say, "Not usually. Most of the time I feel like I'm about to be ambushed by Taliban insurgents."

But I didn't. I was too tired. The business with Happy Cimongila owing me $10,000 was driving nails into my skull and I didn't want to fight with my wife. So I just sighed again, tried to concentrate on Jay's monologue. He was saying something about President Bush, which is almost always funny.

"Schreiber!"

I was up out of bed fast, my pajamas trailing my legs. I ran to the kitchen, and saw Helen screaming in the hallway, the light on. The doors to the other bedrooms in the hallway snapped open.

Roaches were crawling through the underside of the front door, the hinges, wherever they could find an opening. They were walking all over each other, making small mountains of filthy brown insects.

"Get a broom!" was all I could think to say.

"I'll get the vacuum!" Helen yelled. She plugged it in as they started crawling all over her legs. She swatted them flat against her legs. I knew she was disgusted by what she was doing, but under the right circumstances, you can adjust to anything, I guess.

Once she got the vacuum going, the roaches started to get sucked in easily. But the problem was bigger than any of us imagined.

My boys ran to the front door as the roaches streamed in. A collective scream went up. Helen threw a broom out of the closet. Jon took it. Richie got his golden Sandy Koufax baseball mitt out of the closet, Max and Mark grabbed pieces of the *New York Times*.

I stepped on dozens of roaches to open the door and turn on the porch light. I thought it would help to have an open space to kill more of them. This was not a good idea.

I'm not sure I can describe feeling roaches crawling and being crushed under your feet. To say that it's disgusting is to shortchange the sensation. Their backs are slick and greasy. Their legs have little stubs extending out. I could feel hundreds of roach legs rubbing against my ankles.

As we fought against them, some took flight and flew into our heads, bounced off and found their way further into the house.

When I got the door open, I stared for a few moments, in shock, as a sea of roaches marched up the steps to our house. They extended back from the lawn and the street. And dozens of them had little yellow squares on their backs.

"It's a freaking army!" Richie shouted.

I was reminded of the scene in the *Starship Troopers* movie when the humans land on the insect planet and the bugs come streaming out of their holes to fight the forces from Earth.

We killed and we killed, but there were too many of them. Battalions of roaches, a number with yellow square backs, made it inside. We were all screaming as we mashed them with our hands and feet. Gee Gee rushed out from wherever she was sleeping and started snapping her mouth. She ate quite a few of them. A number of the roaches ran right over her little hot dog body, which made her shiver and even more frenzied. She became vicious and war-like in her killing.

They streamed by us. Our position was overrun, in Army terms.

One thing that helped is that Jones's pesticide bomb still had some potency. A lot of the roaches died when they got further than the hallway. Their little bug bodies seized up in mid-step and they sank to the floor.

The roaches ran through the kitchen like buffaloes stampeding through the Plains. Some were dropping from the remnants of the pesticide, but most of the roaches took a left turn into the dining room, took another left turn into the living room, then came back through to the hallway and ran off through the front door.

The Schreiber family mashed as many as we could as the bugs took off to the street, but their numbers were so great that it seemed as if we hadn't made much of a dent at all in their little army. Gee Gee swallowed whole some of the dead ones remaining.

One last roach, the size of my hand, ran for the doorway. It had a yellow square attached to it. Richie went to smash the little vermin with his Koufax mitt. He crunched it flat against the door jamb. The antennae twitched. He hit it again. When he lifted the baseball glove, we saw what the yellow square was. It was a Post-it note folded and attached to the roach's brown-plated back with some kind of glue.

I picked the note off of the dead bug, dozens of smashed roaches lying at our feet, a few with yellow square backs too, and I had a sick feeling that The Weirdness was rushing in faster and stronger than ever.

"What's it say?" Max asked. The boys all leaned in to me to see the note.

"Let me read it!" They all shouted at once.

I shared the note with the boys. They crowded around it. The writing had a certain psychosis to it. The lines were jagged, edgy.

Max read it aloud, like he was a teacher making an announcement to the class.

"I am happy living in the 67th Avenue subway station with my friends. My happiness owes you money!"

The boys quickly ripped off yellow paper squares from a dozen other dead roaches, and unfolded them to read the messages, like fortune cookies. They all said the same thing, in the same sick handwriting. The sender had been very thorough—he wanted to make sure we wouldn't miss the point.

"What's it mean?" Mark said.

I inhaled sharply. "It's from your Uncle Derek. He's kidnapped Happy Cimongila."

"We've got to get him!" Mark shouted. He would have been a good actor in the B-movie pulp pictures of the Forties.

"That's not going to happen. You're all helping me clean up this mess."

We obeyed my wife. The clean-up took one hour. Helen vacuumed every room in the house. Max, Jon, and Mark and I swept up the dead into black plastic garbage bags. Richie mopped the floors with Helen's strongest ammonia, diluted with just enough water so as not to completely scar our lungs. Helen mopped over what Richie had done with a scented soap, wiping out the ammonia.

Then it was time for the conversation with my wife. The boys all listened intently.

"I have to go," I said.

In her nightdress, Helen looked at me sharply. "It's the middle of the night. Call the police, Schreiber. You're out of your league."

"He's my brother, my problem."

"He came after us with a gun last time. I don't want to see you killed. I need you alive. You can't leave me alone with these." She swept her hand out at our children.

"You have a point there. But nobody's going to get hurt."

"Oh, really? Every time, every time, Schreiber, you get hurt when you go out there like you're some kind of superhero. You got shot up by the cops when that ghost or whatever it was took over Queens Boulevard. A giant jellyfish almost killed you that time at the beach. You take too many chances. I won't have it. You're just a housing contractor, that's all."

"Happy Cimongila owes me a lot of money. Money to pay Richie's college tuition, and to put food on the table."

"Call the cops."

"Then Derek may kill Happy. He's trying to—"

"Bait you! Don't take it!"

"It's a brother thing. You wouldn't understand."

"The only thing I understand is you walking in that front door every night. Everything else is just craziness to me."

There are moments, and they happen often, when a man has to decide whether he is going to listen to his own animal instincts or allow himself to be politely yet pointedly civilized by his wife. Virtually every day, men are challenged by other men. It happens in business, often. Most of the time, your only weapons are words. But sometimes, something more is required. A glare works occasionally. When it doesn't, a jab to the mouth may be required, or a right cross to the stomach. A hand closing on the throat. A fist in the nose. I could go on.

Most of the time, the man lets his wife lead him. He bows to her superior sense of survival. Let it go. Don't yell at the other driver. He's stupid. You don't want to get into a fight. It's not important.

However, when a man feels threatened too much, too deeply, he may very well throw off all the wifely chains that bind him to state-of-the-art polite society and run off to meet the enemy on the field of battle. And it is his fondest wish to leave that green field painted with the red blood of this enemy.

I looked at my wife, my dearest devotion, and stared through her cat's eye glasses and into her brown almond eyes.

"I'm going to the 67th Avenue subway station."

"Don't do it."

"I'm taking the boys with me."

"Yeah!" Richie, Jon, and Mark shouted, fists pumping in the air.

Max was the only one who wasn't excited. "I have an Earth Science Regents tomorrow," Max said.

Richie laughed. "You make it sound like that's important."

"It is important!"

"You're coming along with us, ding-dong."

Helen looked at me with open-mouthed fear and the words came out of her with no particular logic. "No. It's a school night. Why?"

"Because he doesn't expect it."

"No."

"Yes."

"You're as stubborn as a mule, Schreiber."

"Probably worse. Go to Ruth's house. We have some work to do."

My wife looked at me with disbelief and regret. She walked away to the bedroom. I heard something get thrown against a wall. It might have been our wedding contract, framed, under glass.

"Richie, get your mother's rubber gloves out of the closet."

He did. I put them on and lifted the can of Jones's pesticide up off the floor of the closet.

"Richie, get the keys to the station wagon. Boys, put on your socks and sneakers."

My sons and I marched out of the house, in our pajamas and sneakers, with me lugging the pesticide can, a canvas Boy Scout pack, and a metal snout for the top of the pesticide can. Rich was wearing green and yellow college gym shorts at least, his usual sleepwear. I had forgotten to tell them to change, and I had forgotten as well. We looked like the Vietcong, circa 1968, except my sons' pajamas had pictures of Batman, little Buddhas, and David Beckham.

For a moment I had to wonder about the mental stability of my 17-year-old, Max, wearing Batman pajamas, but I dismissed it to deal with the task at hand. There would be time to take him to a psychiatrist later. My own pajamas were inked with black bowling balls and tumbling pins, which was embarrassing enough without having to consider my son.

But I wasn't going back inside to change. I am scared of my wife at times like these. I admit it. Besides, I didn't want to ruin my exit.

Our little black dog ran out before the front door closed, bounding along the lawn in the darkness after us, pieces of cockroach legs stuck to her muzzle.

"What's she doing here?" Richie complained.

"She wants to come," Max said quietly.

"It's in her nature," Jon said, backing him. "The Buddha would approve."

"She's totally useless," Rich said. "She's stupid."

I agreed. "She is stupid. But stupid could be good here."

"She can eat a lot of roaches," Mark said.

"All right, all right, all right, you douche bags! But she better not get in my way," Richie growled, like a grizzled old soldier about to storm the front line.

We all got in the car, the dog on Mark's lap.

"So, what do we do now?" Max asked.

"First stop, the local pharmacy."

We went to the CVS store right next to the 67th Avenue subway stop. They sold rubber gloves, face masks, and most importantly, Super Soaker water guns. I bought the automatic kind—one squeeze gets off six shots. We purchased five Super Soakers. They were made of solid plastic and came in half a dozen different full-gloss colors, from orange and lime green to purple and yellow.

The guy at the counter, with piercings in his eyebrows, lip and nose, looked at us like we were crazy. Maybe we were. It was about two o'clock in the morning on a school night, we were wearing pajamas and sneakers, and we looked like we were arming ourselves for a massive water fight.

Outside the store, on a side street with little light where I had parked the station wagon, I directed the boys to put on their face masks and rubber gloves, to protect their skin, eyes, and lungs from the pesticide. In the car I had several sets of goggles for my carpenters to use when drilling through wood. We all put on a pair of goggles to protect our eyes.

I stuck the metal snout in the top of the can to open a hole in the pesticide and pour the solution. I armed the Super Soakers with John Jones's pesticide while Richie held the back of the can. After we handed out the Super Soakers to the boys, I placed the can in the canvas Boy Scout pack and strapped it to my back in case we needed to reload.

We walked to the subway stop, just a few steps away from the front entrance of the CVS store. I took the point, my boys behind me.

I made a silence gesture with my finger as we tiptoed down the steps. I didn't see anyone or anything. The station is very long, almost 100 yards in both directions. The subway stop was dead quiet. There was no clerk in the booth. There were no trains rumbling through and no passengers coming or going. As we walked down the platform, we saw the usual two drunks in dirty tee-shirts sleeping on benches. They were extremely asleep, clutched in a fog of alcohol. My sons looked at the bums with contempt. I envied the bums for a few seconds.

If Derek was here, he must be down the stairs, on the platform. I didn't think it would be a good idea to jump the turnstiles. So we walked to the automatic vending machine and I purchased five Metro Cards, round-trips, to get in the subway. I didn't buy one for the dog. I think they can ride free.

I handed a Metro Card to each of my sons, and we all swiped our cards to pass through the turnstile, with the little screen flashing "Go" each time. Gee Gee walked under the turnstile, following us.

We walked down the stairs to the west-bound platform, quietly. We walked all along the platform, but there was no sign of life, not even rats. Gee Gee sniffed the floor, which was splotched black with grease and dirt.

We went back up the stairs and tried the east-bound platform. We found the same nothing.

We were all confused. I took Derek's note out of one of my pajama pockets with my free hand and read it again. There was no ambiguity about it. He must be here.

"Let's go back to the other platform, boys," I said, my voice muffled by the face mask. "We must have missed something."

We started to walk up the steps and there they were. An army of roaches scrambled down the steps to meet us. They crawled all over each other, a stinking, greasy moving mountain of brown insects. Some flew at our heads, which is always fun.

"Shoot! Shoot! Shoot!" I shouted, but I didn't need to. The boys were yelling too and pumping their Super Soakers as fast as possible. The dog, brave or stupid, take your pick, charged right at the roaches.

The roach bodies piled up fast, but the survivors were faster. Dozens climbed up our pajamas. It was a sickening feeling.

"Run up the steps!" I shouted. The roaches had the high ground and the high ground is always the best place to be in a fight, even if you're an inch-long insect.

The boys followed me as we stepped on dozens of roaches coming at us.

Gee Gee tried to follow us, but she was covered in roaches. I shot them with the Super Soaker and hoped I didn't hit her directly with a shot of pesticide.

With my help, she shook them off and came up the stairs behind us.

Now that we were on the same level as the roaches, it was a lot easier to kill them off in bunches. The brown vermin kept running at us and we fired and fired into the swarm, madmen, crazy with fear of the bugs. We used the pump action in the water guns and laid waste to most of the herd. But there were still thousands running around on the station floor.

Then we ran out of juice in our Super Soakers. There was only a little residue left in the barrels, a few ounces at most, and no time to reload. I decided to take radical action.

"Boys, move back!"

I took the can out of the canvas sack and poured it on the floor. The solution burned the station ground and it wasn't even close. The thousands of roaches caught in the circle inhaled the stuff and collapsed on the floor. The dozen or so that tried to fly away were caught inhaling the juice and fluttered a little before succumbing to the fumes.

We didn't have much time to enjoy the triumph. Out of the pesticide mist came Derek, walking with a .45 Magnum glued to Happy Cimongila's head. I thought he would be disappointed at the almost-complete loss of his cockroach army. Back to wearing a leather motorcycle jacket, with long brown hair, unwashed of course, he was strutting across the greasy killing ground of the subway station, the flat light making his head look like a burning candle. The scar on his nose looked worse than ever, as if he had dug a new line in the purple ridge with a steak knife. Maybe he had.

"You've brought me all the little Harold clones! What a night!"

I took off my face mask so Derek could hear me clearly.

"I see you've graduated. Last time you had a P22, a toy compared to what you've got there."

"Harold, help me!" Happy shouted, panicky, his shark fin nose shriveled up in fear.

"Yes, Harold, help him. He owes you a great deal of money, I understand."

"How'd you know about that?"

"I'm good at sneaking around, finding out things."

I stared at him. "Yeah, I believe you, Derek. We've got laws against stalking."

"Oh, I'm worried, Harold."

"What'd you do with the subway clerk?"

"He's tied up."

"That's five years upstate right there, for assaulting a transit employee."

"I'm crazy, remember?"

"How'd you get the cockroaches into our house?"

"You're changing the subject. Rather abruptly, I might add."

"I'm just curious. I'd like to know, in case, you know, this ever comes up again."

"I don't see this ever happening again. Well, actually, it could, if you and your boys manage to live through this night."

He was drifting off-topic, and even though I felt stabbed in the chest with that threat, I really wanted to know what he had done. It's part of my problem. I can't just find out the time—I have to find out how the clock actually works.

"You're a smart guy, Derek. Very smart. What did you do to the roaches?"

"So easy. You don't see it?"

"I have my theories, but I'd love to hear you brag about it. I live to hear these arrogant spewings from you."

Loving brothers forever.

"All right, Harold. I'll feed your obsessive curiosity. I seeded the streets leading up to your house with increasing amounts of pheromones. Sweet smelly stuff, to lure the cockroaches, right up to your front steps and beyond."

He had given me the ammunition for the point I was trying to make.

"You've shown cruelty and calculation, but not insanity. Any decent prosecutor would drive that argument in court and you may find yourself in prison instead of Creedmoor. That's a whole other barrel of crab apples."

Derek looked at me thoughtfully. "You know, Harold, that was actually an intelligent thought. You surprise me."

"Where'd you get the bugs?"

"I had them shipped up from some outfit in West Palm Beach, told them I was doing biological research."

"I don't think you're crazy at all. Psychotic, maybe, but not crazy."

"Flattery will get you everywhere but out of this."

He pressed the gun to Happy's temple with a very intense face. Happy squirmed and groaned.

"Let's stop screwing around. The games are over."

"We're getting too old for this, Brother."

"Speak for yourself, Brother."

I sighed and my boys sighed with me, their heavy exhalations coming through their face masks, yellow rubber gloves rising and falling with the slight heave of their bodies.

"Shoot him, for all I care. He's not going to pay me anyway."

Happy shouted, "No!"

"I think you do care, Harold. Why would you come here if not for him? You're still a little Eagle Scout bitch."

I raised the barrel of my purple and yellow plastic Super Soaker to his face, two precious ounces of pesticide sloshing around in the back of the barrel.

"Drop the gun, Derek."

"You have a sense or humor too, Harold. Who knew?"

Knowing Derek, he would want to engage in this playful, mocking talk half the night. But I couldn't afford to wait. The bullets in the Magnum held very big threats. And the boys had school the next day.

I squirted the Super Soaker. The juice flew. My brother ducked, but he was hindered by the bulk of his hostage. The pesticide found a home in Derek's right eye. Max had once squirted his own brother in the eye with a nasty chemical, in a demented little boy fit. Now I found myself copying him.

Derek didn't shout or scream, which surprised me. The burn from the gun must have been very painful. He staggered, but held on to Happy. I gave him credit for tenacity.

Now he was hanging onto Happy, the Magnum swinging around Happy's mid-section. Happy turned and hit my half-blind brother in the stomach with an enormous fist and ran off.

"You owe me $10,000!" I shouted at him as he ran up the steps, but I knew I wouldn't get a reply.

Derek staggered around, waving the .45 in the subway air. My boys scattered behind blue metal subway posts, not exactly hiding their pajamas and sneakers.

Gee Gee was the only noticeable thing in his line of sight. So he shot the dog. It wasn't a clean hit, but the enormous bullet took off a piece of her right back leg.

She fell to the floor screaming a little dog scream, blood gushing from her side, and that really got me.

I squirted the gun at his face again, but I had nothing left in the barrel.

Derek raised the gun at me, still dangerous, but weaving. His afflicted eye looked like it was smoking a little. I stared at him and considered backing off to one of the metal beams.

A juice bullet came out from one of the subway posts and hit my brother on the lips. By reflex he swallowed some of it.

Brother fired the .45 Magnum again and the bullet hit the ceiling. I ducked behind a post. A police siren sounded from far away.

Another juice bullet sliced through the air and smashed into Derek's nose. The pesticide on his jagged scar got him screaming.

The dog was thrashing against the ground and I really was shocked and upset by it. She may have been a stupid dog, my oldest son may have roped her once like a calf being captured for the slaughterhouse, but she was my dog. Blood and muscle and ligaments spilled out of her leg onto the subway station.

A bullet full of wounded pet owner fury blasted Derek in the cheek, under his right eye. Off balance now, he brought the gun up to fire it again. A gush of juice hit his right hand and you could see the trace outlines of where it hit his flesh. He brought the gun down and massaged the wound.

Our black dachshund was screaming even more loudly now and the mental pain of it was incredible to me. I didn't think I could be so upset about a dog.

Derek started to seize up. He was coughing and spitting out whatever bit of pesticide he had swallowed, stumbling forward.

The barrel of a Super Soaker got jammed into his neck, courtesy of my oldest son, Richard, bringing my brother down on the concrete floor.

Mark, my 13-year-old, raced out from behind a post, which took my breath away in fear for him. Armed with the last little molecules of Super Soaker juice, he shot Derek in his other eye. Derek started to scream, drowning out the dog.

I jumped out and stamped my sneakered foot down on Brother's hand, breaking the bones attaching to the fingers. The Magnum came loose and so did a new scream.

Max took the gun.

"Don't touch it!" I shouted, frightened as hell of what a gunshot with a .45 Magnum would do to my accident-prone son.

Max didn't listen to me. He threw it hard with his rubber glove, sending it off in the air, sailing barrel over grip, landing with a clink against a metal beam 20 feet away. It fired on landing, hitting the beam and taking out on the ricochet a chunk of the subway wall and a movie poster of Adam Sandler's crotch coupled with a giant blow dryer. Adam's groin was completely blown off. Oh, dear God.

Mark tossed off his gloves and mask and took our bloodied dog in his arms.

"Don't die, Gee Gee. Please don't."

She whimpered and looked up at him. He tried to put her muscle back where it belonged, canine blood snaking over his hands and arms. I was heartbroken.

Max picked up Derek's head by the hair and smashed his pesticide-infested scar of a nose into the greasy concrete.

"Stop," Derek said, almost whispering. But it didn't matter. My sons were going to humiliate their enemy in the best way they knew.

As my brother lay twitching, feet away from a hill of thousands of dead cockroaches, Richie unlatched a round, jet-black New York City garbage can near the turnstiles. Inside was a smaller garbage can which actually caught all the trash. He dragged the metal can, made of corrugated silver metal, out of its hidden place.

"Hey, come here," he said to Max and Jon. "Help me lift this thing."

They went over to him and the three of them hoisted the can over their heads, brought it over to Derek and emptied its full contents on their uncle's head. Newspapers, soda cups, cans, candy wrappers, gum trays, and a single wingtip shoe smashed down on the back of his skull.

Then they threw their empty Super Soakers at Derek's head. They ripped off their face masks, then their gloves and threw them on top of the garbage over his defeated spine. He lay very still, as if dead.

The three older boys looked at the mess they had made of Derek. "What an asswipe," Richie said. I had to agree.

The police sirens rode closer. Helen must have called them.

"Let's get the hell out of here. I don't want to deal with the cops, at least not tonight," I said, grabbing in my bowling pajama arms the Super Soakers, gloves and masks from the top of the pile of garbage. I didn't want to leave direct evidence for the cops. There wasn't enough time to take the pesticide can, though. We had to leave the .45 Magnum too, but that was really Derek's problem.

We all ran up the steps to the station wagon. Mark, his eyes full of grief, carried Gee Gee, blood leaking from the dog onto him. He looked at me with his big brown eyes as I opened the car with the keys in my front pajama pocket, and popped the locks to let them in. He got into the front seat with the dog.

I threw the Super Soakers onto a ratty old blanket in the back seat. I tried not to tear away from the sidewalk.

"Where are we going?" Max asked.

"Kleinfeld's, the vet."

"I need to go to sleep. I have the Earth Science Regents tomorrow!"

"What a dilemma!" Richie yelled out, filling the car with leftover adrenalized sarcasm. "Either we try to save the dog or you don't do well on your test."

Max, yet hurt again by his brother's salvo, said, "Of course I want to save the dog. Unlike you. You don't give a damn about the dog. You said she was useless, remember?"

"True. I would much rather go get a beer than anything right now."

"I don't think you're Buddhist material," Jon told Richie.

"What about Gee Gee?" Mark sniffed.

"Pet cemetery?" Richie asked.

"Shut up, girls!" I shouted while gunning the car to 80 mph on Queens Boulevard. "Richie, call Kleinfeld on the cell, wake her up, tell her we're coming to her office. Max, go to sleep in the back seat. We are saving this dachshund!"

Two weeks later I was talking to Happy Cimongila on the phone.

"I can't pay you back, Harold. The money's not here. Malinka still owes me."

I don't know why, but I couldn't just say, "I saved your freakin' life, Happy. You can and should give me the money."

What I did say was firm, but still within the realm of politeness. "You've go to do something, Happy. This is a lot of money."

"I'll send some things over to your house."

Silence means consent and I wasn't quick enough to protest.

That's how we got some furniture we really didn't need, like a round wicker footstool. Jon liked to put it over his head and walk around the house, shouting, "I am the God of Wicker Furniture!"

We also got an upholstered chair which had metal slides for legs. I put it in the living room near the picture window. Nobody would sit in it but me.

The most useful thing we got was a plexiglass table with triangular metal sawhorses. Max liked to read and do his homework on it. He got only a 74 on the Earth Science Regents, so he decided he needed to study more, even during the summer. He was still mad at Richie for insulting him about caring about the test, so studying more was his way to get back at his brother. (Yeah, Max, that should really get him back.) Mark, who was spending lots of time looking at electronics magazines, used the table to assemble his own computer.

After he successfully put the computer together, Mark came to me and said, "Dad, I can help you save money on the electric bill if you open up the walls and let me put in new wiring."

The kid's 13 years old and he wants to re-wire my house.

The best thing about my not pressing Happy for the money is he felt so guilty about it that he had us over for dinner with his family twice a month. He put out quite a spread—steak, grilled chicken, hot dogs, hamburgers, lots of exotic breads, and pasta stuffed with potatoes. Sometimes, he took us out to my favorite diners—the Nosh and the T-Bone. That helped Helen and me save some real money.

Derek was in the hospital ward at Creedmoor. My father had gotten the call from the police. They had found him in the 67th Avenue subway stop, a few feet away from a small mountain of dead cockroaches, buried by the contents of a garbage can.

The boys in blue also found the subway clerk, alive, thankfully, hog-tied in his booth. He told them what Derek had done to him, but couldn't explain the dead roaches or the pesticide job or

Derek's injuries. The cops rousted the two drunks in the station at the time, but they had slept through the whole thing and just seemed confused when the police questioned them.

A detective investigating the case, out of the 612th Precinct, came over to the house to talk to me and I looked at her blankly.

The Super Soakers, rubber gloves, and face masks were sitting in a landfill in rural Virginia. I also made the boys throw out their cherished pajamas and gym shorts and sneakers. Too many pesticide fumes clinging to their clothes.

The back of the station wagon was thoroughly cleaned out as well. Slats of new lumber sat in the back seat.

"You understand, Mr. Schreiber, we're trying to figure out what happened," the detective, with the noble Irish name of Harren, long black hair pulled back in a bun and piercing blue eyes, said to me. Sometimes I wished I were Irish. But I'm not even close—I'm just a Schreiber.

"Sure, of course. I'll try to help you however I can."

"We have files on you and your brother. You were arrested for trespassing at Creedmoor, while you were looking for your brother, more than 30 years ago."

I didn't want to talk about the past.

"I was a juvenile. The charges were dropped. How is that relevant to this case?"

The detective looked at me sharply.

"You don't seem very respectful, or cooperative, Mr. Schreiber."

I sighed the deepest of sighs.

"I'll try harder."

"Alright, I'll try to take you at your word. There's a history of violence between you two. We know your brother attacked you and your family six years ago. We're wondering if it happened again."

I looked at the ceiling for a few seconds, like I do when I'm a little stuck. I considered what I could possibly tell the detective that would make any sense. That my brother had commandeered an army of cockroaches to attack our house? That he had also kid-napped a business associate of mine? And that we counter-attacked with pesticide-loaded Super Soakers in the 67th Avenue subway station?

A number of police scenarios floated through my head. As-sault and battery (on my brother)—unlikely, but possible. De-struction of MTA property (the subway station garbage can)—definitely. Endangering a minor, three charges (Richie was 19 and legally, if not mentally, a man)—likely. Obstruction of justice (not calling the police in the first place)—certainly.

"My brother is very troubled. I basically raised him. Maybe I didn't do such a hot job, but I tried my best. I'm sorry he's so screwed up. But I can't explain what he was doing in the subway station. I wish I could tell you more."

Detective Harren breathed shallowly and looked at me as if she might not believe me, but didn't know what else to do. I thought she would certainly try to talk to my brother, but I didn't think Derek would talk. It was too humiliating for him. And he had a lot of trouble with authority. I could imagine him in his room at Creedmoor trying to play with the detective's mind, but not giving her one real hint of what happened.

Humiliation was the same reason I didn't think Happy would talk either. As a home builder and a Russian in Queens, you can't afford it. You need respect or people will walk all over you.

"Here's my card, Mr. Schreiber. If you can think of anything else that might help, call me."

Dad, checking up on Derek at Creedmoor with a phone call to the hospital's administration, told me my brother had lost sight in one eye. The other eye was saved. His scarred nose was broken. His right hand was smashed up pretty good. I felt bad about his injuries, but I came around to the point of view that they were unavoidable. When it's brother against brother, the fighting can get very ugly.

As he healed, the subway people, the Metropolitan Transit Authority, were considering putting him on trial for what he had done to the subway clerk. The police found Derek's handprints on the Magnum, so gun possession was added to his potential legal trouble. The forensics guys dug .45 Magnum bullets out of the subway walls, Adam Sandler's groin, and the station ceiling. There was the foundation for two more possible charges—discharging a firearm in a subway station and property damage.

If Derek was deemed fit for trial, and found guilty, he would go to Rikers Island off the northern edge of Queens, which is one of the toughest jails in the state. Then he might be shipped off to a prison upstate, one with a dreaded name like Dannemora or Sing Sing.

I had very mixed feelings about that. I veered between the idea of justice and the idea of charity. As far as justice, he had done a lot of bad things. He didn't have to go down that road. But maybe he couldn't help himself. Derek was really sick. He was my brother. And he really needed a lot of help. I just didn't know if he would allow himself to be helped.

However I balanced the scales, I couldn't come up with an answer.

I went to sit in Happy's gift chair as the summer sun came through the picture window in the living room. Gee Gee was lying on her side, soaking in the heat, her leg bandaged and healing. Kleinfeld was able to put some semblance of it back together. The dog saw me and gave me her most pitiable look. I picked her up gently, with an arm under the damaged leg, and she fell asleep in my lap. I stroked her long ears and petted her head. I wondered if she would ever run fast again.

For several weeks after the incident, my wife didn't talk to me. I kind of wished she would yell or shout about all the terrible things I had done, so we could get over it and move on.

I added her silence as another burden of my husband-hood. Helen didn't really need to speak. I knew what she would say. We could have called the police. I had endangered my children and my own life. Any of us might have been killed. What would she have done then? What was I thinking? I was an Eagle Scout, remember?

Well, Eagle Scout was a long time ago. And whatever I had been, I was bent by The Weirdness into something I would not have recognized when I was a kid. I could say the fault was with my mother, my father, my brother, the neighborhood, or the Ozone Park Ladies' Garden Club. Maybe they all contributed their little bits to my personality. But I can't really blame them.

No, I have to take responsibility for my own violent tendencies. I may be an Eagle Scout, but there's an animal inside me trying to get out. I try to wear the armor of responsible son, husband, father, home building entrepreneur, and small business person, and it's a good cage, solid as iron most of the time, but ultimately, it can't hold the wild energy which infects and burns through me.

Most of the time, the cage contains the spirit in a well-steeled box. But if trouble finds me, my eyes go wide and the blood beast comes out.

I'm not saying I'm the toughest or most vicious guy on the block. I'm no James Bond character. I'm not Stallone or Schwarzenegger in their primes, or even Vin Diesel. I inherited my father's shoulders and slaughterhouse arms. That's something, but not a huge advantage. But I've learned to take The Weirdness and put it on my side of the ledger when needed.

After all they've been through, all I've put them through, The Weirdness now envelops four part-time crazy boys. I started out trying to protect them from the ravaging, greed-filled world, but I screwed it up, like I screwed up with Derek. Despite their outward appearances of sarcastic wit, bookish loner, Buddha follower, and mop-headed electronics whiz, if they think you've put them in a corner, they will collapse their personalities into the same type of little Schreiber fighter.

ABOUT THE AUTHOR

Michael Gold is a freelance writer who has lived in three boroughs of New York City over the last 25 years—Brooklyn, Manhattan, and Queens. He has two bachelor's degrees, one in political science from Binghamton University in Upstate New York, and one in journalism from the University of Oregon. He lives with his wife and daughter in Forest Hills, Queens.

Early in his career, he delivered newspapers, washed dishes, filled sandbags, made auto transmission kits, and worked on an assembly line loading glass tomato sauce jars. He later became a reporter, writing for small-town newspapers and industrial and specialized business magazines. He has written public relations and sales materials for computer, graphic arts, and industrial companies.

One of his major causes is to eliminate the letter "P" from the alphabet.

He hasn't been making much progress, but still longs for the day when humankind can be rid of the power and predominance of "P."